RENATA

&

THE FALL FROM GRACE

The Gustafson Girls #2

BECKY DOUGHTY

BraveHearts Press

To enigmatic married women everywhere.
You know who you are.
God knew what He was doing
when He made
You.

ONE

"So, Juliette darling, what diabolical deed could you have possibly committed?" Phoebe wound a black tendril of hair around her forefinger as she glanced pointedly at the clock on the wall. "Whatever it is, make it quick. I've got a date tonight." The dark-haired artist was resplendent in a scarlet kimono dress paired with thigh-high stiletto boots. A pointed toe dipped up and down in time to the music playing in the background, one of Juliette's beloved 80s' movie soundtracks.

"What on earth is there to do on a Tuesday night in this town?" Renata asked from across the room. The question was out before she could stop it. Phoebe liked nothing better than to flaunt her wild lifestyle, and Renata had just given her leave to do so.

Phoebe's smile became sultry. "I don't think you want to know, Rennie. Let's just say it probably isn't your cup of tea." Then she raised both her bangled wrists above her head and did a slow and sensual gyrating motion.

"You're going to hell, Phoebe Gustafson."

"Oh, I'm well aware of that, thank you very much. You, on the other hand, may be headed for the pearly gates, but at least I'm having fun along the way."

"Hey, you two. Cool it." Juliette's soothing voice cut through the mounting tension, and Renata took a deep breath, hating the tightness in her chest when Phoebe mocked her faith. But Juliette didn't look very happy, either. "What time do you have to leave, Phebes?"

"You've got me for thirty minutes. Brandon is picking me up at my place at six and I still have to fix my face."

"What's wrong with your face?" Gia asked, her back to the entertainment center, her fingers buried in Bob's scruffy fur.

Bob, once Tootles, was the beloved dog Juliette had rescued from the park with Renata's help last fall. Although she brushed him regularly, Juliette had given up on taming her dog's coat.

"I can tell you what's wrong with her face," Renata quipped unkindly.

"Please." Juliette held up a hand, an uncharacteristic scowl on her face. "If I had known we only had half an hour, I would have waited to call a G-FOURce. I have something pretty serious to talk to you about."

"That's not for like two hours, Phebes. You look fantabulous already. Do you really need that much time?" Gia asked, her curls spilling down her back in a riotous waterfall of autumn hues. The youngest of the four sisters, she was the only Gustafson girl who still lived at home with Grandpa and Granny G, but she'd obviously forgotten the epic Battle of the Bathroom that took place every morning when they'd all shared the same room.

Renata rolled her eyes. "Don't be silly, Georgia. It only takes her ten minutes to actually get ready. The rest of the time, she's just admiring her own reflection."

She was feeling especially snarky today, and Phoebe had been on her nerves since Christmas. Besides, for various reasons, January was always a difficult month for her. Putting away holiday decorations and giving the house a thorough cleaning gave her a satisfying sense of accomplishment, but it never lasted. No matter how hard she tried, within weeks, she'd broken all her New Year's resolutions. Particularly the resolutions involving coffee, gummy bears, and the cookie dough in a tub she kept stocked in her freezer year-round. Once the boys were off to school in the morning, she could hear the little chocolate chips calling her name.

Not that she would have thought of that herself, but right before the big family Christmas meal last month, Phoebe had been sent out to the garage freezer for a bag of ice. She'd taken four-year-old Judah with her, the two of them chattering away about how much lizards and aliens look alike. They returned shortly, a bag of ice in Phoebe's arms, and one of the chocolate chip cookie dough tubs in Judah's.

"I didn't ask for cookies," Renata sighed. "Just ice. We're almost ready to sit down."

"I know. But the poor little chocolate chips were calling us, weren't they, Jude-Dude? Their tiny sad voices cried out, 'Phoebe! Judah! We're so cold in here, so c-c-cold.'" Phoebe peeled off the lid and began chipping away at the frozen lump with a fork from one of the beautifully set places around the table. "We knew just where they'd get nice and warm very quickly."

She winked at the little boy and they both shouted gleefully, "Belly-town!"

Phoebe's fork slipped and a huge chunk of dough plopped onto the clean, white tablecloth and rolled a few inches, leaving a discolored smudge in its wake. "Oops!" Before she got to it, Judah reached under her arm, snatched it up, and popped it into his mouth, then dove under the table so Renata couldn't get to him. Phoebe laughed out loud.

"Great. Thanks for spoiling his appetite," Renata groused. She didn't want to fight with Phoebe, not on Christmas of all days, but it seemed inevitable no matter how hard she tried not to.

"Did I just make you lose your appetite, Jude-Dude?" Phoebe lifted the edge of the tablecloth and peeked underneath at the boy.

Judah chortled gleefully, but shook his head, then crawled out to prove that everything, including his hunger, was still intact. Telltale brown streaks ran down the front of his white shirt as he stood in front of Renata. "I'm starving, Mommy! I'm starving for salad, and smashed tater toes, and... and turkey bird, and corn." He continued to list the items he could see as he craned his neck to get a better view of the dishes on the table. "My appetite didn't get lost. It's right here." He patted his tummy, leaving even more smudges.

"Oh, dear. Let's go wash up and change your shirt, shall we, little man?" Phoebe shoved the tub of dough into Renata's already packed refrigerator and grabbed the boy's hand. The two of them disappeared down the hall, and Renata frowned after them.

Now here she was, sitting across from Phoebe, picking fights with her again, and it occurred to her that she was breaking yet another resolution: *I will not fight with Phoebe.* "Sorry," she muttered. "That wasn't nice."

"Maybe not, but it's true." Phoebe wasn't going to allow her to be gracious. "I practice my pucker, my blink, my surprised look." She put both hands on her cheeks and shaped her mouth into a perfect scarlet 'O.'

Gia grinned at her antics from her spot on the floor, and Renata wished the girl wasn't so easily impressed with Phoebe.

"I even practice my 'come hither' look," Phoebe continued. "Because there's always a chance that I might meet Hither while I'm out and about."

"Cute, Phoebe. But enough. I really do need to tell you about something," Juliette cut in. "I just don't want to feel rushed." She shifted in her favorite corner of the two-toned beige sofa. She'd added some new throw pillows, Renata noticed, in plum shantung silk and a gorgeous apple green. She saw traces of the same colors around the rest of the room, too. Even the black and white Ansel Adams prints on the walls were now accented with pieces that looked like some of Phoebe's artwork; bold, swirling colors against serene blue backgrounds. Renata had to admit she approved.

Juliette spoke again. "Nor do I want anyone to leave until we've talked things through." Her tone sounded the slightest bit foreboding, making Renata's Mom radar start dinging.

"Fine," said Phoebe from the other end of the sofa. "If it runs too long, I'll just call Brandon and make him wait. It'll be good for him. He's getting a little too comfortable." Phoebe took a long sip of her iced tea and turned to Gia. "Get on with it, little sister!"

As the youngest member, it was Gia's job to begin the pledge. "Welcome Empress Juliette, Empress Renata, and Empress Phoebe." She pressed her hands together in a prayer-like manner and nodded her head to each sister accordingly.

"Welcome, Empress Georgia." The other three spoke just as somberly, nodding back at her.

They clasped hands, formed a circle, and began the G-FOURce pledge, a time-honored tradition that had somehow survived adolescence into adulthood.

Let the words of our mouths
Be necessary, kind, and true.
Let the secrets we share
Be kept safe amongst us few.
Let the decisions that we make
Be brave, noble, and wise
Oogie-boogie-doggy-loogie

Wiggly-jiggly-fries!
G-FOURce unite!

They didn't collapse into giggles the way they used to, but none of them was quite grown up enough to give it up. The pledge was like an unbroken cord weaving through their lives, binding them together. They released hands and settled back into place, and Phoebe turned laughing eyes on Juliette.

"So? Does this have anything to do with our favorite police officer? Has he put you on house arrest?" She wiggled her ring finger in the air. "Did he ask you to marry him yet?"

Juliette didn't smile, and that niggling sense of foreboding settled more heavily around Renata's shoulders at the look in her older sister's eyes. She laced her fingers together in her lap and held her breath.

"No," Juliette shook her head in emphasis. "He doesn't have anything to do with this. Not exactly, anyway."

Renata unclenched her hands and took a sip of her tea, relieved. Juliette had fallen madly in love with a local police officer, Victor Jarrett, last year, and although Renata could see how happy he made her, she still wasn't so sure about the man.

Sometimes, when Officer Jarrett looked at her with those foggy-morning gray eyes, it felt like he could see right through her, making her self-conscious and uncomfortable. Her boys adored him, her husband thought he was the best thing that had ever happened to Juliette, but Renata had butted heads with him from the very beginning, and he'd made her feel silly and foolish and incompetent, all things she didn't like feeling. She couldn't find anything wrong with him except for how he made *her* feel, and she wasn't against Juliette loving him. She just didn't want to be around him, herself, any more than she had to be.

"What is it, Jules?" Gia brought her knees up, resting her chin on them. She wrapped her arms around her legs, and Renata thought maybe her little sister felt the same wariness Renata felt.

When Juliette raised her eyes again, they were glistening with unshed tears. "It's about Angela. Angela Clinton. I-I wrote to her a few weeks ago. And she wrote back."

TWO

"You what?" Phoebe's hushed voice cut through the silence like a dull knife, ripping and tearing, rather than slicing cleanly, the way it usually did. Her tone, despite its brevity, held accusation, anger, betrayal, and something else Renata couldn't quite place. Fear? "You did *what*?" she repeated. Then she turned on Renata. "And you? Were you in on this, too?"

"No!" Renata held up her hands. "I knew nothing about it." But she did know something about it, and Phoebe must have read it on her face. That day in the park, when Juliette had rescued the starving Bob from under the hedge, she'd seen Juliette's notebook open to the page with Angela's name scrawled at the top. She'd asked her about it, and they'd talked briefly about how difficult it was to just write the girl's name.

She did not, however, know that Juliette had succeeded in moving past the salutation to the actual letter itself. And she'd had no reason to believe her sister would actually send it.

In fact, had she known of Juliette's intentions, she would have done everything in her power to prevent that letter from going out. Short of committing criminal acts, that is, lest she be forced to deal with Juliette's policeman.

"She didn't know, Phebes," Juliette swiped at a lone tear that tracked down her cheek. "I didn't talk to anyone about it except Victor—"

"Victor? Officer Jarrett? You talked to him about writing to Angela before you talked to us?" Now it was Renata's turn to raise her voice. "What business is it of his? And just how long have you two known each other now?" Little currents of electricity sparked behind her eyes, making it difficult to connect her thoughts together.

"Ren, please. Don't make this about Victor."

Phoebe was on her feet. "Uh, *you* made it about Victor, Jules. Not Ren." She began pacing the floor between the back of the sofa and the arched opening into the kitchen. "What were you thinking? And why didn't you talk to us before you did this?"

"I—I couldn't. I couldn't talk to anyone about it."

"Really? Because I don't remember you having any trouble talking to me about it last year," Renata retorted. "And you obviously felt you could talk to Victor." His name curled her lips into a sneer.

"So, you did know?" Phoebe stopped pacing and glared at Renata.

"No. I mean, we talked about *thinking* about writing to her a long time ago. But I had no clue she'd actually go and do it." Renata glanced over at Gia and sighed. The girl had her forehead resting on her knees, her folded legs hugged tightly to her. She turned back to Juliette. "Why didn't you just talk to us first?"

Juliette took a deep breath and pushed her long, dark hair away from her face with both hands. "I'm sorry I didn't. I should have. But it was such a strange process. I tried so many times to write to her. I'd start with her name and then... *nothing*. I did that countless times." She looked pointedly at her, and Renata looked away. She, too, had experienced the same struggle and had admitted as much to Juliette. "But then when the whole thing with Mike happened, his meltdown—"

"His assault, you mean," Phoebe interjected.

"Phebes, please. He wasn't himself."

"Right. He has that wolf disorder." She rolled her eyes. "Apropos name, I'd say."

"Wolff-Parkinson-White syndrome," Juliette corrected quietly.

"Stop making excuses for him," Renata said. She could tell Juliette was trying to remain calm, but how could she defend the guy? How *could* she after he'd broken into her house and hurt her? Renata was still appalled at his behavior. She'd always liked Mike, at least until he'd broken Juliette's heart, but Renata wasn't in any hurry to let him off the hook because of some obscure diagnosis.

Juliette clamped her lips shut for a few moments, her fingers toying with the strings of a tassel on the cushion she held in her lap. Then she straightened her shoulders. "I'm not trying to excuse him, but it doesn't matter, anyway. The point I was trying to make was this. Something happened when I chose to forgive him. It was like a light got turned on inside of me, shining into the corners of all these locked rooms in my heart. Rooms that harbored all this ugly stuff, you know?"

Renata made a real attempt not to roll her eyes. Ever since Juliette had climbed on the back of Trevor Zander's motorcycle, she'd turned into a Christian cliche queen.

Light shining in the darkness. All things made new. Forgive and forget. Washed clean. God's will.

Whatever. Renata had heard them all. She'd used them all—in fact, she still did among certain circles, and sometimes just to goad Phoebe—but she knew each word and phrase for what it was. A nice way to say, "Life is hard, but now that you're a Christian, suck it up."

She tuned back into what Juliette was saying.

"In a way, forgiving Mike freed me to forgive others I never thought I could." Juliette took a deep breath and let it out slowly, hugging the cushion to her chest. She spoke firmly, but she didn't make eye contact with any of them. "It was like this dam broke loose, and suddenly the words just came out of me in a rush." Her eyes were bright, still fixed on something just above Gia's head.

"That's all fine and well, Jules," Phoebe stated. "But why didn't you talk to us then? Why couldn't you wait and talk to us before you sent her anything?"

Juliette blinked twice, slowly, then shrugged, looking more like the noncommittal Juliette they all knew. "I—I guess I was a little afraid to tell you because I had no idea how this would all turn out. And," she chewed her lip, then continued, her voice dropping to just above a whisper. "We've never really discussed Angela before, you guys. And I... I didn't want anyone trying to talk me out of writing to her."

"Well, that's exactly what we would have done," Renata exclaimed. She stood up and crossed over to where her youngest sister sat on the floor, her head down on her knees, long red hair spilling around her like a veil. She dropped down to sit beside her. "You okay, Georgia?"

Renata had a difficult time using the nickname her little sister preferred: Gia. There was a part of her that wondered what was so wrong with the names they'd been given. Why change them? Juliette was Juliette, not Jules, not Juju like her best friend, Sharon, called her. Just Juliette. Phoebe was Phoebe. Not Phebes, but Phoebe. And Georgia was Georgia. 'Gia' sounded like the name of a Victoria Secret model, or something racier, and it bothered her calling her sweet baby sister by a name like that.

Gia lifted her head and nodded. "I'm fine."

An awkward silence settled over the group, and although she was no longer pacing, Phoebe didn't sit down. She stood with one shoulder against the wall, almost as though she were separating herself from the rest of them.

Finally, it was Gia who spoke. "Do you have her letter with you?"

"Of course. Would you like to read it? Or I can read it out loud."

"I want to know what you said to her first." Phoebe pushed away from the wall, and to everyone's surprise, crossed over to the two sisters on the floor and sat down on Gia's other side.

Four against one, Renata thought; even the dog stayed curled up around Gia's feet.

Juliette must have been dying inside, but Renata wouldn't look at her, not directly. From the corner of her eye, she watched her oldest sister sitting all alone in her spot on the couch, not moving, not speaking, just studying them, sizing up the situation. Renata knew that if she were in Juliette's shoes, she would be on the verge of kicking everyone out. Juliette wasn't like that, though. Although she was stubborn and a little stand-offish when she was hurting, she would do everything in her power to make sure the rest of them were all right. Which is what made this whole situation so surreal.

"Well," Juliette began slowly, testing the weight of each word. "I told her I forgive her for what she did to me. I didn't speak for anyone else. And I asked her for forgiveness, too."

Another long silence, then Phoebe's husky voice asked the question the others longed to. "For what, Jules? What did you ever do to her?"

Juliette snorted softly, a sound so derisive that Renata did look at her now. "I think a better question would be 'What have I *not* done to her?'" She set aside the pillow and leaned forward.

It was just a coffee table and a few feet of floor space between them, but it felt like a chasm to Renata, with Juliette on one side, the look on her face raw and ferocious, the three of them on the other, disbelieving, betrayed.

"I have run her down, run her over, shoved her off the Golden Gate Bridge, thrown her into an abandoned well. I have left her stranded in the middle of the Mohave Desert. Naked." Juliette clamped her mouth shut as though to put a halt to the litany of atrocities spilling out of her. Her nostrils pinched as she breathed in, then said, "I have spent the last fifteen years hating her, wishing she were dead, and coming up with a million ways to off her. That, my sisters, is what I've done to her."

Renata was shocked. She shouldn't be, because she'd struggled with her own rather ugly feelings about Angela, but this was Juliette. Sweet Juliette, who wouldn't hurt a fly. Literally. The girl would rather shoo one out the back door than break out the flyswatter. Yet here she was admitting to contemplating all forms of murder for Angela Clinton.

"I have wasted so much of my life wishing her dead, you guys," Juliette's soft voice was loud in the stunned silence. "And it has kept us both trapped by that horrible night. Not just Angela, *both* of us! I've had her locked inside the jail in my heart, and every time I thought of her or heard the name Angela or Clinton, I'm back in that dark place, standing on the other side of those bars, *hating* her. Wanting to kill her was killing me."

Juliette's eyes were overflowing now, the tears falling freely as she reached for a tissue from the box on the coffee table. "It's as though my life stopped that night. I've just been walking around like the living dead, waiting for satisfaction so that I could go lie down and die for real."

Renata could feel her throat tightening as Juliette bared her soul to them, but she would not let herself cry. The others needed her strength; even Phoebe, although she'd never admit it. Renata cleaned up the messes and held the pieces together. It was her role in their little circle, and she did it well. They didn't always love her methods, but she was the go-to-girl when it came to getting things done. She was the backbone of this little family of orphans.

She looked around at her sisters. Juliette was the level-headed glue, the oldest, Gia, the peacemaker, the youngest. Phoebe, not quite two years younger than Renata, shared the middle sibling slot with her, so she resisted being categorized. If nothing else, she brought the entertainment, the fuel, the fire. Phoebe gave them a reason to kiss and make up.

It had been this way since they were children, even before Gia showed up, a bonus baby late into Maman's and Papa's parental careers. When it was just the three of them, it was always Phoebe who pushed first and hardest. Renata would rage and tattle and pout until Juliette stepped in the middle to sort it all out.

When Gia was born, Renata seemed to find her place in the family at last. She loved being a little mother and she doted heavily on the baby who responded with sweet coos and slobbery nuzzles. Gia was the kind of infant who smiled and chortled far more than she cried, who raised her arms to anyone who looked twice at her and wanted desperately to be right in the middle of things. While Juliette was planning her future, and Phoebe was planning her evenings out, Renata was planning out a home and family of her own.

When she and John had their first baby, Reuben, she didn't care that he didn't have tiny red curls and no eyebrows like John's baby pictures, like Gia's. He still cooed and nuzzled and wanted to be nowhere more than tucked into the crook of her arm.

Simon arrived two years and two months later, solemn and scowling, mostly silent, his brow often furrowed even in slumber. Renata loved to stand over his bed while he slept and watch his constantly moving features. One day, she just knew, when he finally figured out all the things he really wanted to say, a torrent of amazing words would flow from his lips, and he would change the world.

Then Levi was born, and Renata thought if there was ever such a thing as a perfect baby, Levi was it. He smiled for the sheer joy of it. His internal clock coincided perfectly with hers, and if she didn't put him to bed by 7:30, he'd fall asleep in his highchair, his swing, or curled up in a corner of the play area, usually underneath or behind something, throwing her and John into a momentary panic.

Judah made his entrance into the world roaring like a little lion cub, and he hadn't stopped since. He was the last to fall asleep, the first to wake up in the morning. His cries were the loudest of all the boys', and his belly laughs shook him so hard he often fell over. When he was angry, he did not want to be comforted with hugs and snuggles. No, he preferred to crawl into a corner and complain, sometimes in irritating whimpers, other times in endless yowls, until he either got tired of tormenting everyone around him or fell into an exhausted sleep.

It was with the birth of Judah that Renata started to wonder if God was no longer listening to her. Every time she became pregnant, she begged for a baby girl, for their own John and Renata Dixon version of Gia, and every time another son was born, she fell in love with him and agreed to wait until the next time. But four years after Judah, it was still Renata and her family of boys.

Now, as she looked around Juliette's living room, she again felt that spiraling ache, that emptiness in the deepest part of her belly, that longing for a baby girl to love, to cherish, to dress in pretty polka-dots and lacy socks.

And suddenly, an overwhelming sense of being rudderless and adrift washed over her, even as she sat with her hip and arm pressed against Gia, her feet tucked under the warm body of Juliette's dog. She felt alone and always, always on the outside, even as she sat there surrounded by her beloved sisters.

She wondered if Angela Clinton felt the same way in prison; lost, untethered, and alone.

THREE

Angela Clinton killed Maman and Papa. On the night that Angela and Juliette and the rest of their senior class were to walk the aisle and flip the tassels on their cardboard caps, Angela Clinton got plastered, then climbed behind the wheel of her classic 1970 El Camino, a sweet-sixteen present from her daddy. She drove full speed through a red light, plowing into the side of the Gustafsons' Buick Park Avenue Sedan, making Maman's head snap back so hard against the passenger door window that the impact killed her almost instantly. Papa, on the other hand, lasted nearly an hour, but not long enough for any of the girls to say goodbye. At least Grandpa had gotten there in time to hold Papa's hand as he slipped away to join Maman.

Renata attended the same high school, two years behind Juliette and Angela. The girls weren't friends, but they weren't enemies, either, because Angela was kind to everyone. In fact, Angela had few enemies, only those who couldn't tolerate kindness from someone as popular as she was. She was the brightest star in their school, and Renata could still remember the first time she'd seen the girl perform.

The voice that flew out of her mouth was like nothing she'd ever heard before—or since—and Renata sometimes wondered if Angela still sang. What kind of opportunities did prison offer a girl who looked like a pixie with flaxen blond hair, dreamy eyes, a brilliant smile, who had a voice that brought people to the brink of euphoria?

Angela. Why, of all days, of all people, had Angela Clinton been drinking? Alone? She stated at her trial that she'd been at home in her room, drinking her bottle of whiskey all by herself. According to Grandpa and Granny G, Angela gave no real reason for her binge, only that the alcohol was available, so she took advantage of it. But what would cause a girl with so much promise to drink alone on the day of her high school graduation?

Angela had turned 18 three months earlier, so was tried as an adult. Her sentence required her to serve two consecutive sentences of 10 years each. It would be 15 years this coming June, and Renata wondered how the parole system worked, if Angela might be eligible. Did her family still live close by or did they move away to begin a brand-new life where the visage of Angela wasn't hanging over their heads? And if they had stayed local, what would that mean for Angela when she was released?

What if Angela came back to Midtown? Renata shook her head briefly, not ready to think about what that meant.

But Juliette had opened a can of worms with Angela's name on it, and they were all being forced to stare at the grotesque contents against their will. Juliette sat waiting, holding a pale sheet of stationery in her hands, offering to read the words Angela Clinton had written, words that would bring the girl back to life in a very real way.

Renata didn't want to know what the letter said. She didn't want to feel sorry for Angela. She didn't want to feel anything for the girl. And from the expression on her face, neither did Phoebe. For once, the two of them were in complete agreement.

"I don't know, Jules." Phoebe shrugged, feigning nonchalance, but not fooling anyone. "Honestly, I'm not really interested in what she has to say to us, to you. I'm more interested in the unbelievable fact that you took it upon yourself to contact that woman in the first place, especially without including us." She pushed herself up off the floor and brushed her long-fingered hands together, the bracelets on her wrists jingling prettily. "I need to get going. I don't think it's really fair to Brandon to leave him hanging after all. So," she turned around and held out her hands to Renata and Gia. "I don't know how you two feel about this, but I'm ready to call it a night. Come, say goodbye to me."

Gia stood up, her pale skin mottled with color. She flushed in patches when she was upset, and Renata could tell the girl was despairing over the way their meeting had completely unraveled. When Phoebe made up her mind, though, there wasn't any budging her, and this time, Renata didn't feel like arguing with her. This time, in fact, she agreed with her. She turned to Juliette, who still sat curled into the couch, hands clasped over the letter folded in her lap.

"Phoebe's right, Juliette. You should have included us long before now. And I'm not going to let you put Gia on the spot about this. We're going to call it a night, so we all have a chance to think things through a little. We can get back together over the weekend. Maybe Saturday night."

"That will work for me," Gia murmured.

"I'll have to check my calendar." Phoebe clearly wasn't ready to commit to anything yet.

"I'm sorry. I didn't mean for it to go like this." Juliette looked at each one of them, imploring, her eyes revealing the truth of her words.

Renata sighed deeply and shook her head. She couldn't imagine what had motivated Juliette to act independently of them, especially over something so pivotal in each of their lives. "I'll call all three of you tomorrow to set up a time. A good night's rest should clear the air a little." She stepped forward and reached for Juliette's hand, pulling her up to stand as well, the corner of the coffee table still between them. She still held tightly to Phoebe's hand, even though the younger woman tried to pull away. "Let's do this right, okay?"

As we go our separate ways,
As we ponder what's been said,
May we keep each other's secrets
Lest we all wind up dead.

It was a terribly morbid way to end this meeting in particular, in light of what had been discussed, but they brought their clasped hands toward the center of their circle, then let go of each other, lifting fluttering fingers high overhead.

"Oogie Boogie," they muttered in unison, voices flat.

"I'm outta here. Thanks for the coffee, Jules. We'll talk soon." Phoebe was never really angry with anyone except Renata, but she didn't fake her feelings, either. If she wasn't happy, you didn't have to guess why. She hugged Juliette quickly, bending over the top of the coffee table. "I just need time to process, okay? You threw me for a loop with this."

Juliette just nodded.

Gia circled the table and hugged her, too, then quickly followed Phoebe without saying anything more.

Renata stood with her arms crossed and watched them leave, waiting until the door closed behind them. Then she rounded on Juliette.

"What were you thinking, Juliette Gustafson? Why didn't you say anything? At least to me, so that I'd be prepared to support you." She pressed a hand to her chest. "I feel like you tried to manipulate me into backing you up. Like you thought I'd be okay with this because we'd talked about it once last summer."

Juliette didn't answer at first, and Renata momentarily regretted the harshness in her voice. But when she did speak, Renata stiffened defensively.

"I think the point of breaking up this G-FOURce prematurely was to *not* talk about this now."

"Excuse me?" Renata's eyebrows rose in astonishment. "Don't get all snippy with me. I'm not the one who stirred the pot, you know."

"No, you're not. And it isn't your job to clean up the pot, either." Juliette made quotation marks in the air as she used Renata's words. "It's your job to go home and think things through a little. Get a good night's sleep on it, remember? Those were your words." Juliette picked up the purse from the floor by the armchair Renata always sat in and handed it to her. "I have to take a shower. Can you lock up behind you?"

Renata snatched her purse out of Juliette's hand and glared at her. "What on earth is your problem? You're acting like Ph—"

"If," Juliette interjected, crossing her arms, her eyes bright again. "If you tell me I'm acting like Phoebe, so help me, Renata, I will stop speaking to you altogether. I am acting like *me.* This is how I act when I'm not happy with how things are going. I'm not angry, but I *am* trying not to be rude. I love you, but I don't really want to talk to you about this right now, especially since the others aren't here. Just let it go for now."

Renata was livid. No one seemed to care how hard it was for her to always be the bad guy, the one to take the hits. Phoebe could just up and walk out of a room without so much as causing a ripple, her silky voice soothing any frayed nerves, her looks intimidating everyone into compliance. Georgia? Well, no one could be upset at the girl, not for more than a second or two.

But Renata? It was as though people *looked* for reasons to be angry at her. And always found them, no matter how hard she tried to keep things from getting out of hand.

She clamped her lips shut, slung her bag over her shoulder, and marched to the front door. "Fine," she tossed back at Juliette. "Why don't *you* call everyone tomorrow, then, and arrange the next G-FOURce. I wouldn't want to interfere with your plans. I was just trying to help, you know."

Juliette nodded, her tears gone, her cheeks flushed. Renata was accustomed to her big sister's tears, but not this dry-eyed, slightly haughty version of her. Was this Officer Jarrett's doing?

"I'll call you tomorrow, Ren. And I'll call Phoebe and Gia, too. You shouldn't have to worry about always cleaning up the messes we make. We're all big girls now. Even Gia. She can make her own decisions, too." Juliette took a step toward her. "Sometimes messy is actually a good thing, you know."

Renata let out a derisive snort, then stepped out into the cold January air, pulling the door shut behind her a little more forcefully than she'd intended.

Don't worry about cleaning up after them? About fixing things? Well, who was going to take care of business if not her? It was what she did in this family. Nothing would get done if she, Renata Gustafson Dixon, didn't take the bull by the horns and deal with it. Phoebe would walk away, Georgia would dissolve into the floorboards, and Juliette would curl into a fetal position, bawling her eyes out. Someone had to be responsible, and that left only her. They needed her. They just had no clue how badly they needed her.

FOUR

"They take me for granted."

John could tell Renata was trying not to give in to the tears that were making her eyes glisten.

"They have no clue how much I do for them. They have no idea how hard I've worked to keep things together all these years. They think I'm bossy because I like to be, but if just one of them would step up and stop acting like selfish babies, I wouldn't be forced into this role. Then I could be self-centered and ridiculous like them. Georgia, at least, has an excuse. She's still practically a kid."

Across the table from her, John just nodded as he methodically cut and ate uniform bites of the baked potato in front of him. He knew better than to contribute to her rant. Anything he said could be used against him when she got this way.

"Have you heard anything I've said?" She glared at him, her eyebrows raised. Clearly, not saying anything could be used against him, too, but at least it was the lesser of two evils.

"I heard you, Mom. You're bossy, and they don't like it." Simon, nine years old, expressed himself in short, declarative statements that often left those around him deflated. It really bothered Renata who thought he was too young to be so opinionated. But Simon's directness was refreshing to John. It reminded him of Renata—how, at least in the early days, he'd never had to guess what she'd been thinking.

"Actually, no, you clearly did not hear me, Simon." She turned toward her son. "I said they *think* I like being bossy, but I'm not. It's because of them that I constantly have to step in. They force me to take charge because if I didn't, nothing would ever get resolved in this family." She turned narrowed eyes on John, and he knew what that look meant. *Why aren't you defending me?*

The thing was, John did defend her. Everyone knew better than to say a negative word about her to his face. When she was being attacked, in any way, shape, or form, he was there by her side, at the ready, the moment she needed him. But more often than not, he'd step in too early and then get yelled at for treating her like a child. Or worse, like an idiot. He never intended to do either, and he didn't like being accused of it. He would lay down his life to defend her, to cover her, to protect her, but she made doing so the biggest challenge in their relationship.

Lately, he'd opted to err to the side of caution, so he often kept silent, waiting for just the right moment to step in... and inadvertently leaving her high and dry and on her own. It was a fine line to walk, and he constantly listed to one side or the other these days, according to his wife.

She plucked the napkin from her lap and tucked it neatly under the edge of her plate. Did that mean she was leaving the table? She'd barely touched her food.

John sat back and studied her, waiting for her next move. It never ceased to amaze him the inner workings of his wife's mind. On the outside, she was beautiful, incredibly sexy with her sleek black hair and a mouth God shaped for kissing, eyes the color of summer rainstorms. But what went on behind those eyes, well, sometimes it was like standing at the edge of the bottomless Loch Ness and wondering if the creature in its depths was a timid, gentle Nessie... or a beast that would swallow him whole.

When they'd first met and then early into their marriage, she had burst into bloom under his affection, a flower so exquisite he was sometimes afraid to touch her lest he bruise her very soul. But somewhere along the way, something had bruised her anyway, and like a cactus blossom at the end of the day, the delicate petals folded in on themselves, leaving nothing exposed but prickles.

Oh, he knew her heart was breaking for a baby girl. He understood. He, too, had dreamed of a pink-cheeked daughter, chubby fingers reaching for him, a miniature of Renata. But it was more than that. His wife held on to things like no one else he knew. She didn't give second chances. Not even to herself.

He looked around the table at their boys, studying each one for a moment or two. Reuben, suddenly a tween, was listening to music in his head. He didn't need wires hanging from his ears to hear it; it came from inside of him. When he wasn't doing homework or playing soccer, he was working on a song. Usually it was someone else's music, but more and more often now, when they asked him what he was humming, he'd answer vaguely, "Just a song I'm writing."

Levi watched everyone with that half-smile he had yet to outgrow. With his big gray eyes and coal-black lashes, his coloring was the most like hers. Even his hair, straight and thick, grew as quickly as his wife's did. They called him Harry Potter sometimes, which he didn't mind, because as soon as Renata trimmed his hair, it seemed to grow back the very next day.

Levi, however, was most like John in his temperament; tolerant, patient, and quiet. The kid said only good things about people. His favorite new saying was "You slay me!" and even though John didn't think he knew what it meant; it was pretty funny coming out of the gap-toothed mouth of a grinning seven-year-old.

Judah. Well, all that could be seen of him at the moment was his hand gripping the edge of the table. There was more food spread in an eight-inch swath around his plate than could be credited to what had originally been on the dish, and his cup lay on its side, thankfully all but empty. How could one child create so much chaos? The rest of him was rooting around underneath the table where he was either retrieving runaway food or trying to sneak away so he wouldn't have to eat the orange Jell-O melting on his plate. He didn't like the stuff, but for some reason John couldn't fathom, Renata felt compelled to keep trying to convince Judah otherwise and served it to him every time she made it.

Simon, still stoic and often scowling, always seemed to be listening. Always alert, aware of what was going on around him, even when they were certain the conversation topics were over his head. They'd learned the hard way that they couldn't talk freely around him; he had the embarrassing tendency to ask questions at the worst possible time, especially when Renata's sisters were around. John was pretty sure he did it intentionally, just to be cantankerous. And because his calculating little mind knew exactly what went on in his mother's head when he did.

Sometimes Renata admitted to John that she wondered if Simon did stuff like that just to be mean to her.

His eyes fell on his wife, having made a full circle around the table, and he smiled at her, hoping she'd soften and stay. He wanted to tease her, but he didn't dare. She didn't use to mind when he did. She used to blush and bury her face in his neck. But lately, she often accused him of ridiculing her, of thinking she was just a silly girl. He'd pull her close and kiss her until her knees gave out, reminding her that the best gift she ever gave him was laughter. She couldn't argue with that, but she did anyway.

"John?"

"Hm?" Dang it. He'd forgotten the question.

When she pursed her lips and raised her eyebrows at him, waiting for a response of *any* kind, he swallowed and took a sip of his iced tea. "You'll figure it out, Sweetie. You girls always do."

• • • • • • • • • •

RENATA LAY IN BED, her back propped up against her pillows, reading the latest Ella Robbins novel. She was a fan through and through. Ella could craft a story like no one else, maybe not even her beloved Agatha Christie. Of course, she'd never admit that to anyone. Ms. Christie's books were classics. They were Literature, with a capital L.

Ella Robbins' novels, on the other hand, were purely Pleasure. With a capital P. They were predictable stories that started with a bang, roared through the pages at a heart-thumping, break-neck speed, included plenty of passionate entanglements between the heroes and heroines, and ended with earth-shattering revelations Renata could see coming from the very first page. She loved them anyway. In fact, she loved them because of that. Ella wasn't going to pull the rug out from under her feet. Ella wasn't going to surprise her with anything but a happy and blood-pounding, climactic ending. Yes, Ella's love scenes included rather explicit details, but Renata tolerated them for the sake of the story.

Granted, she wouldn't want John opening one of the books to any of those scenes—or anyone else, for that matter—which is why she kept her collection tucked neatly into shoe boxes in her closet, amidst the myriad of other shoe boxes... containing shoes. Besides, she really didn't have to worry about John. He knew she read them, but he never bothered to open one. He didn't read anything except hunting, fishing, and various other outdoorsman magazines.

He also read the Bible, she admitted, and more often than she did, eyeing the worn leather-covered book sitting on his bedside table. Although he rarely read in bed, he kept it there for the morning when he'd slip out from the cocoon of their 1200 count Egyptian cotton sheets, scoop it up, and pad off to the kitchen. While waiting for the coffee to brew, he met with the Lord. Then he'd return to their bedroom with two steaming mugs and warm wake-up snuggles.

She loved those languid morning moments with him, before the world around them stirred, before the boys awoke and realized they wanted something immediately. Lying in the circle of his arms, curled against his solid man-strength, the faint bergamot of his aftershave still lingering on his skin from his shower the night before. Sometimes they talked about the day ahead, or of some other pressing matter. Other times, rather than words, they communicated with the whisper of flesh and bone.

On nights like this, especially, when the sink of dinner dishes seemed bottomless, and the boys' bedtime rituals lasted far longer than they should, Renata wanted nothing more than to escape into someone else's story, preferably one with an idealistically happy ending.

John, too, seemed quieter, deeper, like still water, and Renata tiptoed around him, not because she didn't want to disturb him, but because she wasn't so sure she wanted him to disturb her.

She heard the bathroom door open and peered at him over the top of her book, watching him as he crossed the room to their bed. His short hair was still damp and rumpled from drying it with a towel after his shower. He wore only his boxers and socks, his chest and limbs pale with the winter months. Come summer, he would absorb the California sun into his skin, turning every exposed part of him a golden brown.

He noticed her eyes on him and winked, then did a slow soft-shoe shuffle toward her. She smiled appreciatively, but waved her book at him, held open in her right hand.

"You already know how it's going to end, Renata." When John was especially tired, his voice took on a husky quality that made her skin tingle. She let her long hair fall forward a little to hide the blush.

"No, I don't. This one is brand new." She turned the page purposefully, even though she couldn't remember a thing she'd just read.

"I wasn't referring to the book. I meant the competition." He eased himself under the blankets and slid over beside her, snaking an arm around her middle, jostling the book in her hands. "Who will make your heart race tonight? Will it be Ella Robbins and her paperback pirates? Or John Dixon, in the flesh?"

"In the cold flesh!" Although she knew he was like a furnace and would be hot to the touch in moments, his skin, even through her nightgown, was chilled after his shower. She tried unsuccessfully to nudge him away. He reached up, took the book out of her hand, then tossed it over his shoulder. It landed on the floor and slid beneath the tapestried slipper chair in the corner of the room.

"Hey! You shouldn't treat books that way." She stuck out her bottom lip and crossed her arms, feigning petulance.

"I love that glint in your eyes when you don't get what you want." He leaned over and braced his hands on the bed on either side of her, his face mere inches from hers. She could see the goosebumps on his skin, feel the fine reddish hairs on his forearms stiffening beneath her fingertips as she ran her hands up to the smooth curve of his shoulders. She laced her fingers through the damp hair at the back of his head and pulled him toward her, the book forgotten for the moment.

"Who says I'm not getting what I want?" She whispered the words against his mouth.

FIVE

"Mommy, my tummy hurts." The little voice rasped in her ear, and Renata turned away from it, not wanting to awaken from the dream she was having. "Mommy!"

"What? Hm?"

"Renata. Wake up, honey. It's Levi." From her other side, John's hand on her shoulder tightened, shaking her gently. "Levi needs you."

"Mommeeeee!" Levi's voice rose sharply just before he threw up all over her side of the bed, splattering her neck and cheek with warm chunks.

"Wha—? Oh, Levi! Yuck! How could you?" She sat bolt upright, screeching in her shock and disgust, resisting the impulse to throw off the sheet. Without intending to, she'd fallen asleep in John's arms after making love, and she wasn't dressed. "John, help! I'm covered in vomit! Argh!" She clenched her teeth and wailed, trying not to breathe in through her nose. "Do something! Get him out of here!"

John was already out of bed, slipping into his pajama bottoms. He flipped on his lamp and hurried over to pull a weeping Levi away from his mother. "Come on, son. Let's get you into the bathroom."

"Not in ours! I need it. Take him to theirs," she demanded, her voice shrill.

John, his hair sticking up in funny spikes on one side of his head, scowled at her over his shoulder. "Cool it, Renata. He's the one who's sick."

"Yes, and I'm the one who's covered in his sickness!" She waited until John pulled the door closed behind him, then climbed out of bed and stripped the sheets from it. Everything would have to be washed, including her down comforter she'd paid a fortune for, even with the huge discount, during last year's Black Friday sales. In the meantime, what was she supposed to do with it? Disgusted, she rolled everything up in a huge ball, shoved it into the hall outside the bedroom door, and stormed into the bathroom. She'd deal with it in the morning; at least nothing had soaked into the mattress. She got straight in the tub and stood at the far end while the water got warm, shivering and angry, trying to hold back her own dry heaves and tears.

· · · · **·** · **·** · · ·

BY THE TIME SHE was out of the shower, her wet hair wrapped in a towel, John was standing helplessly in front of the linen closet, eying the carefully organized stacks. He clearly had no clue what he was looking at, or for, and she impatiently nudged him out of the way.

"We use queen sheets, remember? Grab that blanket up there." She pointed to the comforter they'd used two winters ago, shoved into a plastic case on the top shelf.

When John followed her back into the bedroom, she asked, "Where's Levi?"

"He's in bed."

"Is he asleep?"

"I don't think so. He feels awful about puking on you. He wants to apologize before he falls asleep." John grabbed one side of the fitted mattress pad and slipped it over the two corners on his side of the bed.

Renata eyed his work, sighed with frustration, and came around to do it herself. "If you don't do it right, it'll all come off while we're sleeping, and you'll end up lying directly on the mattress."

John stepped back with both hands in the air.

Renata rolled her eyes. "Did you give him anything for his tummy?"

"No. I thought you might want to check on him first." He now stood with his arms crossed over his chest, his eyes squinting a little in her direction. "Do you think you might be checking on him anytime soon?"

"Of course, I will." She unfolded the top sheet and with a flick of her wrists, sent the fabric billowing out across the bed. John didn't even bother trying to catch his side of it, but just stood watching as she smoothed out the creases, then tucked in the bottom, making perfect hospital corners on each side. "As soon as I'm done getting your bed ready."

"I didn't ask you to make the bed for me, Renata. In fact, I was just getting ready to make it myself, if you recall."

"Oh, please. You didn't even know which sheets to grab. For all we know, you might have tried half a dozen sets before you found the right one, then wadded the wrong ones up and shoved them back in the closet, or even worse, in the dirty clothes for me to wash. And let's be honest. You wouldn't have remembered a mattress pad, would you?"

"Good grief, woman. I'm sorry you find me so incompetent." John turned and left the room, calling over his shoulder. "I'll go let Levi know you're coming to see him soon."

Renata took a deep breath and blew it out in a huff, dropping her head into her hand. Why was she being so awful to John? Why was she angry at poor Levi?

"I'm a terrible mom," she muttered, but stubbornly refused to leave the bed half-made. She quickly finished stuffing their pillows into new cases, all except the one she'd been resting on. She was relieved to see no sign of vomit on it, but she wasn't going to take any chances. She'd send it to the cleaners along with the down comforter.

Out in the hall, she scooped up the ball of linens and headed toward the boys' rooms. Levi and Judah's twin beds were against opposite walls in their sky-blue room, headboards centered beneath windows draped in American flag curtains. A navy peg-board chair rail circled the room, from which hung an assortment of boy paraphernalia. An old-fashioned braided rug in red, white, and blue covered the floor between the two beds; a war zone of maple building blocks transformed into decimated towns, complete with Hot Wheels military vehicles, and plastic green soldiers holding position in mid-battle.

Renata glanced over at Judah first. If he awoke, he would not go back to sleep, and that meant Renata wouldn't be able to either. But Judah was nowhere to be seen.

In a panic, she turned to John, who grinned, and pointed at the heap of blankets mounded at the foot of the bed. She noticed then the top of a straw-covered head poking out from the pile, and realized Judah was there, sleeping soundly, butt up in the air. Sometimes, he still slept that way, and it always softened her mommy's heart to find him so.

John sat on the edge of Levi's bed, and she shoved the bundle of their bed linens into his arms. "Here. Can you take these out to the garage for me? I'll take care of them in the morning."

John wrinkled his nose at the aroma wafting up from the bundle, stood, and turned to wink down at Levi. "I'll be right back. You tell your mom all about your tummy, but don't forget about that problem you have with the slimy green fuzz, okay? She'll want to know all about that."

"Ew. Actually, I don't think I want to know about that." Renata took John's place and reached over to press a hand against Levi's neck, his cheek, his forehead. "It doesn't feel like you have a fever, Levi. How's your tummy?"

"It feels good. Daddy thinks I just ate something rotten. I'm sorry, Mommy. I didn't mean to barf on your face like that." Levi looked like he was about to cry again, and Renata shushed him.

"It's okay, Levi, honey. I know you didn't mean to. And I'm sorry I freaked out like that. It did kind of startle me. I wasn't mad. Just surprised." She brushed the damp hair away from his forehead; John must have completely hosed the little guy down.

"You seemed pretty mad, Mommy." Then he grinned.

"What are you smiling about?"

"I just called you 'Mad Mommy.' That can be your pirate name." His gray-green eyes were starting to drift shut. "You did say 'argh' like a pirate."

"Did I?" She smiled, slightly abashed that it was Levi who was soothing her spirits, not the other way around. "Well, my wee matey, it's off to the land of dreams with ye, y'hear?"

"Aye-aye, Mad Mommy," Levi murmured. He turned onto his side and tucked his hands under his cheek.

Renata sat and watched him drift away. All was at peace in Levi's world; now she had to face her own.

She turned to find John standing in the doorway, watching them. Even though one side of his mouth was hitched up in a half-smile, she could see that his brow was furrowed.

"He doesn't have a fever. Maybe just a little flu bug or something he ate. I'm not going to make him wake up for medicine; he probably just needs to sleep. I know I do." She didn't want to talk; not right now, anyway. Being awakened in such a sudden and disturbing way had her feeling completely out of sorts, but not in a way that would keep her awake much longer. She just wanted to go back to bed and try to pretend this had all been a bad dream.

"Okay." John kept looking at her, waiting for something.

"What?" She stood up and arched her back, her long, wet hair leaving a chilled patch down her spine. She reached up and lifted it away from her neck, wishing she'd at least braided it. Now she'd have to change her top again.

"Nothing bugging you?"

"Just a barfing kid and not enough sleep." She crossed the room and tried to slip around him, but he reached out an arm to block her, his hand gripping the door frame.

"You reacted pretty harshly. Levi thought he'd done something wrong." He spoke softly, so as not to wake the boys, but his tone demanded an explanation.

"I know. And I feel terrible. But I apologized, and Levi understands." She pushed a shoulder against his forearm, but he wouldn't budge. "Let me through, John. I need some sleep. If he's not sick, then the morning will be that much busier because I'll have to get him up for school and he'll be exhausted. If he is sick, then it'll be a miserable day for both of us here, trying to keep Judah busy and quiet and away from him."

John let go of the door frame, but slipped his arms around her, pulling her up against him. His chest was still bare, but his skin radiated heat and she leaned against him, tucking her cheek into the crook between his neck and shoulder.

"Baby," he murmured, his hushed voice loud against her ear. "You've been so wound up. I'm worried about you."

Renata didn't lift her head, but she scowled as she listened to the constant rhythm of his heart working beneath the muscles and bones of his chest.

"I know you're still hoping, baby, but maybe God doesn't want us to have a little girl. Maybe our little family is perfect just the way—"

"Good grief, John. Levi woke me up out of a sound sleep by throwing up all over me. Don't you think a little freaking out is to be expected? I said I was sorry, okay?" What on earth made him assume this was about her wanting another baby? Besides, she didn't want to talk about it. Not now, anyway.

She thrust out her chin toward the now-softly snoring boy. "Levi got over it; maybe you should, too." She pushed against his chest with her hands, harder when she realized he wasn't planning on releasing her. "Let me go. You're making a mountain out of a molehill, and you're going to wake up the boys."

At an impasse, the two stood frozen that way for a few moments, eyes locked, his probing, hers resisting. Then he released her.

For the second time that night, John raised both hands in the air in mock surrender. Suddenly bereft of his warmth, she crossed her arms and hugged herself, then scurried back to their own room where the bed awaited, fresh sheets and blankets emitting a faint French Lavender and vanilla scent from the potpourri packets she kept tucked into the linen closet. It made her think of her mother.

SIX

RENATA STOOD AT THE kitchen sink, listening to the chatter behind her. The four boys were seated on the two benches of the built-in corner breakfast nook and were discussing the latest superhero movie they'd seen. At least Simon and Reuben were. Judah had his feet on the bench and was sprawled across the table on his stomach, stretching for the sugar bowl just out of his reach.

"What do you need sugar for, Judah?" Renata didn't rush over to stop him this morning; she was too tired.

She'd lain in bed beside the instantly sleeping husband of hers, wide awake and plagued by his words. Of course, her heart ached with the unfulfilled desire for a little girl, but it didn't change the way she felt about her other children. She loved each one of their boys immeasurably. What exactly did John expect, though? That she wasn't going to mourn their decision to stop trying? It felt like giving up. It made her feel like a failure.

"I jeswanna eat some sugar." Judah was nothing, if not guileless.

"We are not having sugar for breakfast."

"But it's on the table." Judah propped his chin in one hand, still staring longingly at the sweet treat he was missing out on.

"Get off the table, Judah. Now."

"I want some sugar," he grumped, but shimmied backward until he was back on the bench. Renata hoped there hadn't been anything on the table beneath him; it would be all over his shirt front now.

"Mom, Levi looks like he's going to hurl." Reuben and Simon were both leaning away from Levi, who did, indeed, look a little green around the mouth. His eyes were watery and now his cheeks looked flushed. He'd seemed fine an hour earlier when she'd gotten him up.

Renata hurried over to the table, lifted Judah out of the way, and reached for Levi's hand. "Let's see if we can make it to the toilet this time, okay?"

But as he started to slide out of the bench, he lifted tear-filled eyes to her face, and brought both hands up to cover his mouth.

To no avail. Levi, once again, vomited all down the front of her.

"Levi! What is *wrong* with you? Why did you wait so long?" She stood there, arms akimbo, glaring at her son.

The room fell silent as the other three stared up at her in shock. Levi just sat curled in a ball on the edge of the bench, sobbing quietly, head down, his soggy hands held out in front of him.

"I'm sor—sorry, Mommy. I didn't know fast enough." She almost couldn't hear him; he spoke so softly.

Reuben slid out from the opposite side of the bench. Without a word, he headed for the bathroom and returned shortly with a wet washcloth for Levi. "Come on, dude. I'll call Dad."

"Excuse me, young man. You will *not* call your father. I'm right here."

"Yeah, Mom. I know. But you just yelled at Levi for puking. Just like last night." Reuben didn't turn around to look at her when he spoke, and Levi followed solemnly, holding the wet washcloth to his face.

Renata wanted to rebuke him, but she couldn't find the right words. She just stood there, her mouth opening and closing like a disgruntled goldfish.

"This place sucks."

"Simon! Watch your mouth!"

"Fine. This place stinks. It smells like rotten barf." Then he, too, slid off the bench, leaving his dirty dish on the table, and headed down the hall to join the other boys. Only Judah remained, still standing just behind her where she'd set him. When she turned to look at him, she saw a funny expression on his face, then his eyes got really wide.

"Mommeeeee!" Judah screamed, a high-pitched keening wail, as his body heaved, then emptied itself of everything the boy had just eaten for breakfast.

Renata scooped him up and followed Reuben and Levi into the boys' bathroom. Standing Judah in the tub next to Levi who was shivering and crying, she turned to Reuben.

"Reuben, honey, you're right. I'm sorry I overreacted. I'll take care of them from here. Why don't you go wash your hands—with soap—in my bathroom. Can you call Aunt Georgia to come pick you and Simon up for school, please?" As an afterthought, she added, "And check on him, will you? Make sure he's not sick, too."

Reuben didn't say anything, but turned and left the room. She had no doubt he would do exactly as she asked. She just didn't know whether or not he'd call John, too. Or what he would tell him if he did.

Renata climbed into the tub with the two boys and reached for the hose attachment on the shower head. Turning on the water, she waited until it was warm, then began to rinse all three of them down, clothes and all.

An hour and a half later, the two sick boys were sound asleep in their bedroom. Renata was trying to work up the courage to tackle her bedclothes from the night before, but she was so tired of body fluids and bad smells that she didn't move. The kitchen was completely sanitized; she'd hosed things down with a bleach mixture and followed up with an antibacterial room spray on everything. She could hear the thumping of Levi's sneakers in the washing machine out in the garage and she tried not to focus on the unsteady rhythm as she sipped on her third cup of coffee. At least this one she might actually finish before it got cold.

SEVEN

"Two of them down. Two to go. And that's if you and I don't catch it." Renata sighed as she flopped back on her pillow at the end of the day. John was already in bed, scanning the pages of a new magazine he'd received in the mail. How he could sleep shirtless in the middle of January always confounded her. "I'm exhausted. I hope I'm not next. I hate throwing up."

"You'll be fine. Just get some sleep tonight. I'll get up if someone needs a parent." John absentmindedly reached over and patted her shoulder, not taking his eyes off the page he was reading.

Renata turned to look at him, his words reminding her of Reuben's. "Hey. Did you talk to Reuben last night? Did he wake up?"

"Yes. Briefly."

"Briefly... he woke up? Or briefly you talked to him?"

John closed the magazine and looked down at her over the top of his reading glasses, but he kept his forefinger marking his place. "Actually, both. He woke up briefly, asked what was wrong, and I answered briefly. Then he went back to bed. It was all done very briefly."

"Huh."

He blinked slowly, still eyeing her. "And what does that mean? Say what's on your mind, Renata. I can't read it."

"It's nothing. Don't worry about it." She turned on her side, her back to her husband, but softened her rebuttal by turning to look at him over her shoulder. "Goodnight, John-Boy."

"Oh, no. Don't pull that with me, woman. I'm tired, too, but this is no way to end the night. Turn back over and tell me what's on your mind. Besides...." He pointed at the handmade picture frame on his nightstand that held a photo of the two of them on their honeymoon, lips locked. In

Renata's flowery script, she'd written "Always Kiss Me Goodnight" along the bottom of the frame, and it had been a hard and fast rule in their marriage. Even on the rare nights they spent apart, John took it upon himself to call her and describe in detail how he would kiss her in person when he returned home. It was almost as delicious as being kissed for real. Almost, but not quite.

Renata let out a long-suffering sigh and rolled back over to face him. John scooted down in the bed so that they lay looking at each other. "What's going on in that sexy head of yours, wife of mine?"

"Am I a terrible mother, John? Do the boys think I'm awful?"

When he didn't immediately respond, she closed her eyes, unable to watch him trying to come up with a kind way of telling her the truth. Because the truth he *would* tell, she knew that for a fact. And he'd do it in love. But even truth in love usually still stung.

John reached over and cupped her cheek with his long-fingered hand, his palms rough against her soft skin. "Hey, we've been through some tough stuff lately. The boys know you're sad. No one thinks you're a terrible mother."

"But today Reuben said something that made me feel like he thinks I'm not doing a good job. I'm trying, John. I really am."

"I know, baby. We all know that. The boys may not completely understand, but they know you love them. Give yourself a break, okay?" He kissed her on the nose, then the lips, then pulled her close, holding her comfortably against him. "You know, maybe you should do just that. Maybe you should take a break. You haven't done anything for yourself in a long time, why don't you call up your sisters and plan some time away. When was the last G-FOURce weekend?"

Renata pulled back, propping her head up on her hand. "That sounds like a terrible idea right now."

"Why? They love you, Renata. Don't think they haven't noticed you're struggling. Juliette asked me the other day if you—"

"Juliette talked to you about me?" How *dare* she? "Why didn't she ask me?"

"Let me finish, Renata."

She pushed herself up into a sitting position and crossed her arms over her chest. "I can't believe that she, of all people, would gossip about me to you. And you let her."

"Let me finish, Renata," he repeated. "She asked me if you and I were doing anything for your birthday next month. She said the girls want to do something special, but they didn't want to step on my toes if I had made plans already. That's why she asked me and not you." He lay back and laced his fingers behind his head, gazing up at her with hooded eyes. She hated that look, and his words made her feel even worse about herself.

"Apparently, I'm a terrible sister, too."

"No, you're not, but I really believe it would make things better if you talked to them, if you told them about your miscarriages."

"I can't tell them. They wouldn't understand. None of them are married, none of them have children. I don't even know if any of them *want* children. How can they possibly understand my pain? Besides, they'll just think I'm trying to manipulate them into feeling sorry for me so they'll be nice to me right before my birthday."

He didn't speak, but from the corner of her eye, she could see him frown.

"You don't know my sisters, John."

"Actually, I do know them, and I think you're being ridiculous. Not even Phoebe would think that about you."

"I'm not being ridiculous. Don't call me that. Juliette's in love and doesn't need my woe-is-me news. Phoebe could care less, and Georgia? She's too young to understand how devastating miscarriages can be when you so desperately want a baby. *Our* miscarriages, by the way. Not *my* miscarriages, *our* miscarriages," she clarified.

"Our miscarriages." John nodded, sat up, and slid his legs out from beneath the covers.

"Where are you going?" She glared at him, angry that he was walking out on their conversation. In the winter, he lost some of the coppery highlights that the sun painted into his hair, but the ends still shone burnished in the lamplight. He looked like a torch lit by banked embers, and she wondered what was going on inside his head.

"To get a shirt. I'm cold."

"Oh." But she knew that even if he wasn't going anywhere physically, she'd already lost him. "I can help keep you warm."

"I'm going to check on the boys, too." He threw on the brown t-shirt he'd been wearing before bed, the one that said, *We interrupt this marriage to bring you HUNTING SEASON.* Renata hated it; not just because of the stupid words on it, but because Phoebe had given it to him for Christmas. She'd given Renata a long-sleeved black one with the term *Hunting Widow* emblazoned in pink rhinestones across the chest; like she'd ever be caught dead in something like that. And she wasn't about to let John wear his in public, either. She compromised by letting him wear it as a pajama top. He usually took it off before crawling into bed next to her... but not likely tonight, it seemed.

She glared at his back as he left the room, then flopped over on her side, facing away from the door, her back to the empty place where he would lay beside her. She really did not want to wake up and see those words first thing in the morning.

And she really did not want to think about Phoebe first thing in the morning, either.

· · · • · • · • · · ·

WHY COULDN'T SHE JUST talk to her sisters? This whole situation was driving John crazy. He had become her only sounding board, and he didn't know how much more he could stand of her roller coaster emotions. He loved his wife to distraction, but lately, the lovely woman he'd married had become harder and harder to find. Oh, she was still incredibly beautiful to look at with her thick, black mane of hair against her porcelain skin, her well-toned body kept in shape with regular workouts and healthy meals. She didn't go overboard with that stuff—she never served him wheat grass or flourless bread—but it was important to her, he knew, and frankly, he enjoyed the benefits of having a wife who didn't mind taking her clothes off in front of him. She didn't try to convince him to join the gym with her... although she teased him about his little love handles every once in a while. It didn't bother him, though, because he knew they didn't really bother her, either.

He was in pretty good shape for a guy in his mid-thirties. He didn't drink beer, he didn't stop at the doughnut shop on his way to work in the mornings, and his job required him to be pretty fit.

As an electrical engineer, he spent much of his time climbing, crawling, digging, lifting, and performing various other strenuous tasks. His physical condition played a huge part in his efficiency and focus at work, but also in his extracurricular activities, too. He wasn't a big guy—he had no delusions about being some muscle-bound jock—but he knew he could hold his own when and where it counted.

Like in the woods.

The adrenaline rush of taking down a Blacktail deer at 200 yards was something else. The band of brothers he hunted with made the trips that much better. They were all believers, so there was never an issue about partying or any other rough living; instead of BFFs, Phoebe called them JFFs. Jesus Freaks in Flannel.

He'd take it. Life was so much simpler, so much easier to enjoy to the fullest, when you didn't have to worry about keeping secrets from your wife.

Last September, right after school started up, when he knew he wouldn't be leaving Renata with a house full of high-on-summer boys, he and the guys took off for Amador County, just this side of Sacramento. Tim Larsen, his closest friend, grew up in Sutter Creek, and his family still owned a chunk of land with a cabin in the woods. Everything operated on a generator and propane, but that was what made it so perfect. Man-fest. They usually scheduled at least two trips during hunting season, but last year, he'd only gone once.

It was during that trip that Renata started spotting, and a few days after he returned, she miscarried. Again. It was the third one since they'd decided to have one last try for a girl back in March. "A Christmas baby," she'd cooed hopefully, her eyes soft and dreamy.

Even with reservations—Judah was a poster child for birth control—he couldn't say no to her when she looked at him like that.

Much to Renata's dismay, and John's guilty relief, the doctor had recommended that they wait at least six months before trying again. Three miscarriages in a row were hard on a woman in so many ways. Dr. Flynn had even offered to write Renata a prescription for anti-depressants when she started crying, but his stalwart wife refused, assuring the doctor that she was sad, not depressed.

Now, three months later, John wasn't so sure.

How he loved her, but how she frustrated him. And he could see that she was beginning to frustrate the boys, too. John pushed open the door to Reuben and Simon's room. Both boys were sprawled across their twin beds in almost the exact position, on their backs, arms up over their heads, mouths open. Reuben had one foot stuck out from under the blankets.

"That's my boy," John murmured, a smile playing across his wide mouth. Reuben did look the most like him, even though Judah was the closest to John's Scottish red coloring. Reuben's hair was straight and nearly black like Renata's, but that's where the similarity to his mother ended. The lop-sided grin that was too big for his face, his bottle-green eyes, his full, slightly thrusting jawline, even his posture and the way he walked; it was all John. No one could deny his oldest son's parentage.

Simon turned onto his side and snorted, but didn't wake up. John chuckled at the frown between his brows. "And that, my friends, is Renata's boy. Just like her in every way." Then, slightly abashed for thinking it, for saying it aloud, he crossed over to Simon's bed and brushed the too-long black hair from his forehead.

Uh-oh. He felt awfully warm.

EIGHT

Renata sat across the table from Reuben, who stared solemnly back at her, his clear gaze not wavering. Just like John, she thought. It hurt that the boys were pulling away from her these days, and she needed to clear the air between them. She knew the other three would follow Reuben's lead, and if she could make him change his attitude toward her, they would, too.

"Honey, I'm sorry I've been so crabby lately. I haven't been feeling well on the inside, but that doesn't give me the right to be ugly on the outside, does it?"

"Are you sick, too?"

"No, not like your brothers, anyway. But I'm sad." She wondered for the umpteenth time if he was too young to hear any of this. But she'd always felt that they should be honest with their children about life. They didn't pretend things were all right when she and John argued, mainly because they felt it was just as important for the boys to know how to resolve things as it was for them to know that disagreeing was normal. They didn't want them going out into the world with unrealistic expectations about relationships, with unbalanced ideas about how to work together with those they loved. "Your dad and I really want to have another baby, but it just doesn't seem to be what God has in mind for us."

"Gross." He looked away. She could feel his foot thumping against the base of the table, suddenly nervous.

"I know. But I thought you should know why I'm sad so you don't worry."

"Okay." He still didn't look at her; he slid the zipper on his hoodie up and down repeatedly, in time with his swinging foot.

"Okay." She stood up, not wanting to push him. He tended to clam up when she did. "Aunt Georgia will be here to take you to school in a few minutes. Are you all ready?"

"Yep."

She waved goodbye to him, grateful again for Gia's willingness to help out whenever she needed her. They lived just up the block from each other, and with Gia's hours at Café Rico's not usually starting until after 9 a.m., she often proved to be a very convenient back-up plan for mornings. Not one to be beholden to anyone, Renata made it up to her, much to Gia's delight, with gift cards and movie tickets. It worked well for both of them.

She was not looking forward to another day of sickness. She stared out the window over the kitchen sink into the backyard. It was winter in Southern California, but the grass was green, and the rosebushes were in bloom. If they had a freeze, Renata would clothespin some old sheets over the top of her salvias, begonias, and geraniums; the plumbago didn't seem to mind, and neither did the vining lilac. But everything looked tired, worn down, the way she felt all the time these days.

She used to enjoy getting up to make breakfast for John before the boys awoke, but now she dragged herself into the day, her mind sluggish, slow to respond. By mid-afternoon, her body wanted to shut down; she could hardly keep her eyes open after lunch. And she dreaded the three o'clock pick-up from school because she was so cranky by then and didn't think she could handle a back seat of babbling, battling boys. At least while they were in school, even on the days Judah didn't go to preschool, she could put him in front of the television and sit uninterrupted in her favorite chair in her room.

In fact, since the New Year, she'd actually gone back to bed a few times on the days that Judah was gone. She blamed it on the cold wet weather, but she didn't tell anyone about it.

And now the day loomed ahead of her like a black cloud. "I don't want to be a nurse today, Lord. I don't want to think about anyone, worry about anyone, or clean up after anyone today. I don't want to see or smell vomit. I don't want to cook; I don't want to do laundry." It seemed like once she got going, she couldn't stop. "In fact, I don't really feel like being a mom today. Or a wife, for that matter."

Someone took a deep breath behind her and she turned guiltily, afraid one of her boys had slipped out of bed and overheard her words. It was only Harry, sighing contentedly on his dog pillow in the family room. He lifted his head to look at her, Sally followed suit as she always did, then both Labradors dropped their heads back onto their front paws again. Renata covered her face with her hands, relief washing over her.

"Oh God, I feel like such a failure." She pressed her lower back against the edge of the counter and dropped her hands. She gazed down at her nails which were long overdue for a manicure. "I just want to run away from me," she whispered.

Sally opened her eyes to look at her and thumped her tail on her cushion a few times.

An acute silence settled around her and Renata's ears began to pick up the myriad noises of the house; the whoosh of the heater as it kicked on, the mechanical hum of the refrigerator, the gurgling of the coffee-pot as it prepared to turn itself off.

The sounds swelled, filling her senses, until Renata thought she could hear even the bumblebee buzz of electricity coursing through the wires in the walls. She stood transfixed, poised; for what, she didn't know.

"Mommy!" Renata's heart skipped at the shrill call, the air around her exploding into activity as both dogs leapt to their feet and went scuttling down the hall to heed the call of their buddies. "I need a drink! And a cookie!"

That, she thought, was a good sign.

Three hours later, she was back at the sink. She gazed out the window at all three boys bundled in sweats and hoodies. She'd banished them to the back yard to play while she made their lunch, hoping to wear them out enough that they'd settle down for a nap, or at least a movie after they ate.

Simon was sullen, but that wasn't anything out of the ordinary, and he sat at the picnic table with his arms crossed, glaring at the other two who were fighting over the tether ball. Which is why she'd kicked them out. They'd been arguing and bickering non-stop for the last two hours, and Renata thought she might harm someone if she had to listen to it any longer. Even though Simon still wasn't feeling well, he had no problem coming up with mean things to say to antagonize Judah who was always ready for a fight. It wasn't just the little guy's auburn hair and flashing eyes that were so like John's. His temperament had to come from his father's Scottish roots, too. John claimed a direct line through the Dixons to the Douglas Clan of Ayrshire. He liked to brag about his forefather being William the Hardy, one of William Wallace's first supporters. Renata could totally see Judah jumping into the fray of that blue-faced lot, no holds barred, roaring at the top of his lungs.

Levi, although he didn't really argue, was a good counterpart for Judah, because he simply stood his ground. He didn't fight dirty, he didn't cry, but he didn't budge either. It drove Judah into a frenzy at times, but Levi's levelheadedness almost always won his little brother over.

Today, however, Levi's fever had been replaced by frustration. He was feeling better, but not well enough to feel good, and he was taking it out on Judah by keeping the ball circling the pole just out of the little boy's reach. Judah was putting up a good fight, but he was losing hope, along with his grip on his temper. Simon continued to glare, but she could see a nasty smirk of anticipation on his face. Any minute now, if she didn't step in, the back yard would go up in flames.

She turned away from the window. "Let them burn."

She left three pita pockets stuffed with turkey, sprouts, and cream cheese, three piles of carrot sticks, and three oatmeal cookies on three plates next to three glasses of unsweetened apple juice at their assigned stations around the table. If they survived the tether ball war, their hunger would bring them back inside. Renata headed back to her bedroom to wait in peace, her chair beckoning her. If she was lucky, she'd get another half hour of reading in before someone shoved open her door.

She picked up the novel she'd tucked in between the armrest and the cushion and opened it to the pages she'd been reading earlier. A third of the way through the book; there would be a sex-scene coming up any minute. She hadn't read this author before, but she hoped it was a good one. Maybe the stimulation would get her blood pumping enough to wake her up.

But the high seas adventure—the abducted English princess with skin like rose petals blossoming over the top of her cleavage-baring satin gown, the shirtless buccaneer leaving her with no doubts of his intentions—none of it was even holding her interest. Closing the book and shoving it deep into the chair again, she rested her head against the high back and listened to the noise coming from the kitchen. She could hear Judah's high-pitched, non-stop chatter, Levi's even-toned responses, and Simon's abrasive one-liners. What was she going to do with that kid? But at least all three were alive, and now were being fed, and hopefully, would all keep it down. Whatever the bug was, it didn't look like it was much more than a 24-hour thing. She sighed resignedly and got up to go do the mom thing.

· · · · ● · ● · · · ·

WHEN JOHN ARRIVED HOME at five, Renata was on the phone. A cold rain had begun to fall, so he stood just inside the front door, removed his damp coat, and gave it a good shake out onto the porch. He eyed his wife, gauging her mood, then made a wide circle around her to the living room to greet the boys, whose voices could be heard over the noise of the television.

It wasn't a normal scene; at least it hadn't been up until recently. Renata rarely let them turn on the television until after dinner. "If there's daylight, there are things to do outside. If the weather won't allow it, there are games to play and books to read and rooms to clean."

But since Christmas, things had shifted. Since the last miscarriage, actually. He knew that was the problem, but he kept hoping she'd come around, she'd come back.

As the boys leapt up to greet him, he kept one ear tuned to the conversation she was having.

"No. No! I already told you I had no clue she was going for it. I would have made her talk to the rest of us first if I had known!"

Thankful for the movie that quickly drew the boys' attention again, he wandered into the kitchen where Renata now stood over the sink, her free hand turning on and off the water in her mindless agitation. He quietly made his way around her to the coffee pot, brought it to the sink and held it under the flow of water, grinning at her. She smiled back briefly, waved her fingers at him, and walked away, leaving the water running. He'd been acknowledged... and dismissed. Prettily.

A bit too aggressively, he finished making the coffee and followed her down the hall to their bedroom. He didn't miss the frustration in her eyes when he came in, but he just shrugged and began to undress. With his back to her, he peeled off his long-sleeved thermal shirt, then turned and caught her watching him. He grinned, wiggled his brows, and swiveled his hips suggestively. She rolled her eyes and turned away, but he saw the smile playing on her lips. That was all he needed.

Renata. Her name meant light. And she was his light. Oh, he knew she was hard; he knew she was a little too tightly wound for her own good, but when she came apart in his hands, he knew there would never be anyone else for him. Like glass, she was, and she trusted him to pick up the pieces every time she shattered.

The fact that God had given him, John Daniel Dixon, the only backstage pass to the real Renata, blew his mind. When she set aside all her hang-ups and all her preconceived notions about everyone else's expectations, she lit up his world. He took seriously the responsibility of being the one and only person who really knew how to make her shine.

He crossed the room to stand in front of her in just his jeans and socks, refusing to be ignored any longer. She didn't look at him, so he placed both hands on her armrests and bent forward so his face was less than a foot away from hers. When she kept her eyes averted still, nodding solemnly at something the other person was saying into her ear, he grabbed her free hand and brought it up to his jaw, rubbing her soft palm along his two-day stubble. She jerked her hand away and turned to scowl at him, and he pressed his mouth to hers, completely catching her off-guard. She tried, halfheartedly, he could tell, to pull away, but he gripped her chin gently, and kissed her deeper.

"Rennie? Are you there?" He recognized the caller immediately, Phoebe's voice like butter even over the phone line.

He grabbed the phone and spoke into the mouthpiece. "She's kissing her husband right now. Can she call you back?"

"Hey, John. Glad to be home?" she purred into his ear. "Kiss her once for me." Then she hung up. John set the phone on his wife's lap and cupped her face with both hands.

"I'm home, woman. Now kiss me back."

And she did.

NINE

WHEN JOHN LOOKED THAT good, and kissed even better, it was hard to remember her name, no less the conversation she'd been having before he so rudely interrupted her. And now, her face red from rubbing against his, she watched as he sauntered into their bathroom, obviously feeling quite pleased with himself, leaving her sitting in her chair, completely disarmed. It was hard to stay worked up over the situation with her sisters and Angela Clinton when she felt like this. She sat and listened to the comforting sounds of the water come on in the shower, to his humming—she couldn't quite make out what song it was—and closed her eyes.

How she loved that man.

When he emerged from the bathroom again, his hair still damp, but his face smooth, wearing a pair of flannel pajama bottoms and a plain black shirt, she smiled softly at him. He bent over her again, but this time, he just rubbed his jaw line against her cheek. "Better?"

"Mm. And you smell good, too."

Grinning, he straightened. "I'll keep the boys busy while you call your sister back. And get yourself looking respectable again."

"What do you mean?" she asked, looking down at her blouse, wondering if she'd come undone. "I look perfectly respectable."

"No, you don't. You look perfectly kissed. Scandalous, my love." He drew a circle around her mouth with his finger, winked at her, and left the room. He knew just how to make her melt. Suddenly, she didn't want him to leave her alone, even sitting in her favorite chair. She wanted to be near him, close to his soft touches and heated gaze.

She'd call Phoebe back after dinner.

Dinner was spaghetti, a family favorite for the variety of ways one could eat a noodle. The options were endless; with or without the sauce, olive oil with garlic salt, butter with salt and pepper, even ketchup for Judah who liked to dip each noodle individually.

Reuben seemed relaxed and had no signs of illness, for which Renata was happy. Simon looked tired, but claimed he no longer felt nauseous, and the two younger boys were clearly back to themselves.

Renata, on the other hand, couldn't focus on anything. By the time the kitchen was cleaned up and the boys were taking turns in the bathroom, she had no desire left to talk to Phoebe. She didn't want to think about her sisters, or Angela, or why on earth Juliette would take it upon herself to contact the girl. Why didn't she at least ask Renata what she thought of it before she up and sent that stupid letter.

Forgiveness. Well, Renata had forgiven the girl for killing their parents years ago. She didn't harbor any bad feelings toward Angela, not really, but that didn't mean she wanted to usher her back into their lives. Renata agreed that Angela probably needed some closure, and that it would be good to hear that the Gustafson family had endured and survived and thrived, but to open the door for her to contact them, to have any kind of relationship with them? That was totally unnecessary.

And not Juliette's call to make on her own.

"What were you thinking, big sister?" she muttered to her reflection in the mirror over her dresser as she put away the pile of socks and underwear she'd brought in from the garage.

"Are you talking to yourself?" John came up behind her and put his arms around her, watching her face in the mirror. "Hey, Beautiful," he said to her reflection.

"Hey, Handsome," her reflection replied, but she didn't expound. There was a time when she might have talked to John about Angela, but lately when she shared difficult stuff with him, he seemed to get distracted. His eyes would get that glazed-over look, as though he was listening out of obligation rather than because he was actually interested in what she was saying.

And sometimes, she had to admit, the things she had to talk about were unimportant, boring, and even tedious.

But then, so was her life. Besides the tragedy of the miscarriages, the most exciting thing that had happened to her in the last year was organizing the Monday ManDates to help Juliette find a new boyfriend. How pitiful was that? And the only reason she considered it exciting was because of the way Victor Jarrett got her blood boiling in all the wrong ways. He seemed to see right through her and wasn't intimidated by her at all. They'd gone head-to-head over Juliette after a terrible episode with her sister's ex-boyfriend, and Renata had come out feeling silly, and childish, and *ridiculous,* and she didn't like to feel any of those things.

Why couldn't Juliette have gone for Tim? Or even Trevor? Trevor had led her to Christ, so why would she pass up a guy like him to settle for Officer Jarrett? What made it worse was how much John and the boys liked him. No, worshiped him. At least the boys did.

"Let's do something, John. Just you and me." Once the words were spoken, she realized she meant them. "Let's do something crazy. Like go sky-diving or hot-air ballooning. Or let's go to Japan. Or Scotland!" She turned in his arms and toyed with the seams at his shoulders, but she didn't meet his eyes. She didn't want to see his reaction.

"Wow. Where did this all come from? Skydiving? In January?" He leaned back and dipped his head to look at her face. "You okay?"

"We don't have to go sky-diving. Just something. Anything. Something different. Crazy."

"You said that. Crazy. So, what brought this on?"

She heard the wariness in his voice and shook her head to reassure him. "I'm not crazy, John. And I'm not depressed. I just need… I need to… I don't know. I just feel squeezed right now." She looked up at him then and read the concern in his eyes. "I feel a little like I have cabin fever or something."

He chuckled and shook his head. "I'm not surprised. After being shut up with those boys for two whole days? I'd be going crazy, too. You don't need skydiving. You just need some peace and quiet around here. Take Judah to preschool tomorrow. Curl up in here with a good book."

She darted a glance at her chair with disinterest.

"Or get out of the house. Get your hair done or something." He swayed a little, side-to-side, making her move with him.

Her heart sank at his words. He thought she was joking, being silly.

"Did you call Phoebe back? What were you two talking about that had you so worked up?"

Worked up. He thought she was being ridiculous, like he'd said the night before.

"No. I'll call her in the morning after the house is quiet. Then I won't disturb you when I get all worked up." She pushed out of his embrace and turned to leave the room.

"Hey." John grabbed her arm and tried to stop her. "Where you heading in such a rush?"

"Let me go, John. I need to check on the boys." She tugged her arm free and left him standing there, a bewildered look on his face.

Why wouldn't he listen to her? Why did he not care about what she said? She didn't *want* peace and quiet. She wanted excitement. She needed something juicier than a romance novel to get her going again. She wanted to feel lit up, the way Juliette looked right now, as she basked in the glow of her police officer's adoration. She wanted to look like Phoebe did all the time, like she had an incredible secret that was just a sigh away from being released. She wanted to see life like Gia did, eyes wide with anticipation.

She trudged into the living room where Reuben was sprawled on the couch, reading the newest book in the YA amateur detective series he loved so much. He read as voraciously as she did, and it always made her smile to see him so engrossed in his books. Judah and Levi were playing with model cars on the racetrack rug in the corner of the living room, all the engine noise coming from Judah's sputtering lips, while Levi quietly built bridges and ramps with blocks and assorted books from a shelf behind them.

"Where's your brother?" she asked no one in particular.

Judah pointed at Levi, Levi looked around the room, and Reuben didn't even acknowledge her, so focused he was on his book. Finally, Levi suggested she look in his room.

Sure enough, Simon had put himself to bed and was sound asleep, his back to the door, the blankets pulled up over his head, just his mouth and nose sticking out to breathe. She smiled down at him, wishing for his sake he wasn't so obstinate, but loving him for it, anyway. Bending over, she kissed his forehead, glad to find it cool and dry.

Back in the living room, she read to the two younger boys while Reuben brushed his teeth and changed into his pajamas. Then John took Judah and Levi to the bathroom to brush their teeth with him, as they did almost every night. The ritual usually included dollops of shaving cream on noses and cheeks, and more laughter than Renata thought conducive to proper dental hygiene, but John always assured her that everyone was scrubbed and fresh-breathed by the time they exited the bathroom.

When the boys were tucked in, prayed with, and kissed goodnight, even Reuben, who still let her kiss his forehead, Renata headed to the kitchen to make herself a cup of tea. She would sit in the living room for a while and watch television, a rare treat for her in the evenings.

"May I join you?" John dropped onto the sofa beside her and reached for the hand she wasn't using to flip through the channels. He laced his fingers with hers and waited in silence for a response from her.

"Of course." Her eyes never left the television screen.

"What are you going to watch?" He didn't sound very curious. More like he just needed to talk to be heard.

"I don't know. Probably something on PBS. If there's anything good this time of night."

"Or you could come to bed with me. We could pick up where we left off before dinner." He stroked the back of her hand with his fingers, but she pulled away.

"I just want to relax for a little while before going to bed, John. I need some peace and quiet, remember? The house is quiet...."

"And now you want me to leave you in peace." He finished the statement for her. She didn't argue. "Look, Renata. I'm sorry if I said something to upset you. We were talking about how stressed you were, and I suggested you do a little pampering for yourself. I don't know where I went wrong with that, but I'm sorry. I certainly meant it to be a good thing, so please trust my motives and not my words."

"But it was your words that made your motives clear, John. You were just trying to pacify me." She stopped flipping channels when she found the station she wanted, but still didn't look at him.

"I was not," he said, his voice sharp and indignant.

"Um, I beg to differ." Her eyes were bright, eyebrows up. "You didn't really hear me at all. I didn't say I needed a day off alone to do nothing. I told you I wanted to take some time off with you—*not* by myself—and actually *do* something. I don't want my hair done. I need a manicure and a pedicure, but I don't *want* either, because if I have to sit still for one more activity, I'll probably scream."

As she spoke, John's expression changed. His eyes grew dark, his brow furrowed, and he began to chew on the inside of his cheek.

Great. Now he thinks I'm psycho.

"Okay." He leaned forward and propped his elbows on his knees, lacing his fingers together in front of him. "Have you given any more thought to doing something with your sisters? Did you mention that to Phoe—"

"Good grief, John." She cut him off. "If you don't want to do anything with me, just say so. Stop trying to foist me off on my sisters. For the last time, I don't want to go somewhere by myself. I don't want to do something with my sisters." She crossed her arms tightly around her middle. "I *wanted* to do something with you, but now, no thank you. Tomorrow, I'll go out, spend some money to get pretty again, and I'll come home feeling like a new me. I'm sure that's all that's wrong with me." Her voice dripped with sarcasm and she unmuted the television, turning up the volume in an obvious dismissal.

"Renata, come on. This is no way to finish this conversation."

"What conversation? This wasn't a conversation. This was just you trying to butter me up so that I'd crawl under the covers with you. Well, forget it. I'll come to bed when I'm tired. But don't let me keep you up."

"Aren't you overreacting just a little?" John didn't raise his voice, his tone didn't change, nor did his posture, but she saw his knuckles whiten as he gripped his hands together tightly.

"No. I don't think so," she retorted, turning the sound back down a little so she wouldn't wake the boys. "I think you, my dear husband, are under-reacting. I think you would like it if I just shut up and came to bed like a good little wife. But I don't want to come to bed. I don't want to be quiet. I don't want—" She broke off, remembering her rant from the morning and her list of things she didn't want. She shook her head and snorted dryly. "Actually, I'm done."

"What does that mean?" He splayed his fingers out, and she watched the color seep back into his knuckles.

"I'm done complaining. I do just want some peace and quiet after all. I'm going to watch this show and then, if I'm tired, I'll come to bed." The man had no clue what was going on in her heart. He had no idea how desperate she felt right now. He had no desire to understand any of it either; she knew that just by watching his hands.

Without another word, John rose and left the room.

TEN

The next morning, Renata pressed back into John's warmth, forgetting briefly that she was angry with her husband. When he pulled her close and whispered into her hair, "I'm sorry I didn't listen to you last night," it all came rushing back and she had to force herself not to stiffen. He sounded sincere. He sounded like he wanted to make things right.

But he didn't offer to take her anywhere.

He slid out of bed, returning several minutes later with their coffee and the devotional they read each morning, and climbed back in beside her. He went through the motions of their morning routine as though his apology had set everything right, and she didn't correct him.

As soon as she dropped the boys off at their respective schools, she hurried home to make a few phone calls.

"Hi, Phoebe. I'm sorry I didn't get back to you last night."

"You don't have to apologize, Rennie. I love that John lets you know who's the boss. Who am I to stand in the way of a demanding—and hot, I might add—husband just home from work? You're a lucky woman, Renata Dixon." Her throaty chuckle raked across Renata's nerves.

"Yes, I am. I know. Listen. Juliette hasn't called you, has she?"

"No. What for?"

Renata rolled her eyes. This was why she had to take control of things. "We need to schedule a G-FOURce and figure out this whole Angela thing. I don't want to talk in circles on the phone with everyone. We need to get together soon and make some decisions now that Juliette has started this ball rolling. I can meet tomorrow after dinner, or Friday before six. Will either of those times work for you?"

"My, my. Aren't we business as usual today? Either one is fine. I have a dinner to go to on Friday night, but it isn't until 8 p.m. I don't know why it's so late. I'll be starving by then. Maybe I'll eat before I go, then I can impress people with how little I eat in front of them."

"Phoebe," Renata said sternly. "This conversation isn't about your dinner on Friday."

"Of course. Either works fine for me, but tomorrow evening is better."

"Fine. I'll call Juliette and Georgia, then let you know what time we decide on." She checked Phoebe's name off her list. "I'll talk to you soon."

She spoke to Juliette, then Gia, and both agreed to meet Thursday night after dinner. Gia offered to make coffee wherever they met. "Practice, Renata. I'm becoming one of Rico's favorite baristas. I have to keep working my skills, though, if I want to stay on top."

"That's fine, Georgia, but coffee skills or not, come prepared to talk about how you feel about Angela Clinton. Got it?"

"Got it." She sounded deflated, but Renata had no time to coddle her.

"Don't be late. We'll probably meet at Juliette's again unless Phoebe begs to hold it at her place."

"Yeah, right," Gia giggled.

"Yeah, right," Renata echoed, smiling herself.

Phoebe's place was always a disaster. Costumes and fabric strewn about over every surface, paint samples, sketches, and colored pencils were scattered across her small dining table, and canvases propped against furniture, the walls already on the verge of collapsing under the burden of all her mounted art. It wasn't just her own work; her place was a haven for her artist friends. They brought food; she provided the workspace. It worked well for the artists, but left little room for anything else, including family gatherings.

"Yeah, right," was Phoebe's response when Renata called her back and asked if she'd like to host.

The last two phone calls she made were appointments, one at the nail salon, the other with her hairdresser. Then she checked her purse for her stash of credit cards, poured herself a cup of coffee to go, and headed out the door after saying goodbye to the dogs. They stood in the side yard and watched her through the wrought-iron gate as she pulled out and drove away. She knew they'd run around a bit, then head back in through their doggy door to find their doggy pillows and wait patiently for their family to return.

When she picked up Levi and Simon from elementary school, the boys both hesitated before climbing into the car, staring at her with wide eyes. Levi started to tear up, and Simon scowled. Once they were buckled in behind her, Simon said, "I don't like it."

"I didn't ask you, did I?" Her retort sounded much more unaffected than she felt, but it was Levi's tearful silence that really got to her.

When Reuben climbed into the front seat beside her, he actually lurched away, startled at her appearance. He hadn't even spared her a glance until he was inside with the door closed. "Oh, my gosh! Mom! Dad is going to kill you!"

"Well, hello to you, too, son. And how was your day?" She would not let herself cry.

"Fine," he muttered, but he kept his face averted, staring out the passenger side window instead. When they reached the privately owned and operated preschool that Judah attended, all three opted to wait in the car in the little parking lot.

She returned shortly, Judah in tow, his mouth going a mile a minute. He hadn't even noticed. The moment he was buckled in, however, Simon poked him. Hard. Before he could start crying, Simon asked, "What do you think of Mom's boy hair?"

Judah stared at her, stunned into silence. Then he suddenly burst into tears. "I don't want you to be a boy, Mommy. Who will be our mommy then? Who?" He was inconsolable the whole way home, weeping and shaking his head in despair.

Even Harry barked at her when she first came in the front door. "*Et tu, Brute?*" she muttered, heading for the kitchen as the boys disappeared down the hall, all four slipping into Reuben and Simon's room. At least Judah was no longer sobbing hysterically.

She laid out yogurt cups and peeled orange sections at each place at the table, along with spoons and glasses of water. No one answered when she knocked on the closed door, and after a few moments, she pushed it open just enough to take account of all four of her sons. The room went dead silent; only Judah met her eyes, his expression one of utter betrayal. "Your snack is ready. I left it on the table. I'll be in my room if you need me." Then she pulled the door closed again and headed down the hall, closing her own bedroom door behind her.

Sagging against it, Renata finally let the tears spill. Her long, beautiful hair. Chopped off in a fit of... what? She'd assured Cynthia that she wanted it off, that she wanted to donate it to LoveLocks, an organization her hairdresser supported, and she'd found a perfect spiky new hairdo that would complement her features well. Cynthia had eyed her hesitantly, then after being reassured three times, had gone at her hair with gleeful abandon. The result looked exactly like the magazine photo because Cynthia was that good, but Renata had teared up, anyway.

"Oh, sweetie. This is just like in that Steel Magnolia movie. Please don't cry, Renata. Don't cry. You'll make me cry, too, and I'm not wearing my waterproof mascara today."

Renata pulled it together, just like in the movie, too, then went shopping. Her bed was covered in bags of clothes, shoe boxes, and a new leather jacket she'd found on the discount rack. Even at half-price, it had cost her more than any other jacket she'd ever purchased, but something about the way it looked with her new hairstyle convinced her to take it home with her.

Now she stared at it mournfully, wondering what had gotten into her. She heard Reuben's voice in her mind. "Dad is going to kill you!"

When John walked in the front door, his eyes lit up, but not in surprise. Reuben must have called to warn him.

She had made every effort to look her best, despite her dramatic new style. She'd applied her makeup with extra care, then slipped into a new ankle-length, slim, black knit skirt topped with a silky wide-necked blouse. It was a casual style, but the pieces accented her trim shape and feminine curves quite nicely. John noticed; she could tell by the way his eyes drifted over her.

ELEVEN

IT HELPED THAT SHE had dinner in the oven and the house smelled almost as incredible as she looked. John approached her slowly, taking in everything about this new version of his wife, from her painted toenails on her bare feet, up her legs to her round backside clearly defined by the skirt she wore, to the shirt that kept trying to slide off her left shoulder. Her neck, so much longer than he'd realized, drew his eyes again and again... or was he afraid to let his gaze linger too long on her cropped hair? He didn't hate it. He didn't love it, either. In the 14 years he'd known her, she'd never had hair shorter than her shoulders. Even when she wore it up, it seemed long. This choppy, tousled look suited her spitfire personality, he silently acknowledged, but he selfishly wasn't so sure it suited him.

He was glad Reuben had called to warn him. He couldn't imagine how he would have reacted if he'd come home without being prepared.

Then his eyes found hers. Hopeful, challenging, pleading, daring, it was all there for him to see. How she wanted him to approve, and how she expected him to disapprove. Did she really doubt him so much? It was only hair, for Pete's sake. He may have preferences on how she wore it, but even if she shaved her head bald, he would love her just the same.

He let out a low whistle. "Wow. You look amazing." He reached out a hand, and she put hers into it. He spun her around, making a show of looking her up and down again, this time for her benefit as much as his own, then turned to the four sets of eyes watching them from the living room floor. "Isn't your mom the most beautiful woman in the whole world, guys?" Then he swept her close and kissed her soft cherry-colored lips thoroughly, much to the dismay and disgust of their sons.

"Do you think you can find a babysitter on such short notice? I'd like to take you out tonight." He whispered against her skin as he planted kisses along the newly exposed column of her neck. She sighed softly and settled into his embrace, obviously relieved at his reaction.

· · · · ●· ●· · ·

GIA AGREED TO COME spend the evening with the boys. "I have some new music I want Reuben to hear. Taz sent Ricky a couple of albums, and I think Reuben might get into some of this stuff." She hesitated on the other end of the line. "It's not all Christian stuff; is that okay? Do you mind?"

"Is it music about sex? Doing drugs?" Renata asked, sounding censorious even to her own ears. This was Gia she was talking to.

"Oh, gosh, no! This is from Taz and some of his friends. You remember him, right? Juliette's date?"

"Yes, of course I know who Taz is, Georgia. I trust you, so if you think it's fine for Reuben to listen to, then I'm fine with it."

The reminder of Juliette's conversion during her date with the Christian musician, Trevor Zander, still rankled her a little. It wasn't because Juliette had become a Christian; no, Renata was truly thrilled about that. But last year, she, Phoebe, and Georgia had set Juliette up on a series of blind dates with some of the most eligible bachelors they knew. The shy Juliette had inadvertently sabotaged their well-laid plans by first falling in love with Jesus, thanks to the introduction from Trevor, then by falling in love with a police officer who, in Renata's opinion, was a little overzealous about his job, at least where Juliette was concerned. He had not been a contender on the list of Monday ManDates, and Renata still felt a little cheated that the intervention plan had been axed before John's friend, Tim Larsen, had his chance. She thought he was a much better fit for Juliette than the enigmatic Victor Jarrett.

One could still hope. Juliette wasn't wearing a ring yet.

"Cool! What time should I be there? And what's the occasion?"

"As soon as you get here, we'll head out. The occasion? I cut my hair."

"What?" She could tell Gia had expected something far different.

"I donated it to LoveLocks today. So, don't scream or freak out when you get here, okay? The boys are finally beginning to speak to me, and I don't want to get them all stirred up again."

"Ooh! I'm so excited to see it! I'm heading out the door right now!" Gia paused, then asked in a low voice, as though afraid he could hear her, "Does John like it?"

"He does."

"Whew! I wondered if you were including him when you said, 'the boys.' That could have been *awkward*." The way she said the word reminded Renata that her little sister was just barely out of high school and she smiled.

"Yes. Going out tonight was John's idea. He wants to show me off." She felt her cheeks flush as she met her husband's eye across the bedroom.

"That's fantabulous! I'll be there in a few minutes."

And she was. She did squeal when she saw Renata's new haircut, but she kept it muffled behind her hand. "I *love* it, Rennie! I love it. You look like a pixie! Oh my gosh, Jules and Phebes are gonna freak when they see it! I mean, in a good way!" She wrapped Renata in an exuberant hug, then turned to hug John, too. "Your wife is a hottie, mister!"

"That she is," he agreed, tugging on one of Gia's corkscrew copper curls that made her look like she was related to him rather than Renata.

John surprised Renata by taking her to a movie. At first, she was a little disappointed, but when she heard him request the tickets from the vendor, she impulsively stretched up to kiss him on the cheek. He grinned, and explained to the teenager behind the glass panel, "Chick flicks are worth every penny when you're with the right woman, my young friend."

After the movie, they headed to a little restaurant that boasted scrumptious pastries and secluded booths. They sat on the same side, pressed together, sharing each other's calorie-free-on-date-night desserts, and talking about the movie, about the boys, about Renata's day out. When she asked him how his day had gone, he grimaced a little.

"All-in-all, it's good, but I'm working with a general contractor who's pretty full of himself. I could handle that if he knew what he was talking about, but when it comes to electricity, he's liable to get someone killed if I don't stay on top of things every minute. Makes it hard to keep my head when I'm around him. They don't pay me to babysit, but I can't afford not to."

"Oh, John. I'm sorry. That makes for a long day, doesn't it?"

"Yeah, but it makes coming home to you even better." He lifted her hand from the table and brought it to his lips. "I'm glad I have you to come home to, Renata Charise Dixon."

"And I'm glad you come home to me, John Allen Dixon." It had been a long time since they'd exchanged those words; sweet nothings they used to say to each other all the time. Renata smiled, feeling content in a way she hadn't in a long time, either.

"Let's go home, shall we? I'm sure the boys are in bed. We can continue this date in our bedroom." John murmured in her ear, his chocolaty breath warm and promising against her cheek.

"I need to change my hairstyle more often," she teased, running her fingers up his thigh under the table.

"Let's get outta here."

TWELVE

The next morning, they sat across the breakfast nook from each other, still enjoying the afterglow of a night spent investing in each other. But John's brow was furrowed.

"What's wrong, husband of mine?"

He took a long sip of his coffee. "Renata, I didn't want to spoil things last night. I would love to get away with you for a couple days, go somewhere, get away for your birthday, but right now, with this big project I'm on, I don't know if I can do it any time soon. I mean, it won't happen in the next two months, minimum. When this one is over, and it's slated to be finished by mid-February, then I have the Farmhouse Development. That's going to take me weeks. I want to do something when the air is cleared, but I'm worried that you're going to be disappointed you have to wait. I really wish you'd consider doing something with your sisters next month."

And back to that again. Suddenly, the euphoria of last night evaporated. "Well, we do have a G-FOURce tonight—you'll be home on time to watch the boys, right? I'll think about it and maybe bring it up at our meeting."

"Going to do a little showing off of your own, are you? They'll love your new look, Renata." He stood up and circled the table to pull her out of her seat, drawing her up against him. She thought he blushed when he continued, "It was like being with a new woman last night. Still you, but different. Kinda sexy."

"John!" she reprimanded, blushing herself. But she understood what he meant.

She thought briefly about filling him in on Angela Clinton, but decided against it, letting him think the G-FOURce was about a haircut and a few new wardrobe items. Once she and her sisters talked, she'd know better what to tell him, anyway.

By the time the day was over, Renata wasn't looking forward to talking to her sisters about anything, especially not Angela. She couldn't get her hair to look the way it did when Cynthia was done with it, the new boots she'd bought pinched her little toe painfully after wearing them for an hour, and Sally had chewed up one of her favorite bedroom slippers.

"You haven't chewed anything in a long time, you bad girl. What were you thinking?" She couldn't help wondering if this was the dog's passive aggressive response to her new haircut. Although Harry had barked once sharply this morning when she emerged from the bedroom, the moment she spoke, he'd hurried to her side and thumped his tail against her leg. Sally, on the other hand, had eyed her balefully, her uncertainty surprising Renata this morning since she'd seemed unaware or unaffected the day before when Renata first came home.

The boys seemed louder and more obnoxious than usual, but maybe it was because she was in a bad mood. She tried to ignore them, but when Reuben threw his shoe at Simon, who ducked, and it hit Judah in the head instead, she sent them all to their rooms to play until dinner.

John arrived home late and scowling, and she could see that his day hadn't gone any better than hers. She didn't offer comfort, though, as she was feeling fragile herself. The last sparkling remnants of their romantic night out blinked once or twice, and then faded away.

"There's chicken casserole in the oven. The boys haven't eaten yet. I banished them so I could have a little peace and quiet." The words sounded ugly, like she was mocking him, but she hadn't meant them that way. John looked up at her, exhaustion evident in the dark circles under his eyes, his wary gaze studying her.

"What about you?" he asked. "Did you eat already?"

"No. I'm not really hungry. Besides, knowing Juliette, she'll have something totally inappropriate and delicious set out on the table and I'll indulge. I'll just feel guilty if I eat before going over there. I thought she'd lay off the pastries once she met a man, but that hasn't happened." Her new coat was draped over the back of the sofa and she scooped it up and slipped her arms into it, fastening the belt snugly around her waist without bothering to button it first. "The funny thing is that even with the holidays, she looks better than ever. Maybe that officer is good for her after all."

"Victor? Yeah, he's a good guy." John was leaning against the kitchen counter watching her, his hands wrapped around a hot cup of coffee.

She almost asked him about his day, but stopped herself before she did, not certain she could handle two weighty conversations in one night.

Besides, he hadn't bothered asking her about hers.

"So, homework is done, the three younger boys are bathed. Reuben will argue with you, I'm sure, but he needs to take a quick shower. He's at that age. And remind him about deodorant, okay?"

John nodded absentmindedly, still holding her gaze, but Renata could see that the wheel was turning but the hamster was miles away.

"Good. I'll try not to be too late. Don't let the boys wait up for me, but I should be home by nine at the latest."

• • • • • • • • •

WHY DIDN'T SHE JUST cross the room and slide her arms around him, instead of into that coat? He needed her to come to him tonight; he barely had the energy to hold himself upright after the day he'd had. *Acknowledge me*, he wanted to demand. *Remind me why I do what I do, day in and day out. Tell me I'm your hero.*

But she didn't. And he didn't ask out loud. He just watched her drawing invisible lines, pulling away as she pulled inside. The eyes that had flashed so brightly for him last night were shadowed and dark again. He couldn't read anything there tonight.

Scott McCain was driving him crazy. He couldn't turn his back on the man for a second, it seemed. Every time he did, wires were rerouted, shoved aside, even removed altogether.

Why did the guy even bring him into the project if he didn't need an electrician? But John knew the answer to that. McCain *did* need an electrician. He just had a hard time admitting that to anyone, himself especially. So, John had to go around behind him, double-checking all his adjustments to the project plans, making sure his own work still met code, even if McCain's left a little to be desired.

But the guy wore him out, and after the late night he and Renata had shared, as amazing as it had been, he was short on patience and kindness, or any other fruit of the Spirit today.

So, to come home to a distant and reserved Renata, especially after she'd been like a live wire in his arms just twenty-four hours before, left him numb down to the bone.

"I'm glad I have you to come home to, Renata Charise Dixon." He spoke the words without emotion today, wishing they carried the potency they had last night.

"And I'm glad you come home to me, John Allen Dixon." Renata crossed the room and patted him on the cheek. "Thanks for covering for me tonight with the boys. We can talk when I get home." Then she stood up on tiptoe and planted a quick kiss on his mouth.

He wanted to reach for her. He wanted to hold her, to find comfort in her womanliness. He wanted to tell her to stay home, to stay with him. But he didn't. He smiled at her, told her she looked beautiful, and walked her out to her car. Standing in the open door of her SUV, he leaned down to kiss her goodbye. "Hurry home to me, woman."

She offered a placating smile. "I'll be back before you have time to miss me."

"I miss you already," he said to himself, as she backed out of the driveway and drove away.

THIRTEEN

"Oh. My. Gosh!" Juliette's stilted exclamation made her hesitate just for a moment. Renata had arrived way early, but she wanted to get there before Phoebe did since Gia had already seen her new look. This way she could face each sister individually and have the support of both Gia and Juliette in case Phoebe reacted cruelly.

"Can I come in or are you going to make me stand on your front steps while you stare at me all night?"

"Oh my gosh, Rennie! You look amazing!" Juliette reached out and touched the spikes on the top of Renata's head. "Wowee-wow-wow! Look at you!" She grabbed her by the shoulders and squeezed her quickly then released her. "Come in!"

"Stop talking in exclamation points, Juliette."

"I can't help it!" she exclaimed, clapping her hands together. "Has John seen you yet?"

"Of course, he has." Renata peeled off her coat; Juliette's condo was warm and smelled like pumpkin spice.

"He must have drooled all over you!" Juliette handed her a hanger from the tiny coat closet.

"Ew. No."

"But he didn't freak out, right?"

"Of course not. He's the one who suggested I do it." Okay, so that wasn't exactly the truth, but why did her sisters automatically assume John would have an aversion to her short hair?

"I just can't stop staring at you, Ren. You look younger, and more... I don't know... fun, maybe? Not so mature." Juliette laughed and rolled her eyes. "Okay. That's not coming out right. You know what I mean, though, right?"

"Sure. I look childish and immature. Got it." But Renata was smiling, too. She knew what Juliette meant, and it felt good to have someone else see the same things she did. She followed the oldest Gustafson sister into the kitchen. "What are you cooking? It smells wonderful!"

"Now look who's talking in exclamation points." Juliette poked her in the shoulder. "So, I whipped up a batch of pumpkin scones with cinnamon cream cheese frosting to die for. I was just getting ready to test one to make sure it was worthy of being served to my favorite sisters. Do you want to be a guinea pig with me?"

Juliette's kitchen was painted in a crisp white, with white-washed cabinets and white tiled counters. But the sliding glass door that led out to the backyard and the bay window over the kitchen sink were topped with crisp apple green cornices. On the walls were black-framed prints from J. J. Jung's Camellia collection, all in shades of pinks, whites, purples, and greens. Juliette had recently discovered a sampler of them in a second-hand bookstore and pulled out her favorites, framing them, and grouping them together on one citrine colored wall. The room looked bright, clean, and fresh without looking too girlie, and although Renata preferred her ambers and reds, she did love coming into Juliette's kitchen. It was like a breath of spring air.

"I'm game," Renata said, her mouth watering at the sight of the tray of pastries on the counter. "We wouldn't want you accidentally poisoning Phoebe or Georgia, would we?" She scooped up one of the still warm scones, then cocked her head before biting off a corner. "Well, maybe Phoebe...."

"Do I need to take away your cookie, Ren? Phoebe isn't even here yet and you're already coming up with ways to sabotage her. Stop it." But Juliette was grinning.

Gia showed up fifteen minutes later, right on time, breezing in on her long legs, her cheeks pink from the cold. "Don't you *love* it?" she asked, without preamble, when she saw that Renata was already there. "I wish I was so brave. I'd look like a boy if I did that to my hair, but you? Oh my gosh, Rennie, you look like a superstar! I can't wait 'til Phoebe gets here."

Phoebe finally showed up almost fifteen minutes late. She crossed her arms and studied Renata, her head cocked to one side. A slow grin spread across her face.

"Well, look at you. Did Judah get a hold of a pair of scissors while you napped?"

Renata balked at first, but then took in the look on her sister's face. Phoebe was jealous! Of *her*! She grinned and played along. "Yep. And you should have seen his hair when I was done with him."

Phoebe obviously hadn't expected her to swing back; she could tell by the raised eyebrows and pursed lips. But her words were kind, even if they were a little forced. "I hope you paid him well." Then Phoebe hugged her tightly, much to Renata's surprise, and told her she looked beautiful.

Phoebe didn't ask about John's reaction, but rather than making Renata relieved, it only made her wonder if Phoebe didn't care, or if she, of all her sisters, knew John best. The thought made butterflies of suspicion dance in her stomach for a moment.

"Thank you. So. How about we get on with things?" She quickly changed the subject, refusing to acknowledge the butterflies, lest they morph into green-eyed giants.

After everyone lavished the essential amount of love and affection on Bob, who was convinced they'd gathered just for him, they found their places around the dining room table in the warm kitchen, armed with Juliette's scones and Gia's coffee.

"Do you want to read the letters?" Juliette got straight down to business, laying a manila folder on the table in front of her.

Phoebe held up a paint-speckled hand. "Actually, before you go any further with this, I have something to say."

Renata suddenly noticed that her sister wasn't wearing fresh lipstick. Her long dark curls, usually at least contained in a semblance of a style, looked hurriedly swept back, as though little attention had been given to how her hair looked. Even her clothes seemed subdued this evening, no extra scarves or belts, no bangles on the wrist. In fact, a closer look confirmed that Phoebe wasn't even wearing earrings. Something was definitely wrong.

"I've thought a lot about this whole situation for the last week, and as much as I love you, Jules, and as much as I can understand your need to deal with this, I've decided that I'm not ready, and I don't really want to have anything to do with it." Phoebe shook her head fiercely when Renata started to interrupt. "Let me finish, please!"

Her words were firm, almost a reprimand, and Renata clamped her mouth shut in surprise.

"Jules, I have no problem if you and Angela want to be pen-pals, nor do I take issue with either or both of you joining in," she added, waving her hand at them all collectively. "But not me. I didn't know her at all, and I barely knew her brother. I think he was in your class, right?" She shot a questioning glance at Renata.

"Oh, my goodness. I completely forgot there was a brother." Juliette's face grew pale for a moment, and Renata nodded.

"Yes. Sean. I had him in several classes the first semester of eleventh grade. He tried to talk to me, but I just couldn't." All three of her sisters turned to look at her.

"I don't ever remember you telling us this."

"It was all too weird, Juliette. You were trying to hold it together for the trial. Phoebe was too busy... being busy, and I didn't really want to think about him, no less talk about him, to anyone." She smiled at Gia. "And you were too young."

"Ren, I'm so sorry." Juliette's heartfelt apology settled on her shoulders like a warm blanket. She knew Juliette meant her words.

"It's all right, Juliette. Things are different now." Several months ago, the two of them had talked for the first time about the period after their parents' death. Juliette had been the only one of the sisters old enough to be in court every day and she'd been like the walking dead for all those months. Renata had stepped up and kept things operating as smoothly as possible, helping out the grandparents with Gia and Phoebe, and covering for Juliette when she struggled to get out of bed each morning.

Grandpa and Granny G had taken in the four orphans with open arms, but it couldn't have been an easy transition for the elderly couple. The senior Gustafsons had been enjoying their retirement, touring much of the US in a refurbished Airstream RV before the girls—aged 18, 16, 14, and 4—moved in. The camper was put on blocks that year. And the next. And the next. In fact, it wasn't until after Phoebe graduated and John and Renata were married that Grandpa had the camper towed to his mechanic's place who gave it a bumper-to-bumper tune-up. Then stowing little Gia at John and Renata's home for a summer, Grandpa and Granny G had taken the first of many road trips since then.

But while it was on blocks in the large side yard, the girls had claimed it, and they'd held their G-FOURce meetings in the comfortable old Airstream.

Even after John and Renata married, after Juliette bought her condo, and after Phoebe landed her huge monstrosity of a home-slash-studio that she'd painstakingly converted from an old, obsolete warehouse, they continued to hold their G-FOURce meetings wherever they could. Sometimes, they even took off for the weekend to a cheap motel by the beach, or up to their grandparents' mountain cabin near Lake Arrowhead, just to get away from the world and remember what it was like simply to be the Gustafson Girls.

Once Reuben was born, however, the trips became shorter, and fewer and farther between. Renata kept promising she'd make their outings a priority again once the kids were a little older, but she kept having more children. Since Judah, though, everyone's schedules had seemed more difficult to work around, so that even G-FOURce meetings were sometimes hard to schedule, no less outings and getaways. The last time the Gustafson sisters had gotten away for a long weekend was to celebrate Gia's 16th birthday two years ago.

John was suggesting she take a trip with her sisters again, like old times. But what John failed to realize was that people change. Lives move in different directions, with different priorities and different motivating factors. As much as she loved her sisters, Renata knew they had very little in common with her. None of them were married, for starters. They didn't understand the first thing about what it meant to live with someone else, to compromise on every aspect of daily life, to take into consideration another human being's feelings every time you loaded the toilet paper roll or folded the laundry. And even though they babysat regularly and loved her boys to a fault, none of them were actually mothers. None of them could relate to that hollow place that opened up when she was away from her children.

And now, Angela Clinton was threatening to divide them even further. Why, oh *why*, did Juliette act on her own? She should have known that this whole thing would need kid gloves and patience and understanding.

On the other hand, Phoebe was drawing a pretty hard line, and Renata felt her hackles rising in defense of Juliette. It was Juliette who had to endure sitting in the courtroom while lawyers dehumanized their parents, turning their devastating loss into statistics and sterile labels: victims, perpetrators, deceased, survivors, alcohol consumption, margin of error, intoxication level, legal, illegal, crime, manslaughter, guilty, not guilty, sentence, ruling.

It was Renata who climbed into bed next to Juliette and held her at night when she didn't even know she cried in her sleep. Phoebe had been too busy avoiding her own pain to comfort anyone, hiding behind her black eyeliner and black book of boyfriends. Nothing had changed, at least not where Phoebe was concerned. Run and hide, play hard to get, and even harder to hold down. Phoebe was selfish, self-centered, and self-serving.

Juliette didn't see Phoebe the way Renata did. Shortly after their parents died, they used to argue about Phoebe because Renata worried for her, while Juliette thought the girl would be fine.

"She's just dealing with stuff her own way, Ren. She seems okay to me. Just because she wants to wear stuff you and I wouldn't be caught dead in, who cares?"

"But she won't talk to me about anything. Not seriously, anyway. She turns every conversation into a sarcastic joke. How will we know she's okay?"

"Maybe she doesn't talk seriously to us, but who's to say she isn't talking to someone else? I don't know that I'd want to unload on my big sisters if I was her. In fact, you don't really share much about your life with me, Rennie."

"But you already know everything about me, because I have nothing to hide. I'm a productive member of society. I'm a senior who actually studies. I bought my own car with money I made from my own job. I have a plan for college and a career. I've got things pretty much figured out, and if I talk about my life, you guys will just accuse me of bragging."

Juliette just shrugged off Renata's concerns. "Maybe that's why she doesn't talk to you, Ren. Maybe she knows she can't measure up."

Juliette spoke softly in those days, but her words had been a double-edged sword in Renata's heart. Why couldn't her sisters be proud of her, of all that she'd accomplished before she even graduated from high school? No, instead, they distanced themselves from her because they couldn't compete with her. She wasn't trying to compete, though. She was trying to move forward, grow up, and take charge of her life.

"I just want the best for her, Juliette." Renata's young voice rang with idealism. But Phoebe continued to challenge the boundaries and push the limits, and Renata knew the day would come when Phoebe went too far, when she would be too wild, and she would end up devastated.

Never in a million years did Renata guess that it would be she who was so badly wounded by Phoebe's games, not Phoebe. The memory of those dark days had her narrowing her eyes at the woman across the table from her now.

"Well, perhaps, Phoebe, you should set aside your own feelings for once and consider Juliette's. I know it's a tall order, but have you thought for even a moment how important closure like this might be for the rest of the family? You're not the only one who lost her parents, you know." She could feel the heat creeping up her neck, and she instinctively reached over her shoulder to draw her long hair around. Instead, her fingers only brushed the spiky tips of her new identity, and she felt inexplicably vulnerable.

"Like I said, Renata, I have been thinking of almost nothing else since our last meeting. I *am* considering Juliette's feelings—*all* of your feelings—by giving you my blessing to go ahead with this. But I'm also asking you to consider *my* feelings by letting me not participate. How on earth is that not allowing for closure here?" Phoebe didn't raise her voice. She didn't squirm, she didn't frown. In fact, if anything, Phoebe looked like a sleepy jungle cat right now; cool, calm, languidly toying with a long tendril of thick, black hair. She gazed unflinchingly as she spoke, and Renata knew Phoebe's relaxed posture was more menacing than any other stance she might take.

But she doggedly pressed on. "This is a family, Phoebe. You're a part of this family, whether you like it or not. And that makes you part of the next step in healing the wounds. Don't you think it's time to grow up?"

"Hold up, Ren. It's okay. I should have—" Juliette put out a hand to stop her, but Phoebe spoke too, her voice a dangerous purr.

"Listen to me, Pixie-cut. I am not your child. I am not your project. I am not your enemy, either. But I *am* tired of you thinking you're so much wiser and more mature than anyone else in this family. You are so full of your own hot air that you can't even hear how pathetic you sound, flapping your little gums at us. 'I'm married and you're not. I have children and you don't. I have a life and you have nothing. I'm perfect and you're a sinner bound for hell.'" Phoebe's purr had turned into a snarl. "You wanna know something, Renata Gustafson? I would sell my soul to the devil rather than be like you."

"Phoebe!" Gia gasped, her amber cat-eyes wide and bright with shock. Juliette just closed her own, her shoulders sagging.

"Dixon. My name is Renata Dixon. Like you said, I'm married." Renata's voice trembled as she responded with the only thing she could mentally grab out of the mushroom cloud in her head.

"No! *Not* Dixon, Renata." Phoebe stood abruptly, startling them all, her chair falling backwards and crashing loudly against the tile floor. Bob yipped and scurried to Juliette's side. "How dare you accuse *me* of not wanting to be a part of this family!" She lifted a finger and jabbed it in Renata's direction, her gray eyes dark as thunderclouds. "You are the only one of us who balks at being called by the Gustafson name. The only one."

Renata sat in stunned silence as Phoebe's words flew at her like buckshot from one of John's guns. She hadn't seen her like this since high school, since the night of that terrible homecoming dance, Renata's senior year. These days, Phoebe teased and toyed, poked and jabbed, but she didn't lash out, not like this.

Not like she used to.

FOURTEEN

Fifteen years earlier....

Halfway through her junior year, about five months after her parents died, Brad Haley sought Renata out. Brad wasn't the biggest jock, or the coolest guy in school, but he had this certain charm that made him popular, and Renata had the same crush on him that every other girl in her class did.

She'd just come out of her Literature class and was making her way through the crowded hallways when a hand was suddenly on her shoulder. She spun around in surprise, and he plowed into her, caught off guard himself, not expecting her to stop so abruptly. In an effort to keep them both from tumbling to the floor, he snaked one arm around her waist and planted the other hand against the locker-lined wall. Renata's school binder was jostled out of her arms and fell, one corner landing on her big toe. She grunted in pain.

"Sorry, sorry!" Brad exclaimed, steadying them both. "I didn't mean for that to happen!" He grinned down at her, holding her against the wall while people skirted around them as though their collision was a common occurrence in the school passages. "Are you okay? Did I hurt you?"

"No. I mean, yes." Completely flustered, Renata stammered over her words. She'd never been pressed up against a young man's body before. Brad was not like her tall, burly father, nor was he anything like Grandpa, who hugged the girls regularly, but with old-fashioned reserve, always keeping his much leaner body angled away. Brad, on the other hand, had no such reservations, confidently thrusting himself against her, using his body to keep her upright. Renata, senses coming alive, felt every inch of

"""

the connection between them. In fact, if he hadn't had his legs firmly planted on either side of hers, she probably wouldn't be standing. His close proximity was doing something odd to her equilibrium.

Brad waited, the knowing smile not leaving his face, his chocolate eyes studying her freely, making her blush.

"I mean, yes, I'm okay, and no, you didn't hurt me." She tried to straighten and pull away a little. He released her slowly, and she had the sneaking suspicion that he liked the way her body had felt up against his, as well. "I'm sorry, too. For stopping right in front of you."

Brad shook his head and abruptly grew serious, as though suddenly remembering something. He stepped back, shoving his hands in his pockets. "It's no problem. Hey. I just wanted you to know that I heard about your folks. I'm really sorry, Renata. I can't even imagine."

If she'd been stunned by his attention, she was even more surprised by his sentiment. Surprised he knew who she was, no less that he knew enough about her to have heard about her parents. Maybe he was a friend of Sean's? But she didn't remember him and Sean hanging out more than in passing.

Maybe, just maybe, he'd been noticing her, too.

The rest of their junior year, Brad had made a game of sneaking up behind her, until she no longer jumped, squealed, spun around, or dropped anything. "Hey, Brad," she'd calmly say, as her heart swelled under his attention. They walked the halls together, he teasing her, she blushing. Why he didn't have a girlfriend was beyond her. He was handsome, gregarious, self-possessed, and he never seemed to lack for friends. One day, as he walked her to her car, where she always had to wait for Phoebe, he asked her why she wasn't dating anyone.

"I guess I can be a little stand-offish. My grades are pretty important and I'm not a cheerleader or anything," Renata replied, after thinking things through a little. "I suppose I'm just not that easy to get close to."

Without warning, Brad grabbed her around the waist with both arms and pushed her gently up against the side of her little Sentra. "I don't know about that. I don't seem to have any trouble getting close to you." Then he lowered his head slowly, while she held her breath, and he kissed her.

His lips on hers were sweet, tender, startlingly warm. Her first kiss. He must have sensed it, because he didn't push her. He didn't try to make her open her mouth; he didn't grope at her backside or squeeze her too tightly. He just kissed her. Three times. Then he stepped back, that grin still eating up his face.

"Ahem." Phoebe stood at the back of the car, a smirk on her sticky-glossed lips. "You call that a kiss?"

What had been so intimate and lovely only a moment ago became tainted. Renata felt like a voyeur, like she'd done something wrong; not only that, but she also felt like she'd done it badly. She knew Phoebe was no novice kisser; she'd caught the girl lip-locked more often than she cared to think about. But to have her own first—and possibly not so great—kiss witnessed and judged by her younger sister made her angry. The possibility that Brad might agree with Phoebe's assessment made Renata sick to her stomach, and she yanked open her car door and climbed in.

Brad and Phoebe exchanged a few quick words that Renata couldn't make out, then Phoebe was pulling open the passenger side door and lowering her scantily clad backside into the seat beside Renata.

"Rennie, I'm so sorry. That was stupid of me to say. I didn't mean it. I was just teasing you two, okay?" Phoebe's apology was obviously heartfelt and sincere, but Renata bristled.

"Whatever. Just sit there and be quiet." She couldn't look at her.

"I mean it. I feel terrible. I could tell you were hurt by what I said. I'm really sorry. I should have just kept my big mouth shut."

"Yes, you should have. Now you can make it up to me by keeping it shut the rest of the ride home. Buckle up."

Phoebe buckled her seat belt, turned to stare out the window, and didn't say another word to Renata for the rest of the day.

Over the next two weeks, Renata walked around on pins and needles. Brad treated her as though nothing had changed between them, but she felt like the earth had shifted on its axis and was holding its breath with her.

A week before school was out for the summer, Brad told her he really liked her and that he wanted to go out with her. Just as her heart stopped, he continued. "It's only that I'm going to spend the summer in Washington with my Dad. He really wants me to move up there with him, but I'm hoping if I spend the whole summer up there, he'll be okay with letting me come back here and finish my senior year."

"Oh. I see." She couldn't tell if he was asking her out or not.

"It wouldn't be fair to you, Renata. I don't even know for sure that I'll be back. And what if you meet someone else and fall in love over the summer?" They walked slowly to her car, an almost daily occurrence. "I don't want to feel like a ball and chain around your ankle. I want you to be free to follow your heart. If it leads you back to me, and you're not seeing anyone when, and if, I come back, well...." He shrugged, his voice trailing off, his hands deep in his pockets.

Renata maintained her composure until she was in the car. Phoebe took one look at her face when she arrived, climbed quietly into her own seat, and the two of them drove away, Renata's silent tears like a wall between them.

They had a G-FOURce scheduled for that weekend already to talk about summer plans and how old little Gia had to be before she could be ushered into their sister society. By the time they sat cross-legged in the Airstream, heavily-doctored coffees in hand, Renata was dry-eyed and confident.

"He doesn't want me to feel tied down, that's all," she explained to her curious, albeit concerned, sisters. "He's trying to be sensitive to me. I think it's sweet."

Juliette sat at the little fold-out dining table, toying with the handle of her cup. She wore a pair of dark blue jeans and a turquoise shirt that made her skin glow under the light over her head. Her long hair was pulled up in a clip, but soft tendrils caressed her face, making her look luminous and fragile. "Sounds like he's a real gentleman, Renata. What do you think, Phoebe?"

"Sounds like he's full of crap, like he doesn't want to be tied down himself." Phoebe's kohl-lined eyes had narrowed as she listened to Renata relay her conversation with Brad to them. "He's been stringing you along all this time and now he's going to string you along even longer so that he can go have his fun while you keep the home fires burning for him."

"Well, aren't we cynical," Renata retorted. "You obviously don't know Brad very well." But she hated the way her scalp tingled in reaction to her little sister's words. Something resonated in her; something she didn't want to face, so she pushed it away by taking jabs at Phoebe. "What do you know, anyway? You're just a kid who thinks she's too big for her britches."

"I may think I'm too big for my britches, but you actually *are* too big for yours. You might want to think about buying a size or two up." Phoebe's voice was cool and low, but so much more deadly than Renata's heated jabs.

"Guys, please." Juliette's calm voice cut in before Renata could think of anything to say. "Look, he sounds like he's being gentlemanly, but even if he was doing it more for his own reasons, isn't it better that he doesn't make some kind of promise that he might end up breaking in the end?"

Renata's heart lurched at the thought of Brad kissing anyone else.

"Besides, we can't know his thoughts," Juliette continued, ignoring the deadly glares being exchanged between the other two. "But Renata, you do know him better than we do, and he sounds nice enough. Maybe we should just take him at his word. All we can do is hope for the best, right?"

Phoebe rolled her eyes, making Renata wish she could poke them out.

Brad did leave for the summer. And he did return three days before their senior year began.

But it wasn't until the end of the first day of school that Renata found out that Brad was back in town. From Phoebe. She climbed into the passenger seat and eyed Renata askance. "What?"

"Nothing," Phoebe responded, turning to stare out the window.

"Why were you looking at me like that?" Renata had dressed so carefully for this day. She'd hoped beyond hope that Brad would be there, that he would sneak up behind her in the hallway, grab her around the waist, and haul her up against the lockers, and kiss her with the sheer delight of a man come home. By the time school was out, she was so tightly wound that she couldn't take Phoebe's furtive glances. "What were you going to say?"

Phoebe turned back and studied her for a few moments. Then her eyes were drawn past Renata and out her window. "I take it you haven't seen Brad yet."

Renata spun around and looked. Brad was crossing the parking lot, making his way casually between cars, his arms around two of his classmates. Both females. They were laughing and carrying on like old friends, and Renata's heart lurched. Where had he been all day? Why didn't he look for her? Why didn't he find her? Didn't he know she'd be waiting for him? Why didn't he tell her he was back?

At that moment, his eyes met hers, and the smile fell away from his face. Then he tipped his head as though to peer past her into the car, saw Phoebe, and hurried over, dragging his friends along with him.

"Turn the car on and leave now," Phoebe ground out between clenched teeth.

"I can't. He's coming. He's already seen us." Renata was at a loss, her hands suddenly shaking so hard she dropped the keys.

"Don't roll down your window, Ren."

"I have to. I can't just ignore him." She was close to tears. Phoebe snaked a bangle-draped arm across the console and snatched the keys off the floorboard, fluidly shoving the key into the ignition and turning it to start the automatic engine. The little car leapt to life just as Brad tapped on the window.

Renata paused just for a moment, then reached for the lever, lowering the glass about halfway. "Hey Brad." Her voice sounded remarkably calm.

"Renata. Man, it's good to see you. You guys know each other, right?" At least he didn't have his arms around Molly and Jenna anymore. The two girls were also seniors this year, and although Renata knew who they were, she was fairly certain they had no clue who she was.

"Hey, Phoebe," Molly leaned over and wiggled her fingers at Phoebe almost in Renata's face. "Are you two related?"

"Hey, Molly." Phoebe leaned forward a little and smiled brightly at the girl. "Hi, Jenna. Yes, this is my sister, Renata."

Jenna blinked owlishly at Phoebe, then turned the same stare on Renata. "Wow. She's as pretty as you are, Phoebe. Hi. I'm Jenna." The tall girl stuck out a soft, limp hand through the window, forcing Renata to roll it down the rest of the way. "Your sister's a jewel, isn't she? It's good to meet you."

Renata shook her hand, overwhelmed by the information being revealed to her in such a strange way, and looked at Brad to see him studying Phoebe. Oh, how she wished she could roll the window back up and drive away. This was not how she imagined her reunion with him.

"Hey Phoebe. Good to see you, too." Brad winked at her, and Renata wanted to scream. She kept the smile plastered on her face. Then Brad reached out and brushed her cheek with the back of his hand. "I'm glad I caught you two before you left. I'll call you tonight, Renata, okay?"

"Um, okay. I'll see you later, then." She nodded at him, then at Jenna, who wasn't even paying attention to the conversation any longer. Then she looked at Molly. She was pretty, petite, with bouncy, brown hair and big blue eyes, and she was frantically mouthing something at Phoebe. When she saw Renata watching her, she stopped and smiled brightly.

"Good to meet you, Renata. I'll look for you in the halls. It's going to be a great year, isn't it?" As odd as it seemed, the girl sounded genuine, so she nodded.

"Sounds great." Brad patted both hands on the top of the car and stepped back, colliding with Jenna, who had her back to him and was watching another group of students across the way. Brad spun around and caught her when she squealed, laughing and pulling her back to his side. She draped an arm over his shoulder and started to drag him away. Untangling himself, but still chuckling, he turned back to blow a kiss at Renata. She winced, and Molly leaned close.

"Don't mind Jenna. She's a flirt, but she's not girlfriend material, if you know what I mean. Too many free samples."

"Ew," Phoebe frowned.

"Yeah. Ew. And Brad knows better. He's just happy to be home. If he said he'll call you, Renata, he will. Don't worry." Then she hurried to catch up to the other two.

The terrible silence that followed was more than Renata could bear. She put the car in gear and drove away, desperately hoping Phoebe wouldn't feel compelled to explain how she knew those two girls. Or Brad.

Brad did call. He talked sweetly to her, making her forget all her reservations. Within a week, they were officially dating.

He started coming by the house, hanging out after school, sometimes even staying for dinner. He often sat too close to her on the sofa, and just grinned cockily when she whispered to him to scoot over a bit. Sometimes his hand would slip under the dinner table and begin a slow glide up her thigh until she was certain her blushing cheeks would catch on fire.

When she walked him to his car at the end of the day, he'd boldly draw her up against him, in plain view of anyone who might be watching. She'd plant her palms on his chest and push as he pulled, his sweet words and sweeter smiles turning her into putty in his hands.

His hands. She loved his hands, but he used them like battering rams against her defenses. She'd tell him no; he'd sweep the word away with his fingers in her hair. "I love it when you wear it down like this, loose and wild around your face." He'd smooth away her resistance with his palms as he cupped her neck, her cheeks, bringing her face to his for more delicious kisses. He'd block her hesitation with his arms as he drew her closer, whispering to her promises of what he could awaken in her if only she'd say yes.

And every once in a while, she'd catch him looking at Phoebe with something in his eyes that made her seriously consider it.

FIFTEEN

There was something about Phoebe that drew people's attention, and Brad was not immune. He teased her incessantly, often to an extreme that frustrated and annoyed Renata. The more attention he plied Phoebe with, even if it was sarcastic jabs and inappropriate innuendos, the less he focused on Renata. Sometimes she wondered if he would even notice if she got up and left the room.

It wasn't like Phoebe blatantly went after him. In fact, she usually rolled her eyes when she saw him. But when he teased her, Phoebe gave back as good as she got, always ready with a saucy little comeback or a well-timed double entendre that would leave him grinning and shaking his head at her. No, back then Renata would not have called it seduction. But back then, Renata was blissfully unaware of the fine art of flirtation and the game called Playing Hard to Get.

October arrived, and Renata bought her first homecoming dress with a fitted bodice in emerald satin and a flouncy full skirt that swished around her thighs when she walked. On the arm of Brad Haley, she felt like a queen.

The Starry Night theme transformed the auditorium into a magical world. Blue and white tulle strung with a million white lights draped the rafters, and yellow paper lantern orbs floated over their heads on transparent fishing line. Even the backdrop of the stage was a monstrous reproduction of Van Gogh's famous painting. The band was a group from their own school, but they were surprisingly talented, playing a good balance of upbeat party songs and slower, couples-friendly dance music. The refreshments were delicious, the bathrooms were kept fairly clean by some unseen attendant, and she loved hearing Brad introduce her again and again as his girlfriend. He seemed to know everyone.

When it was time to leave, instead of taking her home, he drove them to a friend's house, where he wedged his car into a spot among several others. "Where are we?" Renata asked, trying not to sound worried. She didn't want anything to ruin the most glorious night she'd ever experienced.

"My friend is having a Homecoming party of his own. I want to show you off." He grabbed her hand and pulled her toward him across the console between them. He kissed her, hard, then softer, then both his hands were on her face, holding her there while he devoured her lips. "Don't say no, Renata. Not tonight. Let's celebrate."

In the afterglow of the perfect evening spent in the perfect dress with the perfect guy, Renata could only whisper a bright-eyed, "Yes."

Until a few drinks later, and Brad wanted more than a yes. When she tearfully insisted that he take her home, his grin was no longer sweet, but mocking, and a little angry.

"You know, last year, I was cool to hang out with you. I kinda thought you were cute with your big eyes, watching every move I made." He reached out and slid his arm around her just like he'd done that first day they'd collided in the halls and thrust her up against the wall again. "When I left for Washington, I was sure I'd come back to find you making eyes at some other guy. So, when you got all upset at me that first day back at school, I realized I might just have a good thing here. But all you ever say is 'no,' little girl. No, you can't. No, I won't. No, let's not. No, no, no." He chuckled, not a nice sound, leaning so far to the right that he almost lost his balance. "I'm tired of your games. I'm tired of you always saying 'no.' I want you to tell me 'yes.'"

He tried to kiss her, and she ducked her head, mortified and actually frightened. These were his friends, not hers, and she didn't know what would happen if he really wasn't going to take 'no' for an answer. "Take me home, Brad. I just want to go home."

"Nah, I'm not ready to go yet." He nuzzled her neck, his breath hot and moist on her skin.

"Stop it, Brad!" Renata pushed against him and he stumbled a little, then narrowed his eyes at her.

"Fine. Do you think Phoebe's here yet?"

"Phoebe?" Renata was completely taken aback by the question. "What do you mean?"

"Your sister, Phoebe. You remember her, right? Have you seen her yet?" He spoke slowly, but she couldn't tell if it was because he was drunk, or because he thought she was stupid. He spread his arms wide to indicate the crowded room behind him. "Obviously, I have the wrong sister on my arm tonight. I should have brought Phoebe. Now there's a girl who says 'yes' a little more often than you do."

Renata took advantage of the sudden freedom and pushed him away from her. Turning to make her way toward the front of the house, she heard him holler at her over the din of sound, "Run on home to mommy, little girl!"

Renata called Juliette from a payphone at a gas station a block away, thankful she hadn't left her purse in Brad's car like he'd suggested. The walk wasn't too scary since people were coming and going on the street, most of them heading to and from the party she'd left.

Phoebe. Was she really at that party? And just how well did Brad know her little sister?

When Juliette pulled up at the curb, a worried frown on her face, Renata knew the night was going to get worse before it got better.

• • • • • • • • • •

Now here they sat, the G-FOURce, the open wounds of their memories raw between them, and no one said a word. Finally, Phoebe righted her chair and began to gather her things. When Juliette didn't stop her, when she didn't jump in to play peacemaker, Renata knew her eldest sister was asking her to step up. But as adamant as Phoebe was about not being like her, Renata was just as adamant about not giving Phoebe an ounce of grace.

Gia, her eyes still bright with unshed tears, finally spoke. "No one has asked me what I think about this whole situation, but I'm going to tell you, anyway. I don't know Angela like you three did, and I have to admit, keeping her a faceless entity seems like a good plan to me, but that's only because I'm chicken." She tugged nervously on a section of her hair. "I can't even imagine being in her shoes. When I think about being in prison at my age, I feel like I can't breathe. It must be terrible. Are we responsible for her circumstances? No. But can we help? I don't know. I'd like to think so."

She stood up and Renata stared at the black buttons on the girl's brown plaid western-style shirt.

"I don't know Maman and Papa the way you three did, but I do know enough about them to know that they wouldn't be happy with this. I love you. All of you. But sometimes I get tired of watching you punch each other in the head. I don't think I can remember a single time you two have been together when you didn't snip and snap at each other."

Renata raised her eyes to her little sister's face and saw her flushed cheeks and the determined tightness of her mouth. She didn't like looking up at her; it made her feel inferior. "Sit down, Georgia."

"Excuse me? Did I hear a 'please' in that command? Or did you just order her to sit down, like she was one of your children?" Phoebe's voice was tight, angry, as she leaned across the table in Renata's direction. "Gia—that's her name, by the way—is not your child. I am not your child. Jules is not your child. We're sisters, Renata. Equal footing. You don't like it; you can just leave."

"All right." Now Renata pushed up from the table, and without further ado, she scooped up her purse and turned to go.

No one stopped her. No one called her name. She made it to the front door before she glanced behind her through Juliette's living room and into the kitchen where she could see the three of them around the table, Juliette still sitting, head down, Phoebe and Georgia still standing, both staring at the top of Juliette's head.

No one cared when she pulled open the door and slipped out into the cold January night.

SIXTEEN

The confrontation was like hot pokers stabbing into those places she tried to avoid. Renata didn't want to think about that night almost fifteen years ago. She didn't want to replay, yet again, the terrible words she and Phoebe had screamed at each other, Juliette's huge eyes in her pale face as she watched them from the easy chair in the corner of the living room, the raised voice of Grandpa when he'd had enough. Granny G sat on the sofa in silence, watching the familial ties splitting and snapping between the two sisters, as Phoebe stood just inside the front door in her wild get-up, trembling with rage and defiance, while Renata, home for nearly two hours and primed with a different kind of rage, attacked her with scathing accusations and judgment.

"You think you're so wonderful, don't you? You think your looks and your perfect little body are going to get you anywhere in the real world? You're a slut, Phoebe Gustafson, a smear on the good name of this family. You're trash. Your looks and your body and the way you barely keep it covered are going to get you somewhere, I can assure you. On your back, that's where!"

"Enough! How dare you talk to your sister that way, Renata!" Grandpa stormed into the room, his hair sticking up all over his head.

"How dare she seduce my boyfriend right under my nose!" She turned her angry voice on him. "How can you let her out of the house looking like that? Don't you know what kind of a person she is? Don't you care what she's doing to this family?"

Grandpa reached for her, and Renata flinched, certain he was going to strike her for her belligerence, but he only took her in his arms, hugging her closely, unreservedly for the first time that she could remember.

Suddenly, she burst into tears, sobbing against his bony chest, the pain of betrayal and abandonment rising up in her like a wounded animal. How could Phoebe have been so cruel? Why did Brad have to be so shallow? Why did Maman and Papa have to leave them to face the future without them?

And now, fifteen years later, Renata pulled over on the side of the road and wept like she hadn't done since that night, her body heaving, her tears of anger and resentment clawing their way up and out of her.

How dare her sisters dismiss her? How dare they shoo her off like she was an irritating insect? And why didn't Juliette stop her? Why didn't Georgia, her sweet, precious Georgia, come running after her, beg her to stay? And why on earth had Phoebe attacked her so cruelly in the first place?

How dare they change the rules?

How she wished again for a mother she could run to. Granny G was wonderful, but she was Granny G, not Maman. "Why were you always late to everything, Maman? Why couldn't you be on time, just that one time? Ten minutes earlier, and you and Papa would still be here."

· · · · **·** · **·** · · ·

Any other night, John would have gone to bed by ten and slept like the dead, waking up just enough to greet his wife when she crawled in bed beside him. But in the hours that she'd been gone, his need for her had only grown. In the deepest recesses of his mind, he longed for her the way a child does for his mother, the solace of being held to her soft breasts, a soothing voice murmuring in his ear that she loved him and was proud of him. It disconcerted him a bit to think about Renata that way, but it was the kind of comfort he needed tonight.

By 10:30, she still wasn't home, and he began to worry. He didn't want to call her, didn't want to intrude on her time with her sisters, but Renata was the kind of person who, when she was more than a few minutes later than planned, always called him. Without fail.

The show he'd turned on couldn't hold his attention, and the late-night commercials exploiting sex and glamorizing ungodly lifestyles, the ones he could usually tune out, really bothered him tonight. He was a wreck, and he needed his wife.

John flipped the television off and sat in the resonating silence, listening for the low hum of her engine, tires on the driveway. Only the light over the kitchen sink was still on, but it cast a peaceful glow over the open floor plan of their home. His eyes rested on Harry and Sally, knowing the dogs would hear Renata's car long before he did.

Finally, giving in to his growing anxiety, he called her cell phone, but didn't leave a message. Ten minutes later, he tried again and asked her to call him as soon as she could. And ten minutes after that, he called again, and when he still couldn't reach her, he dialed Juliette's phone. In a sleepy voice, she answered. When he told her Renata wasn't home yet, his sister-in-law immediately offered to come stay with the kids while he went looking for his wife.

John was just shoving his arms into his jacket when he heard the garage door go up, then saw headlights flash across the front window. His heart, he was sure, paused to listen, too, and he pressed a hand over his chest in a subconscious effort to remind it to start beating again. He texted Juliette to let her know not to come, then laid his phone, keys, and wallet on the counter. He removed his jacket, tossed it over the back of the sofa, and went to the sink to get a glass of water, his throat painfully dry.

The last time he'd felt this needy, this impotent, was when his wife lay screaming in a hospital bed, trying to deliver a nine-pound baby into the world. He was a man, for crying out loud. His hands weren't supposed to shake and his knees wobble.

She slipped in from the garage, obviously trying to be as quiet as she could, but stopped abruptly when she saw him standing at the sink.

"Oh!" she gasped, her voice hushed. "You're awake."

"Where have you been?" The question came out like a gunshot, and he saw her flinch. "I've been worried sick," he amended, his voice gentler, but still gruff.

"I'm okay. I'm sorry. I didn't think you'd wait up." She kept her face angled away, but he knew her better than anyone, and he could tell she'd been crying. "I just had a few things to think about after our meeting, and I needed a little extra quiet time."

"A little extra time? Renata, you left Juliette's house almost three hours ago! Why didn't you answer your phone?" He took a step toward her, but she turned away and crossed to the closet by the front door, shrugging out of her coat. He followed, taking it from her, and hanging it up for her.

She still wouldn't look at him, but when she spoke, it was his turn to flinch. "I didn't want to talk to you, John. I needed some time to myself. I didn't want to have to explain anything, not in the condition I was in, a condition you're obviously already aware of since you must have spoken to one of my *sisters*." The word came out harsh, full of venom. "I needed to sort things out on my own. I didn't mean to worry you," she said again.

"What did you expect, Renata? We do care about you, you know." She rolled her eyes, but in the low light, he saw them fill with tears again, and he reached for her, pulling her hard up against his chest in a fierce hug, battling with the need to comfort her and attack her at the same time.

"Why didn't you just come home?" he murmured into her spiky hair, so unfamiliar against his cheek. He stepped back and released her, but she didn't answer.

"You could have at least called to tell me you were going to be late." He scrubbed the top of his head with both hands in frustration at the stubborn expression on her face. "I would have left you alone, you know. You could have taken a bath, sat in the room by yourself, whatever. We do have doors here." He turned and crossed back to the sink where he'd left his glass of water. He needed to stop talking. "You could always just *ask* for some privacy and close the door. At least we would have known where you were, that you were alive and not lying on the side of the road somewhere."

"I wasn't ready to come home, John. Give me a break."

He stared at her, the battle heating up inside him. "Give you a break? A break from what, might I ask?"

She just stood there in the entryway, poised as though uncertain whether to come inside or turn and leave again.

"For Pete's sake, Renata! Why do you have to be so selfish? Why can't you think about me? About your family? Doesn't it matter to you that we were all worried out of our minds? Sitting by our phones, wondering, waiting, praying that you're alive! What is wrong with you?" He was pacing again, anger winning this round. "Snap out of it, Renata! You're not an island. You're my wife and I need you. I love you, woman. Your sisters do, too." He gestured down the hall where he hoped the boys still slept. He lowered his voice, but it still rang with his wrath. "And I'm sorry about the miscarriages. I really am. But you still have four other children who need you, too. You're still a part of this family, whether you like it or not!"

Her eyes widened at those words, and he knew he'd gone too far. She blinked once, quite slowly, then turned and walked away from him toward their bedroom. She didn't close the door, and for a moment, he wondered if he was supposed to follow her. He stood there, undecided, but then he heard the door to their bathroom close softly.

When she came out an hour later, he was in bed, wide awake and dreading the early morning looming when he'd have to deal with more McCain. He was in desperate need of a good night's sleep, but he didn't see that happening. He wasn't angry at Renata anymore, not really. But worry had replaced the frustration, and it ate at him in a different way. He wanted his wife back; that was all there was to it, and he was getting tired of clawing through her defenses to find her.

He'd left her bedside lamp on and lay facing her side of the bed, unwilling to let her get in without dealing with him. She moved around the room, putting things away and straightening the few things out of order on her dresser, every action intentional and smooth, but he could tell in the way she held her shoulders that she knew he was awake and watching. The room filled with the fragrance of her, a citrus and rose lotion she used after her baths, one that made him want to press his face to her skin. He resisted the urge to speak first, to beckon her to his side.

"You were right, John," she said without looking at him.

He waited, not breathing. Just waited. Finally, she crossed to the bed, removed her robe, and slipped beneath the covers beside him. She wore one of the silky little nightgowns she liked far more than he did because the fabric caught and snagged on his work-roughened hands. Her face was in shadows now, the lamp shining from behind her, and he reached out and cupped her cheek, bridging the gap between them.

"I'm not doing so well, and I know it. I need to get away. Alone." She covered his hand with her own, then brought it to her lips and planted a kiss on his palm. "I'm going to take a few days up at the cabin, okay? I'll call Gia and see if she can help out with the kids. Maybe she can even stay here. She doesn't mind sleeping on the couch."

John didn't move. If she'd asked him to come with her, he would have said 'no' anyway. His schedule was so tight right now, he couldn't. But something in the way she'd said 'alone' made him feel inadequate, expendable, and it gnawed at him. Knowing the lamp glow was actually lighting his face up, and she could see any expression that crossed it, he carefully kept it blank. "Sounds like a plan, Renata. Let's talk about it tomorrow, okay?" Then he leaned forward, kissed her perfect mouth, and pulled his hand from hers. "I need to get some sleep. I love you, baby. Good night."

"Aren't you going to pray for us?" she asked, as he started to roll away from her. John prayed for them every night.

"I already did." He settled onto his side, pulling the blankets up over his shoulders.

"Without me here?"

"Yes." He kept his back to her, wondering if she'd turn over and read or press her body against him. He felt her shift away from him and he sighed, begging sleep to come quickly.

The lamp went off.

"John Allen Dixon, are you pouting?" And then she was there, sliding her arms around his waist beneath the blankets. "Aren't you a little big for that?" she whispered. "I'm sorry, John-boy. I love you."

He wanted to be done with the turbulence of the night. He needed to turn over and take her in his arms and tell her all was forgiven, that everything was all right.

But he didn't. Instead, he reached back and gave her hip a placating pat over the covers. "I'm not pouting. I'm tired. Exhausted. Work is terrible and I just need some sleep before I have to get up and face another day of listening to McCain bludgeon us all with his know-how, proving his lack thereof. I was hoping for a peaceful evening at home, a little down time with you, but that didn't happen. I'm all good with that. I understand you needed your time to yourself, but I'm not going to pretend that I don't wish things had gone differently tonight. I forgive you, and I love you, too."

He checked his alarm clock one more time, then put his head back on the pillow. "Go to sleep, Renata."

"You need to kiss me goodnight, John. Always kiss me goodnight." Now she was pouting.

He turned briefly, puckered his lips, waited for her to come to him, then rolled back on his side away from her. "I love you, Renata Dixon."

"I love you, too, John Dixon," she whispered in the dark.

SEVENTEEN

The road snaked out in front of her as she listened to the deep-voiced crooner on the radio. Renata had downloaded several audiobooks, knowing she wouldn't be able to tolerate just listening to music during the long hours behind the wheel. The first book she'd put in had been a terrible flop, though. The woman who read sounded like she needed to swallow, and by the end of the first chapter, Renata was so grossed out, she turned it off and put on the music instead. She wasn't daunted; she had four more books to choose from when she was ready, and thankfully, none of them were read by the same narrator.

February in Southern California brought weather as unpredictable as the earthquakes the state was known for, and this week was looking to be right on track. Between dark-bellied clouds casting moving shadows, shafts of sunlight beaconed the wet ground, causing everything to sparkle as though the earth had been sprinkled with glitter. She'd taken the back roads toward the mountains, staying off the dirty, crowded freeways as much as she could. She didn't usually mind them—they were a necessary evil for California residents—but today, Renata had no desire to mingle with humanity, and was enjoying the drive through smaller communities and farmlands, horses, cattle, and even llamas dotting hillsides and pastures.

Grandpa and Granny G had a cabin on the outskirts of Lake Arrowhead, a piece of property they'd purchased before it became a resort town. It was worth a chunk of cash now, but they had no intention of selling it any time soon.

At the back of the property was a small cottage they rented out at a greatly reduced rate to a fellow who looked after the cabin during the

Gustafsons' long absences. Toby had been living in that cottage for as long as Renata could remember, and even though he kept to himself whenever any of the Gustafson gang showed up, he was like a fixture on the property, his presence a comfort and security.

She'd been on the road for over an hour and still could hardly believe she was doing it. The boys, of course, had been shocked and a little dismayed, but John had assured them in his calming way that everything was fine. Renata sighed as she recalled the talk they'd had last week.

"For her birthday, Mommy's taking a little vacation of her own, guys. Kinda like I do when I go hunting."

"She's going hunting? I thought she hated killing things." Simon. Ever forthright. He was sprawled on his back at her feet, hands laced behind his head, staring at the ceiling.

"She's not going hunting. She's just going on a vacation."

"From us?" Levi's large eyes reminded her of Juliette's.

"No, honey. I don't need a vacation from you. It's not that kind of trip." She ran a palm over the top of his head and drew him close. She was sitting on the sofa with Judah on one side, Levi on the other.

"I don't get it," Reuben interjected. "What do you need a vacation from, then?" He was sitting at the counter doing homework. "I mean, when we go on summer vacation, it's cuz we need a break from school. When our family goes on family vacation, we go cuz we need a vacation from normal life, as you always say."

"Reuben, do you remember our conversation the other day? About me being sad? If you need a really basic reason, it's because I need a vacation from being sad. But more than that, it's because I need some time away to sort out *why* I'm sad." She tried not to sound defensive and hoped the boys would accept her answer. She honestly didn't know how to explain it any better.

"Are you going to come home?"

"Of course, Levi. Of course, I'm coming home." She gave his shoulders a squeeze. "I'll just be gone for a week."

They hadn't stopped asking her questions about where she was going, what she would be doing, if she would have birthday cake without them, what she planned on bringing home for them. They were thrilled that Gia was going to stay with them, even though Renata warned them that it was not going to be a week-long slumber party.

When Gia came by to get the last of her instructions and keys, she hugged Renata warmly as soon as she walked through the door. "I'm glad you're getting away, Rennie."

"Oh, I've wanted to do this for a while. I haven't been up to the cabin in ages. In fact, I haven't done anything *alone* in ages and it's kind of exciting, you know?" She sounded overly bright to her own ears, but she didn't want to answer any more questions than she had on the phone earlier. Yes, I'm okay. No, I'm not mad at you, Georgia. Yes, John is fine with me going. He thinks it's a great idea. Yes, the boys know. No, I haven't told Juliette or Phoebe. Why should I?

But Gia didn't seem to notice her forced cheer. "Well, I'm really praying that you have some special one-on-one time with God while you're away. I totally believe He has something special planned. Something He really wants you to hear."

• • • • • • • • • •

It had snowed in the mountains quite a bit this winter, and for that, all of Southern California was happy. The snow brought tourists to the ski towns like Lake Arrowhead, which translated into money and work for the locals, but it also meant water to the valley once the snow started melting. Besides all that, it was just lovely to come up from the muddy, slushy chill of rain in the lowlands to the pristine mountain air, the land covered in white like the frosting on a wedding cake. The snowplows had been through recently, so the roads were clear, and even with the heavy clouds and smattering of sleet, the drive was uneventful and relaxing.

Approaching the cabin, she smiled to see that Toby had shoveled the driveway for her. Grandpa had called ahead to let him know she was coming, and she was pretty sure she'd find the place already warmed by the furnace and a supply of chopped wood stacked by the fireplace to boot.

Taking her keys from the ignition, she climbed out of her Pilot, making certain to step down carefully so she didn't slip. But the grit of rock salt under the soles of her boots told her Toby had gone the extra mile. She glanced down the side of the lot toward the cottage and waved, knowing he was watching for her even if she couldn't see him. Job done, he'd not bother her while she was here.

"Brrr," she muttered, her fleece cardigan not warm enough in the mountain chill.

Renata lugged her suitcase up the front steps, shoved open the sticky front door, and the welcoming warmth of the rustic home drew her like a mother's arms into its bosom.

The open floor plan of the downstairs made the cabin feel large and spacious. A gigantic stone fireplace dominated one wall; furniture groupings broke up the space into the living room, dining room, and kitchen. Area rugs covered sections of the old hardwood floors, lending an added layer of comfort to the ambiance.

Renata started up the stairs to stow her things in the bedroom she and John always used when they came, the room she and Juliette shared when it was just the girls, but three steps up, she stopped short.

"Where do you want to sleep tonight, Renata?" she asked aloud, realizing anew that she had no one to consider but herself. She stood there for several moments, contemplating her options.

Finally, she left her suitcase on the stairs and headed toward the kitchen. "I'll decide later," she proclaimed. "Because I can."

After rooting around a little to see what supplies she'd need for the week, she ate a piece of fruit and some crackers she'd brought with her to tide her over. Then she freshened up a bit, changed into her new leather jacket, and drove the ten minutes into the Village on the lake.

She wandered through the shops for a while, stretching her legs and simply relishing in the detached freedom she was experiencing. It was difficult not to give in to the compulsion to glance over her shoulder for loitering children, or to mentally walk through the afternoon with them at home. What games were they playing with Gia? What was she cooking them for dinner? Was she going to use the frozen meals Renata had prepared, or would she cave and buy them pizza? Who was going to read them their bedtime stories, John? Or would Gia take over that, too? Or would they forget?

"Stop, Renata. You're supposed to be taking time away, remember?" She quelled the rising panic and focused intently on the shop windows she passed and took her time in the boutiques she rarely got to visit when she came with the boys. When she finally made it down to the water's edge, the surface was choppy, stirred by a brisk wind sweeping across the lake. The brooding clouds still hung ominously overhead, but Renata could feel the break coming soon.

The coffee shop she ended up at had a few overstuffed chairs tucked into one corner, and after an early supper of chunky vegetable soup and a pastrami sandwich, she settled into an empty chair and pulled out one of the novels she'd brought along to read.

By the time she was ready to go back to the cabin, she was satiated on good food, hot coffee, and even hotter romance. She was looking forward to calling John after her bath. She wanted to hear him tell her how much he missed her.

When she stepped outside, Renata was shocked to find that the clouds no longer threatened. They'd followed through and it was coming down, slushy rain that would certainly turn to snow in the next hour or two as the day ended and the temperatures dropped. She pulled up the collar of her jacket around her ears and hunched her shoulders, then scurried along the covered sidewalk, head ducked against the nipping wind, until she was as close as she could get to where her car was parked. Then she made a beeline to it, keys at the ready. Clambering inside the vehicle, she shoved the bag of food items she'd purchased into the back seat, then scowled at the neatly folded—and dry—umbrella on the floor of the passenger side.

By the time she made it back to the cabin, Renata was beginning to thaw out, but a hot bath sounded like heaven to her. She put away her few groceries first and made up the deep-cushioned sofa in front of the fireplace with a set of sheets and several blankets, having decided to sleep there instead of in one of the cold bedrooms. Then she filled the tub while she unpacked her suitcase on the big bed in the master bedroom downstairs. Instead of putting things into drawers or closets, she'd leave it all out on the bed in another act of defiance.

"Aah." Sinking into the tub, her sigh was heard by no one else, and tonight, that was such a lovely sentiment. She could stay in the bathroom until her fingers and toes wrinkled, adding hot water as the temperature cooled until she couldn't stand it a minute longer. She'd dry off and smooth on lotion while listening to the throaty Adele sing about fire, cold shoulders, and the boy who will be there for life, then she'd slide between the blankets on the sofa and call her husband in the flickering firelight.

· · · · ● · ● · · ·

WHEN RENATA AWOKE THE next morning, she stretched languidly, without the usual jolt of concern that she was too late, too early, that there was too much to do, and she'd never get it done. She opened her eyes only when she was ready, taking a stab at what time she thought it might be.

"10:42!" Now she did throw back the covers and reached for the robe she'd left tossed across the end of the couch. "I can't believe I slept in so late!" She couldn't remember the last time she'd gotten out of bed after eight. She pulled back the drape on the window and hummed with delight.

"Oh!" The rain last night had indeed turned to snow and the world outside glittered like the inside of a snow globe, so sparkly and white and untouched it seemed unreal. A few soft flakes still fluttered through the air, and icicles hung from the eaves all the way around the porch.

The coffee pot gurgled while she rummaged through her things and got dressed. She'd warm up some of the pastries she'd brought home with her from the Village for breakfast, then maybe take a walk in the snow.

Or she'd sit by the fire and read.

Or she'd take another bath.

Or she'd drive back into town for Mexican food.

Whatever she felt like doing, she'd do.

Renata's sky-blue yoga pants and rust-colored chenille sweater made her skin glow, even in the dreary light coming through the open window, and she smiled at her reflection in the mirror over the vanity across the room. She wasn't going to wear beige or crisp-white or anything linen this whole week.

So, this is what it felt like to be one of her sisters. No responsibility. No compromise. No tethers. She could eat whatever she wanted whenever she wanted. She daintily popped the last bite of an amazing chocolate éclair into her mouth, refusing to feel guilty for her indulgence. She'd probably gain ten pounds this week, but so what? She would just spend some extra time in the gym and eat more salad when she got home. For now, she was free as a bird.

Renata hadn't even called John yet this morning, and the longer she put it off, the more resistant she became to the idea. She didn't want to hear how the kids had managed their first morning without her. She didn't want to think about some other woman, even if it was only Gia, in her kitchen for a whole week, the dishes put away in the wrong places, the spills not quite cleaned up. She didn't want to think about all the responsibilities she'd pawned off on other people for the week.

She didn't want to hear his voice telling her they were all fine. If they were fine, she'd feel expendable, unneeded. If they weren't fine, she'd be able to hear it in his voice, even if he said they were, and she'd feel guilty. She reached for her phone and texted him.

I just got out of bed and ate breakfast. Snowed like crazy last night. Going to venture out in a little while. I'll call you tonight. I love you, John-Boy.

There. That told him she was safe, she was eating, that she had plans for the day, and she'd call him later. And that she loved him.

His return text came almost ten minutes later. *Crazy day. McCain. I love you. Kids did great. Gia's awesome. Talk to you tonight.*

That was it? Did he miss her? The kids did great? Did that mean everyone was doing fine without her?

"Renata Dixon! Stop it. You're supposed to be *away*! He's respecting that." She told her reflection. But a tiny seed of doubt had been planted and it soaked up some of the light from her day.

EIGHTEEN

When the sky suddenly cleared around one, Renata decided to head back into town. Her favorite art gallery had been closed yesterday and she couldn't stop thinking about The Benedict Belgian at The Belgian Waffle Works. She donned her black leather coat over jeans and a deep green sweater, tucked her classic bubble umbrella under her arm, and slipped into black leather wedge boots with fleece lining, a pair she'd picked up on her wild day out. She stood in front of the full-length mirror for a long time, studying this new look. She was still trying to get over the surprise of seeing her short hair every time she caught a glimpse of her reflection, but she thought the bulky boots paired with the comfortable outfit looked relaxed and put together in a very intentional way. Even Phoebe would be impressed.

She was starving after an hour of window shopping and people watching. The sun still held court in the sky, so she made her way to the dockside waffle restaurant and sat outside, in spite of the cold.

"I'm eating breakfast for lunch at three o'clock in the afternoon!" She giggled at the out of character schedule she was keeping. "And I'm drinking too much coffee."

Energized, she decided to head back to the cabin and maybe take a short walk in the snow before settling in for the night. Her feet thanked her; they were beginning to feel the hours spent shopping in new shoes. She was looking forward to another long bath with a good book, a movie on her laptop in front of the fire, and a tub of cookie dough... because the chocolate chips had begged her to bring them along.

As she pulled into the driveway, it took a moment to register what she was seeing.

It couldn't be.

Juliette's car.

Climbing out of her Honda, she glared at the burgundy PT Cruiser, identifiable by the sticker on the back window that said, *Beware of dragons, for you are crunchy and taste good with ketchup.* Phoebe had given it to Juliette the same Christmas she'd given her and John their hunting shirts and Renata thought it was just as tasteless.

Reaching the front door, which was already unlocked, Renata thrust a shoulder into it, expecting the thing to stick, as usual, but it flew open, and she stumbled in.

"Oops. Sorry, Ren. I fixed the door." Phoebe was standing with her back to a blazing fire, Renata's coveted tub of cookie dough in one hand, a giant serving spoon in the other.

Renata righted herself, closed the door behind her, and threw the deadbolt. Shoulders tense, her fists clenched around the strap of her shoulder bag, she narrowed her eyes on the two women in the living room. "Hello, Juliette. Phoebe. Fancy meeting you two here."

Juliette crossed the room quickly, reached out and put both hands on her shoulders, searching her face, then brought her close for a quick hug. "I'm so glad you're okay. We've been worried sick about you."

"Speak for yourself," Phoebe muttered around a bite of dough. Renata could tell by her bored expression that she was not here by her own choice.

"Of course, I'm okay. What are you doing here?" She was having trouble figuring out a good reason for their visit. "Have you talked to John? Does he know you're here?" She was trying desperately to maintain a semblance of control, but suddenly her week away was leaving a nasty taste in her mouth. Things were not sitting well; Juliette and Phoebe's presence didn't make sense.

Then another thought hit her. Hard. "Has something happened?" She snagged Juliette's wrist as panic washed over her. "Are the kids okay? John? What's wrong?" Her voice caught in her throat.

"No, no, Ren. Nothing's happened at home. We're here because of you." Juliette winced as Renata tightened her grip on her arm.

"Are you sure?"

Phoebe had her arms crossed over the tub and projected a calm front, but Renata could see that she was studying her, too, as though looking for signs of some mysterious ailment.

"What is going on?" she demanded, now more curious than ever since she knew there was apparently nothing wrong at home. Then she saw Phoebe's funky carpet bag sitting on the stairs, stuffed to overflowing. She looked from one to the other, anger and wariness warring inside her. "What are you two doing here? Why did you come?"

"Hey, we're allowed to be here, too, you know. Unless you're hiding a lover in the back room and don't want us to—"

"Phoebe!" Juliette elbowed her.

"No! No! This was not supposed to be like this. I was getting away for a few days. *Especially* away from you! How dare you follow me up here in secret. How dare you stalk me like I'm doing something wrong!"

"Renata. Come on." Juliette's eyes were pleading but firm.

"I told you she'd be ticked off," Phoebe quipped, shoveling another bite of dough into her mouth.

"Shut up, Phoebe!" Renata retorted. She snatched the tub from Phoebe's hands, then turned on her heels and headed for the bathroom. Maybe if she stayed in there long enough, they'd take the hint and be gone when she came back out.

"Why on earth are they here?" she asked her reflection, posing the question for what must have been the hundredth time in her head. She sat on the closed lid of the toilet, her purse on her lap, toying with the earrings hanging from her earlobes. She hated surprises, even the good ones, and this one was not a good one for so many reasons.

But face them, she must, she soon realized as she listened to their muffled chatter through the bathroom door. Especially if she wanted them to go away.

She checked her hair, reapplied her lipstick, and stepped out of the bathroom.

Phoebe lay sprawled on the sofa now, paging through one of the books from the pile on the floor, a knowing and quizzical look on her face. Mortified, Renata crossed over to her and snatched it out of her hand.

"Hoo! That's some steamy stuff, Rennie. How does John rate in comparison to the hot-blooded Spanish Conquistador, Raphael Corsico?"

"Get off my bed. Now." Renata stood with one hand on her hip, the other extended toward one of the high-backed chairs in the corner of the room. "I did not invite you here, nor did I give you permission to go snooping through my things."

When Phoebe had pranced her tightly encased self over to the corner, Renata returned the book to the pile, front cover down, and stood so she was facing her sisters.

"Say what you came to say."

"Please, Ren. Sit down so we can talk."

"No." She stared at Juliette, but she paid close attention to Phoebe who clearly did not want to be here anymore than Renata wanted them to be.

"Please," Juliette repeated.

"Fine. But you'd better make this good." Renata smoothed the rumpled blanket, then lowered herself carefully to the edge of the couch and folded her hands in her lap.

Juliette took a deep breath. "We're worried about you."

"You already said that."

"So, we're doing a G-FOURce intervention."

"What?" Renata surged back up to her feet, her mind reeling. "A what?"

"Can you imagine, Renata? An intervention that you didn't concoct!" Phoebe chortled.

"Get out." Renata crossed to the door, but Phoebe was there first, leaning against it, legs braced in a wide stance, hands covering the door handle behind her back.

"Nope. You're our hostage now. Never let the enemy into your sanctuary, Ren, darling. That's something I learned long, long ago."

Renata stared disbelieving at her, then looked back over her shoulder at Juliette. "Are you two serious? You're holding me hostage?" Her voice was tight and high-pitched, her anger putting a chokehold on her lungs.

"No, of course not. But we do need to talk some things out and your little trip couldn't have been more perfectly planned if we'd done it ourselves." Juliette smiled sadly at her sister.

Renata crossed to the bay window and sank onto the cushioned duvet in front of it, a deflated balloon. Gia had been strangely not curious about her trip. Sure, she'd asked several questions, but in retrospect, they'd been questions that a stranger might have asked. "Georgia knew, didn't she? That's why her schedule was so conveniently clear."

This must have been what they'd had in mind when they asked John about her birthday plans. Some birthday outing.

No one denied it. Phoebe returned to a chair by the hearth, unlaced her black, over-the-knee boots, and slipped them off. She stretched her feet and wriggled her toes in her socks, then folded her long legs underneath her. She was settling in for the long haul, Renata realized in dismay.

"And John? Is he in on this, too?" Her voice trembled. Had he pushed her to get away with her sisters because he supported their intervention? How could he betray her like this?

"He is now," Juliette continued softly. "He didn't like it. He argued bravely about this whole thing, but he finally agreed because he's worried, too."

"And because we threatened to pull the plug on Gia's helping out this week if he didn't."

"That's not true, Phoebe. You're not helping here." Juliette came over to sit beside Renata. "Look, Ren. We knew you'd be upset."

Phoebe snorted rudely.

"But when you left the other night, we all started comparing notes, and realized that things have changed with you."

"So, the three of you sat around talking about me."

"Yes. But for the right reasons. You've always been a take-charge kind of person," Juliette said carefully. "But you've become so overbearing that it's hard to even have a conversation with you. And now this sudden change in your appearance, your hair, even your new clothes? We love you, Renata. I love you. You know I wouldn't be telling you this just to hurt you or to make you feel badly. I'm telling you this because this new version of you is not like you. It's clear that there's something wrong."

"Because I cut my hair?" Renata asked. "You think there's something wrong with me because I cut my hair?"

NINETEEN

Juliette and Phoebe stared at her, waiting for her to cooperate. But this was coercion, not cooperation, and she didn't want anything to do with it. It didn't matter if they were right—Renata knew she was different, stretched too thin, unable to cope with much these days. But that didn't mean she wanted to talk to them about it.

She just turned and stared out the window at the night sky.

Finally, Juliette spoke, her voice determined. "Okay, fine. You can play hard ball if you want to, but I took the week off, and Phoebe doesn't have a real job anyway—"

"Hey!"

"So, we're prepared to go the distance with you. In a sense, you really are our hostage, but it's your decision when you go free. We leave you alone when you unload. And just so you know, John isn't going to rescue you. We've asked him to trust us."

Renata stood up and headed back to the bathroom.

"Where are you going?" Juliette asked.

"To slit my wrists. Then we can all go home and be done with this nonsense." She slammed the door behind her and opened her purse she'd left on the counter. She dug through it for her phone, preparing to give John a piece of her mind.

This was so like her sisters, ganging up on her like this. But John. How could he? This was her time away...and he'd sent the dogs after her. She stared at the device in her hands for several minutes, her thumb hovering over the two, his assigned speed-dial number. Finally, she texted him instead.

I will not be calling you tonight. I have unwanted guests. Not cool—feeling betrayed. Hope you sleep well tonight.

A few minutes later, she received a text back from him. *I'm sorry it happened the way it did. I love you. I'm praying.*

She threw the phone at the door, hard, and watched it shatter on the tile floor, a little shocked at her impulsive behavior. It felt good to be destructive, though. "Where's your courage, husband? Praying? Praying?" she snarled at the pieces. "For what? That you'll survive my return? No amount of praying will save you when I get home. I'm going to kill you. Slowly. And with great relish."

"Ren? Are you okay?" Juliette called from the other side of the door.

"Leave me alone!" She was so angry she could hardly stand it and she sank down on the closed lid of the toilet, dropping her head into her hands. *Deep breath in, blow it out slowly. Repeat.*

She'd always felt a bit like an island, ever since their parents died.

That terrible day had changed Juliette from the inside out. Although she still performed all her normal activities, that's exactly how it seemed to Renata, that her big sister was performing, holding back the real Juliette, protecting her, hiding her.

Phoebe, on the other hand, took things to the opposite extreme and went hog-wild. She became obsessed with boys in a driven, competitive way, yet she always seemed to have a plethora of girlfriends hanging around. Phoebe had places to be every day after school, and every night of the week, if her grandparents would let her. They didn't, and she balked. There were some terrible rows between Grandpa and Phoebe in those days, and sometimes it irked Renata that the two of them were like two peas in a pod now. Phoebe's favorite man in the whole world was Grandpa, and Renata could see the light in his eyes burned brightest when he looked at Phoebe.

Renata, unlike either one, continued living her life as though little had changed. She remained driven and purposeful, and she had admittedly few, but close, friends in high school. Over the years, however, those friends had drifted away, either moving, marrying men from other circles, or not marrying at all. John had become her world, and when they became pregnant with Reuben before she was finished with college, she dropped out to be a full-time mother.

But now, tonight, she felt completely alone, abandoned by the last of her allies. She stared at what was left of her phone.

Finally, at her wits' end, she stood up, kicked the pieces of the phone into a pile by the trash can under the vanity, and pressed her ear to the door. Not a sound. Maybe they'd left.

Nope. There they were. Now both of them were thumbing through her books. But Juliette didn't look mockingly scandalized, she looked concerned. So, the little newbie Christian was learning to pass judgment already, huh? Renata crossed to the master bedroom, snatched up her silky pajama set, and grabbed her tablet. She was going to watch a movie while she took a long, luxurious bath.

When she finally got out of the tub, she was shriveled and beginning to get hungry. She had some of the soup left over from the night before, and fixings for cheese and crackers, but she had no desire to sit around the cozy little room sharing soup and *hors d'oeuvres* with her sisters.

Emerging from the bathroom, Renata scouted the room for the infiltrators, but only Juliette was still there. Renata was surprised by how relieved she was, but then she reminded herself firmly that her older sister was leading the charge on this intervention. Juliette eyed her from her place on the sofa. She was no longer reading a novel, but had her laptop propped on her bent knees.

"Where's Phoebe?"

"Upstairs getting our beds ready." Juliette's fingers clicked quietly across her keyboard for a few more moments, then she set it aside and sat forward. "We brought some of Granny G's chili and cornbread for dinner."

Renata sighed. So much for a quiet meal by herself. Against her will, her mouth began to water at the thought of her grandmother's famous chili.

Once they were seated on the floor in front of the fire with their bowls of the aromatic hearty soup, Juliette started talking about herself. It seemed to come from out of nowhere, but Renata was okay with it. At least they weren't attacking her. Yet.

Juliette blushed as she explained that she'd been going through boxes in her garage. "Victor hasn't asked me officially, but we talk about 'when we're married' all the time. I guess I feel a little like if I do this sorting and organizing stuff now, then I'll be able to truly bask when he does ask me. If he asks me."

"Oh please, Jules. The guy is sick-in-love with you. He probably thinks he's already asked you." Phoebe pointed a scarlet-tipped finger at her. "In fact, you might want to hint about what ring size you wear."

"Good grief. I wouldn't do that. Not right now, anyway. He's still trying to adjust to the day shift after so many years doing the split shift. He isn't sleeping well at nights yet, and he says he's been caught a few times napping at his desk or in his patrol car. Poor guy. The last thing he needs to worry about right now is buying me jewelry." Juliette smiled contentedly. "I'm not going anywhere."

Renata studied her older sister over the lip of her water glass as she took a long sip of the icy liquid. She really did look happy, but what Juliette saw in Victor was beyond her.

"So where will you live?" she asked, forgetting that she'd planned on not joining in on any conversation unless she had to. "Your place or his?"

"Actually, as much as I love my little place, I don't really want to stay there unless it's just for a short transition time. Too many memories of Mike." She frowned at the reminder of her ex-boyfriend who hadn't wanted to accept a new man in her life.

"Have you heard from him?" Renata asked.

"Not personally," Juliette replied. "But Victor assured me he's fine."

"Wait a minute. Are you telling us he and Victor have spoken?" Renata's eyes widened with curiosity. She set her glass down and took a big bite of the golden cornbread slathered in honey.

"Yes," Now Juliette looked sheepish. "I wouldn't mind if I never saw Mike again. But I would feel terrible if I thought he'd died or at least ended up with permanent issues because of his collapse at my place. So I asked, no, I begged, Victor to go see him in the hospital and find out what he could just to set my mind at ease. He didn't want to do it. He thought he might kill the guy. But he did it so that I wouldn't have to go myself. He probably realized that I would, too."

"Well, that was very sweet of him," Renata said.

"Sweet?" Phoebe drawled the word like she was talking about iced tea. "That wasn't sweet. That was heroic. There was nothing but bravery and honor in that sacrificial act of love and devotion."

"Oh my gosh, Phoebe. You're so dramatic!" Renata rolled her eyes.

The conversation meandered back over their early years, before Gia arrived in their home, and it was just the three of them and Maman and Papa. They shared a room, they shared clothes, they were each other's best friends. Sleepovers were epic, birthday parties were amazing with Maman's dramatic flair, and family outings were always an adventure with the three of them in the backseat and Maman and Papa in the front, holding hands over the console. They sang old show tunes, the Beatles, some Elvis, and the Bon Jovi songs the girls had forced their parents to learn. "You give love a bad name!" they'd croon at the top of their lungs.

Phoebe pulled from the freezer her favorite ice cream bonbons she'd stashed there when she arrived. They ate the whole carton, enjoying the old camaraderie of their shared pasts, having temporarily shoved the real reason for their gathering under the table to be dealt with at a later time.

It never ceased to amaze Renata how effective good food was for settling the tempest of moods. She'd seen it work on John and the boys repeatedly over the years, and even though she knew they'd be picking up where they left off before long, right now, she was actually enjoying her sisters' company.

• • • • • • • • • •

AFTER CLEANING UP THEIR dinner dishes and putting away leftovers, Renata claimed to be tired, grabbed her pile of books, and headed into the master bedroom. She'd opted to sleep in there instead of on the sofa so she could close the door between her and her jailers. She'd unceremoniously dumped most of the things from the bed back into her suitcase, thinking she'd be heading out as soon as she was able.

Rather than going to their separate rooms, however, Juliette and Phoebe pushed their way into the master bedroom with Renata.

"Seriously, you two? I won't run, I promise. I just don't want to talk right now, okay?"

"Nope. Not okay." Phoebe pulled back the covers on the bed and eased beneath them. "Brrr. It's cold in here. Are you sure you guys don't want to go back to the living room? Renata, get over here. Climb in bed with me so I can warm my feet on you."

For some reason, whether it was the afterglow of their shared meal, the goofy and sweet memories they'd relived together, or just the improbability of the three of them on this rendezvous, Renata did what she was asked. She came around to the other side of the bed and crawled in next to Phoebe. They waited in silence until Juliette emerged from the bathroom.

"You going to join us, or are you just going to stare at us like we're freaks?" Phoebe asked, lifting the edge of the covers for Juliette.

"Um, can I put on some coffee and get my pajamas first? I want to get out of these tight pants. I ate too much. That ice cream was more than the waistband on these could squeeze in." She headed toward the door, then turned back. "Phoebe, do you want me to bring yours too?"

Phoebe turned to look at Renata. "Ren, listen. I've been on the receiving end of these interventions before, and I know they suck. But I also know there's no way to run once they're in play. I trust you. If you would rather that we go to our own rooms right now and leave you alone for the night, we will." She patted her cheek. "I trust you," she repeated.

Renata was momentarily too surprised to respond, but when she glanced at the radio clock and saw that it was not quite nine o'clock, she shook her head. "No. It's still early. Why don't you two go put your jammies on? I'll make some coffee and we'll figure things out from there, okay? I'm not going to guarantee you that you'll get what you want out of me, but I won't throw anything at your heads. I promise."

"Speaking of throwing things, was that your phone—or what's left of it—on the bathroom floor?" Juliette's expression got very serious again.

"Yes. It was time to get a new one, anyway." Renata smiled ruefully.

"Do you need to use my phone to call John?"

"Nope. He knows I'm not planning on calling him tonight. I told him you were here." She might be on the verge of coming to some kind of truce with her sisters, but she felt John's treachery much deeper, and she still wasn't quite sure how to deal with it. She wasn't as angry as she'd been when she first learned of it, but she thought maybe a good night's sleep would give her some clarity on how to talk to him, how to explain what his actions meant to her.

"Okay. But if you change your—"

"I'll ask," Renata interrupted. "Now go get your pajamas, both of you."

The moment the two were gone, Renata felt the evil compulsion to wedge a chair under the door handle and ignore them when they came back. But she did as she promised and started a pot of coffee. She also filled a couple of old-fashioned hot-water bottles and shoved them under the blankets in her bed. Her sisters would be thrilled.

When the knock came, she was ready.

TWENTY

"Who's there?" she hollered through the closed door.

"Eet ees the beeg bad vulfy heer to zuck yoor blud." Phoebe sounded like a drunk Elvira, and although Renata had planned on giving them a hard time in jest, she started giggling, and pulled the door open instead.

Thankful for the king-sized bed, the girls lined up the pillows along the headboard and sat with their backs propped against it. Renata passed each of her sisters their doctored-up coffees after everyone was settled. "This is just like when we first moved to Grandpa and Granny G's house. Remember how huge we thought that bed was? Was it only a queen?"

Phoebe wiggled her hips to make more room for herself. "How did we all fit?"

"It was pretty tight, but I think we needed it that way." Juliette braved the subject, the only one of them willing to open up that can of worms. "Look. I know you two aren't happy with me contacting Angela. I want to clear the air about that before we go on to anything else." She sat between Renata and Phoebe, ever the peacemaker, ever the safe zone in the middle.

"First, I'm sorry I didn't talk to you about it before I mailed her my letter. I think part of me thought surely she'd never respond. So when she did, I was suddenly in a quandary. I'm sorry if it felt like I went around you or behind your backs. That was not my intention."

Juliette turned to face Renata the best she could from her position beside her. "I told Phoebe that she doesn't have to participate if she doesn't want to, and I want to give you the same freedom. I know this can't be an easy thing for you, either. I shouldn't have forced my timing on either of you."

Renata took a sip of her hot drink, then nodded slowly. "It's okay, Juliette. You just surprised me, that's all. You know how I hate surprises."

Then she looked sternly at both of them. "You *both* know how I hate surprises. But that being said, I'm sorry, too, for the way I reacted to you two coming up to interfere—I mean, *intervene*—in my life."

"Forgiven," Phoebe replied immediately. "I would have freaked out even worse if I was in your shoes." She reached across Juliette and squeezed Renata's knee.

"Forgiven," agreed Juliette. "Okay."

The room grew silent, and Renata knew they were leaving the airwaves open for her to fill. She waited, though, not sure where to begin.

"Rennie, what's going on with you?" Juliette tried again, more direct this time. "You're acting differently these days. Something is wrong."

"I know." Renata sighed. Should she tell them about her miscarriages? Would they understand how painful each drop of blood was to her? Would they try to appease her, to pat her on the hand and tell her it would be all right? She didn't know if she'd be able to bear it if they did. But here in this homey room surrounded by tough love, she realized she did want to talk to her sisters. She wanted to let them in for the first time in as long as she could remember.

"I think God is punishing me." The words came out all wrong... or did they? That might not have been what she intended to say, but maybe those were the words her heart longed to release.

"Um, why?" Phoebe, who didn't practice any religion except that of self-idolization, was the first to ask.

Renata was surprised into continuing. "You know how badly I want a little girl, right? Well, every time we get pregnant, God gives us another boy." She toyed with one of the buttons on her pajama shirt. "We've been trying to have another baby now for almost a year, but I can't get pregnant."

Neither sister said anything, and she was afraid to look at them.

"Actually," her eyes welled up, her throat tightening around the words. "I can get pregnant. I just can't stay pregnant long enough to tell anyone about it. Besides John, of course."

Juliette reached over and patted her hand, and Renata cringed, preparing herself for the dreaded words. But they didn't come. "I didn't know you were trying. And here I've made this whole last year all about me and Mike and Victor. I'm so sorry I haven't been more sensitive, Renata."

"Do you remember that day I came over to help you with your dog?"

"The day I found Bob? Yes." Juliette's eyes got really wide. "Oh no! I was really surprised when you were free on a Sunday afternoon. But I didn't even ask if you were okay." Then her hand flew to her mouth. "And when you came out after talking to John, you were crying! Renata!"

"Yeah. I had just lost our second baby that week; the first miscarriage was in April. It was terrible. I was terrible. It was no wonder John took the boys and ditched me."

Phoebe hadn't said a word, but when Renata peered around Juliette at her, she was shocked to see tears streaming down her sister's cheeks. "Phoebe? Are you okay?"

Phoebe nodded and swiped at her tears with the backs of her hands. "Yes. I'm terribly sorry, Rennie. I'm so sad for you, for those babies, for John." Then she turned beseeching eyes on her. "Why didn't you tell us? Why didn't you let us help you get through it? It's a terrible thing to have to go through alone, thinking no one can possibly understand." She sniffed loudly, then continued. "Well, maybe we can't understand your pain, but we do know your heart. And we love you. We're sisters."

"I know," Renata murmured, seriously taken aback by Phoebe's heartfelt reaction. "I—I'm sorry. I just felt so torn up inside, and I didn't know how to talk about it. Then last November I lost a third baby. I was quite a bit farther along with that one, and my doctor told me we had to wait at least six months before we try again." She reached up and covered her eyes with one hand and Juliette slipped her arms around her, pulling her close as the tears began to fall. Phoebe slid out of place and crawled around to sit cross-legged on the bed, facing the other two, resting a hand on Renata's knee.

"I don't think I can go through it again, though," Renata sobbed. "I can't bear the up and down emotions. I can't stand the thought that I might have had three little girls, as precious to each other as my sisters are to me, but I'll never hold them, never smell their little baby necks, never kiss their tiny toes. I feel disemboweled most of the time, like there's just scar tissue inside of me, hard and unreceptive, unnatural, not motherly."

She used the hem of her top to dab at her eyes. "And John. He'd never admit it to me, but I know he's relieved. Of course, he wants a little girl, but not nearly as badly as I do. He didn't have sisters like you growing up." She held out a hand, and they each placed one of their own in hers. "He doesn't know what he's missing."

Her voice dropped to a whisper. "And I can't help but wonder if God is trying to teach me a lesson because I'm hard and unreceptive to people. I'm not a nurturer like you, Juliette, and I'm not fun and full of life like you, Phoebe. I'm hard and stiff and inflexible."

"That's not possible, Ren," Phoebe stated with certainty. "I don't even claim to be a Christian and I know God wouldn't pull that kind of stuff. He may leave you hanging about the why, but He doesn't punish people like that. You know, I used to think that about Maman and Papa, that God was punishing me for being a little too interested in boys at my age, so to get back at Him, I chased them even harder."

Phoebe looked down at their three hands clasped between them. "I learned that people are the ones who punish, Ren, not God. God may discipline, but He isn't cruel. He doesn't punish with a cruel heart." The expression on Phoebe's face was one Renata hadn't seen before, and she wondered where this wild-child sister of hers had kept hidden all this wisdom.

"If you believe that about God, why don't you claim Him?" Juliette asked the inevitable question.

"Just because I think He's fair, doesn't mean I like Him." Phoebe reached over and bumped Renata's knee, effectively changing the subject back to her sister. "So, how long have you been holding this in?"

"We've been trying for a while now." Her voice was dulled by pain. "I don't know what's wrong with me. My doctor says we're both fine. I have plenty of healthy eggs. John has lots of manly sperm."

"Ew. I don't want to know how you know that." Juliette scrunched up her face.

"No," Renata chuckled. "You probably don't. Suffice it to say that John won't look Dr. Flynn in the eye ever again."

"Why not? He didn't like the donor process?"

"Why do you always have to go there, Phoebe?" Juliette poked her with a foot.

"Nope. He hated it. He was mortified when the nurse tried to offer him a girlie magazine. He got all indignant and told the guy to back off. It was a male nurse." Renata grinned at the memory, then sighed. "We've tried everything, but for some reason, we just can't make it stick. And I'm tired of the disappointment every month. And I'm tired of the look on John's face when I have to tell him that there's no baby again." She snorted and smiled through her tears. "Not that he's complaining about having to try some more. He doesn't mind that part."

"Okay, Ren. Ew! Now you sound like Phoebe."

Renata was sure that would get a response, and she wasn't disappointed. Phoebe squeezed Juliette's knee, making her sister squeal.

"Well, I think this trip is my crazy attempt to come to terms with not having any more babies; with not having a girl. I don't ever want my boys to think they're not enough, so I guess I felt like I had to go away and mourn somewhere else. I don't know. I haven't really thought all of this stuff through myself. I thought I'd have the whole week to figure it out," Renata said dryly.

"Okay, you two," Juliette said, leaning forward and reaching for Phoebe, one arm still around Renata. "Group hug."

At first, there were tears, then there were giggles. Then Phoebe released a little belch, and Renata pushed her. Phoebe pushed back. Renata shoved harder, and Phoebe slid off the side of the bed and onto the floor.

"Hey!" Phoebe cried. She snatched one of the pillows off the bed and attempted to thump Renata on the head, but walloped Juliette instead.

The brief pillow fight ended suddenly when Juliette's wild swing took out Renata's half-full coffee cup from the bedside table, sending warm liquid splashing across the wood floor, fortunately missing the braided rag rug beside the bed.

Phoebe hurried to the kitchen for paper towels, and by the time they'd set things to right again, Renata felt a hundred pounds lighter.

"I'm sorry I was so snippy with you this afternoon, you guys," she apologized again. "And I suppose I should call John tonight after all. He's so good to me. I don't know what I did to deserve him."

Juliette reached over and gave her a warm hug. "I love you, little sister."

"I love you, too, Juliette. And you, Phoebe. Thanks for letting me unload on you."

"Actually, we didn't let you. We made you unload, remember? You were our hostage." Phoebe poked her in the ribs as she walked by on her way to the little bathroom. "I'm getting tired, Jules. Can I go to bed now?"

Phoebe yawned, and Renata glanced at the clock again. She was amazed to see that it was nearly eleven o'clock. They'd been talking for hours. "Oh no. It's awfully late. I probably shouldn't call John until the morning." Then she looked at her sisters and spoke softly. "I'm really grateful you came today. I feel much better just having talked it over with someone besides John. I don't have any different answers, but I feel better about facing things." She blinked back tears, then added, "I don't know how I'll feel about all this in the morning, so go easy on me, okay? I do feel much better, but just a little more, well, vulnerable than usual."

Juliette laughed gently and handed Renata her cell phone. "Here. Call your husband tonight. I'm sure he'd be happy just to hear your voice, if I know John." She shrugged and added, "Or call him first thing in the morning, if you'd rather. I can borrow Phoebe's phone if I need to make a call."

"Like to Victor?" Phoebe wiggled her eyebrows.

"Not on your phone, I won't. Then you'll have his number and he'll somehow start getting weird, inappropriate phone calls," Juliette teased.

"Oh. Nice one, Juliette." Renata felt her old spiky personality begin to slip back into place. She didn't mind. Being vulnerable was not something she did well, and she kind of liked her prickles. "That's why I haven't given her John's number."

"Oh, I have their numbers, both of them. Don't you two worry about that," Phoebe murmured. "I know who to call if I need a big, strong man around."

"Go to your room, Phoebe," Renata commanded, half-joking, half-serious. She was tired of the banter, she was tired of her own story, she was just plain tired.

"Good night, then, Ren darling. Sleep well." Phoebe kissed her on the cheek, pranced out of the room, and headed up the stairs. Juliette followed shortly.

Lying in bed in the dark, new tears on her cheeks, but these of relief, Renata decided to wait until morning to call John. She knew this job with McCain was tearing him apart, and he needed all the sleep he could get. She set Juliette's phone on the bedside table within reach and programmed the alarm for six in the morning. That would give John some time to get ready before she called him, but she would still be able to catch him at home. As she turned on her side, she reached out to lay a hand on the empty side of the bed where John's chest would be if he were here with her.

TWENTY-ONE

THE SUN DIDN'T WAKE her as it usually did, because the heavy drapes were drawn across the window. The alarm clock didn't wake her either, because she'd accidentally set it for six p.m. instead of a.m. When the thud of her door crashing against the wall jolted her out of her dreams, she bolted upright and looked frantically around the room, her heart galloping in panic.

"Renata! Wake up! Ren!" It was Phoebe, and she sounded frantic. She looked frantic.

"What is it? Is Juliette—"

"It's Grandpa, Ren. He couldn't reach you on your phone." Phoebe handed her the phone she'd had cradled against her ear a moment ago. Suddenly, Renata didn't want to hear the news he had. She covered the mouthpiece with her hand.

"What's going on? Is Granny G okay?"

Then Juliette was there, too, fully dressed. "I've got our things packed, Phoebe. Go get dressed. I'll help Ren." Then she turned her pain-shadowed eyes on Renata.

In a panic, Renata grabbed Phoebe's sleeve and tried to hand her back her phone. "I don't want to. No. No! I don't—I can't talk right now."

Phoebe tugged free, her eyes suddenly bright with tears, then hugged Renata fiercely. "Talk to Grandpa, Ren. Now."

Renata's hands were shaking as she brought the device up to her ear. "Grandpa? It's Renata."

"Honey." He made no small talk. "John has had a fall at work. He's alive, and he's asking for you, but he's in critical condition. I'm so sorry, Renata honey, but you need to come home immediately."

"Oh God, oh God, oh God." It was a prayer, the words falling from her lips like an overflowing vessel. She almost dropped the phone, her hands were shaking so hard, but she pressed it to the side of her face, desperate for details that would ease her mind. "Is—is he going to be okay?"

"Now you listen to me, Renata." He didn't answer her question, and that scared her more than anything. "You cannot afford to drive unsafely. I am not going to tell you to let one of your sisters take the wheel. However, I'm going to warn you that you may not be in any condition to drive."

"No! I'm driving. I'll be careful, I promise." Renata suddenly jumped into action. She pulled her suitcase out from under the bed and threw it open. There was little left to do but round up her toiletries in the bathroom, which Juliette was already doing, and gather up the few things scattered around the place. "Grandpa? I'm okay. I need to go. I'll see you soon. I love you." Without waiting for his reply, she hung up and hurried into the bathroom.

"Please leave my makeup and hairspray out. I don't want to get there looking like a stray cat. He'll want to see me looking like me." She turned toward her reflection and cringed. "Oh, why did I cut my hair! He loved my long hair!" Then the tears began.

Juliette reached for her and hugged her hard, then grabbed her by the shoulders and shook her slightly. "Renata, chin up, okay? John needs you strong now. Your boys need you steady. Wash your face, put on your makeup, fix your hair. Get it together, you hear? I'll finish packing your stuff. You didn't use any of the upstairs rooms, right?"

"No. I was only in the living room and kitchen and in here." Renata bit down on her bottom lip, the pain a welcome distraction from her panic, but she couldn't stop her hands from shaking and it took her an eternity to get her eyeliner on straight. By the time she was dressed and primped, Phoebe had returned with hers and Juliette's bags, and was standing by the door waiting.

"Ready?" she asked. "Juliette's got your car already started. We'll leave her car here. Grandpa talked to Toby about keeping an eye on it for a few days."

"Okay. Then I'm ready," Renata nodded. She prayed she could keep it together. She had assured both sisters she could drive, that she *had* to drive.

There was no way she could sit in the back seat twiddling her thumbs for the two-and-a-half-hour drive to the hospital where John had been admitted.

The silence in the car as they pulled out of the driveway was filled with uncertainty and fear. Finally, Renata spoke. "Did Grandpa give you any details? Do you know what happened?"

She had both hands on the wheel, her eyes never leaving the road, not even to ask her sisters her questions. Before taking off, Juliette had prayed for clear roads, clear weather, and no traffic to slow them down. Silently, Renata repeated the prayer over and over, adding her own thoughts to it. *Get me home quickly, Lord. Get me home to my John. Keep him alive. Keep him alive. Keep us safe. Keep him alive. Home quickly. Alive. Safe. Home quickly. Alive. Safe.*

"Grandpa didn't know much, but he's on his way over there now. He said he'll call back as soon as he gets some details. The hospital called your home number when they couldn't reach your cell, and Gia answered. She referred them to Grandpa, but they wouldn't tell him much. I don't think they know much yet, anyway. It only happened an hour ago." Juliette was sitting in the front seat with her, and several times, from the corner of her eyes, Renata saw her glance at the phone in her lap.

"My anger. I was so angry last night."

"What do you mean, Ren?" Phoebe asked from the back seat.

"My phone. They couldn't call me because I threw a temper tantrum and destroyed my phone." She caught her breath. "And I... and I didn't call John last night. I didn't get to tell him..... He thinks I'm still angry at him." Her words trailed off, her eyes brimming with tears. "The last thing I said to him—"

"Renata, stop it." Juliette's calm voice interrupted her downward spiral. "John knows you love him. That's what's important. Let's just focus on getting there, okay? Do you want me or Phoebe to drive?"

"No! No, I have to do something. I can't just sit in the back seat and think. At least driving gives me something to concentrate on." She dabbed at her tears with a tissue, careful not to smudge her mascara. "Does my makeup still look okay?" She glanced in the rear-view mirror to see Phoebe watching her, her own eyes big and bright with unshed tears.

"It looks fine. No smears," Phoebe assured her.

"Well, no news is good news, right?" Renata said, her voice shaking.

"That's exactly right, Ren," Phoebe agreed, her hand briefly resting on Renata's shoulder. She was glad she didn't leave it there; she couldn't handle being touched right now.

Fifteen minutes later, there was still no phone call. The girls rode in silence, staring out the windows at the stunning views the mountain road offered of the valley below them, but seeing very little. Each one was awash in her own emotions, and Renata was at first grateful for the silence. Like physical touch, she didn't think she could handle anymore banal conversation than was absolutely necessary. But not hearing back from Grandpa was killing her.

"Can you call him back?" She didn't bother explaining who; she knew Juliette had to be thinking the same thing. "Maybe he's heard something."

"I wonder if Gia knows anything," Phoebe commented. "Why don't I call her, and you call Grandpa, Jules."

The car was silent again while they waited for someone to pick up on the other end of the line. Gia answered first; Grandpa didn't pick up. Phoebe put her on speakerphone.

"Oh, Rennie, I'm so sorry. I can hardly believe this is all happening. Are you... are you...?"

"She's holding up, Gia," Phoebe assured her. "Honey, we called because we need to know if you've heard anything or if you have any details that we didn't get. All we know is that John fell, and he's being treated at the Huntington Trauma Center in Pasadena. Do you know anything else?"

"Oh gosh, yes! A guy named something McCain called here, too, looking for you, Ren. He—he was with John when he fell. John was on a ladder about fifteen feet up and pulling some wires that had been put in the wrong way or something. Mr. McCain was on scaffolding close by and said that John's ladder must have been badly positioned, because at one point, John turned to talk to him over his shoulder, and the ladder started to slide along the wall. The ladder hit the scaffold and John tumbled off, then the ladder came down on top of him." Gia's voice broke, and she paused.

"Georgia, I want to know about John! What happened to John!" Renata spoke sharply, loudly, and Juliette reached over and laid a hand on her arm.

"Don't touch me!" Renata said, shaking her off. "How badly is he hurt, Georgia?"

"I—I don't know, Ren. Mr. McCain said he landed on his back and the ladder came down on top of him. I don't know much more than that. Mr. McCain didn't either at that point. He was calling from the hospital, though. He said he wanted to wait for you there," she finished lamely.

"What?" Renata gasped, her rage making her voice gravelly and harsh. "That man better not be there when I get there. He's been nothing but vile to John from the very start of this job. If he thinks he's going to play Mr. Nice Guy to me, he can think again."

The silence that followed her outrage was almost welcoming to her. She thought about John's frustration over Scott McCain and his ineptitude on the job, his bullish ways and his puffed-up attitude. She imagined John this morning, probably miserable over how things were between him and her, maybe distracted, up on a high ladder, most likely undoing wiring McCain had done wrong.

Phoebe took Gia off the speaker and finished the conversation with her. Renata could hear her soothing their youngest sister.

"No, Gia. Stop worrying. It's okay. Hey, you don't have to sit by Rennie's phone now, so why don't you ask Granny G to pick up the boys for you. Then you can go sit with Grandpa at the hospital to wait for us."

"Let me talk to her," Renata barked, reaching back for the phone.

"I don't think that's a good idea, Ren. You worry about driving, okay?" Juliette spoke quietly, firmly.

"Let me talk to her!" Renata cried out, jerking the car off to the side of the road so suddenly that Phoebe shouted in fright from the back seat. "Give me the phone, Phoebe!"

Turning around in her seat, Renata glared at her until Phoebe said, "Gia, you have my permission to hang up if you feel uncomfortable, okay? Here's Ren."

Renata took the phone and brought it to her ear. "Georgia, I'm sorry I snapped at you. We have at least another hour and a half or more of driving ahead of us and I'm going out of my mind with worry. I shouldn't have taken it out on you, but I need to know anything and everything you know. I don't want to walk in there with nothing."

"It's okay, Rennie," Gia whispered, and Renata could tell she was crying. "I understand. Mr. McCain said it's pretty bad. The ladder is one of those heavy-duty construction ones that extends to twenty-four feet. He didn't go into details with me, but when John came to, he made Mr. McCain promise to let you know he was okay. That's a good sign, right? That he was aware enough to worry about you?"

"I think so. I hope so." Renata closed her eyes and dropped her head so her chin almost rested on her chest. "Do you know if there was any damage to his head?" She didn't know if she wanted to hear Gia's answer.

"Um, the ladder, Mr. McCain said it landed on... on his... his face." Gia's voice was so low Renata had to hold her breath to hear her words.

TWENTY-TWO

"Oh, John." Her shoulders came up and she reached with her free hand to grab the back of her neck, trying to hold everything together. The other two sat watching her, waiting for word.

Finally, Renata lifted her head. "Georgia, I need you to call Tim Larsen. I don't have his number because I broke my phone, but it should be on that list of emergency numbers on the fridge door. Can you please call him and let him know? And give him Juliette's and Phoebe's numbers in case he gets there before you do and can give me some kind of information."

"Of course. I'll do that right now." Gia was trying so hard to be brave, Renata could tell, and it broke her heart. "And Rennie, I'm praying. Real hard. I love you."

"Thanks. I love you, too." She hung up and pulled back onto the highway as carefully as she could before filling Juliette and Phoebe in on what Gia had told her.

"Sorry, Ren. I was worried you'd make Gia feel even worse than she already did. I should have trusted you."

"Let it go, Phoebe. I'm probably not very trustworthy right now. Let's just drive, okay?"

About fifteen minutes later, Juliette's phone rang. She listened to the person on the other end of the line, then said, "It's a lady named Judy from the hospital. She wants to talk to you."

Once again, they pulled over and, without having to be asked, Phoebe traded places with Renata so they could keep moving.

"This is Renata Dixon."

"Hi, Mrs. Dixon. I understand that you're under a terrible amount of strain right now, so this will be very quick. I just have a few questions for you. Does your husband have medical coverage?"

"Yes," she assured the steady voice on the other end of the line. She gave Judy all her pertinent information about their insurance carrier, then abruptly asked, "Do you know how he is?"

"I don't, honey. I'm so sorry. All I know is that he's been checked in, and the trauma team is working with him as we speak. He's in good hands, I promise." Renata fleetingly wondered how often this poor woman had to give those words out to people on the phone. She would hate Judy's job.

"There is one more thing, Mrs. Dixon. Does your husband have a preferred religion? Would he like us to send someone to pray with him?"

Renata was a little surprised by the question. A morbid image of a stranger in a black robe standing over her broken and battered husband flitted through her mind, but she pushed it away. "Yes, he's Protestant. I think he'd like that."

"Oh, good. Today Luke Simons is on duty. He's a wonderful pastor. I'll send him in. He'll want to meet with you, too, when you get here, if you'd like that."

The conversation ended quickly after that and she shared briefly with her sisters, who were just as surprised as Renata was by Judy's personal touch.

"God's already moving, Ren, I just know it," Juliette said softly. "He's going ahead of us."

It was almost another hour before Grandpa called. Renata still had Juliette's phone, and she answered it immediately. "How is he, Grandpa?"

"You're not driving, are you?"

"No, don't worry. Phoebe is."

"Actually, that doesn't make me feel any better. I've ridden with her before." He was trying to make her smile, which scared her horribly.

"Grandpa." Her voice trembled.

"Oh, sweetie. It's not good." He sounded terribly old in that moment, and Renata found it impossible to swallow around the cannonball of fear in her throat. "Can you put me on speakerphone?"

Renata handed Juliette the phone, unable to think clearly. Juliette spoke to Grandpa quickly, then turned up the volume so everyone could hear him.

"Renata, John is in critical condition right now. They still have him in the trauma center; they're waiting for some of the facial swelling to recede so that they can sew up some of the worst of the wounds. Gia told me she'd already talked to you about how the accident happened." He cleared his throat, obviously trying to maintain control of his own emotions. "Rennie, sweetie, the ladder he was on weighs nearly 60 pounds and fell from quite a distance. It landed across his chest and face and did a lot of damage. Besides a partially dislocated shoulder, several cracked ribs, and a broken collarbone, his face sustained some pretty significant injuries. When he fell, he apparently landed more on his upper back than flat, and although that's good news for his internal organs, they're very concerned about his spine and neck."

There was some rustling of papers and murmuring in the background. Grandpa had probably taken notes so he could relay to her exactly what the doctors had told him. "Right now, they're most concerned about trauma to his brain. There are three brain bleeds currently; one at the back of his skull where he hit his head, and two right behind his forehead where the ladder got him. Those are the top priority now, and of course, they're monitoring his spine. He's in a protective brace for now."

"So... you've seen him?" Phoebe asked, her voice steady but quiet.

"Yes, they let me back to see him so he would know someone was here for him. They cut his clothes off him, but otherwise, they haven't done much to clean him up. I want you to be as prepared as possible before you see him. It's going to be quite a shock." He cleared his throat again.

No one spoke for several stunned moments. Renata stared out the window at the sky that was turning gray again, unable to process everything he was saying.

"Can he speak?" Juliette finally asked. "Gia said he was talking to Mr. McCain earlier."

"Yes. Miraculously, he did speak. He's in and out of it right now, but the doctors are very encouraged that he's been fairly coherent throughout this ordeal."

"Is he in pain, Grandpa?" Phoebe questioned. Renata was grateful they were there with her, asking the questions for her. She felt like she was being crushed under the weight of her grandfather's words, and it was all she could do to stay focused on what he was saying.

"He's in shock right now, girls. He's not feeling much of anything. But he's doing as well as possible, all things considered."

"Grandpa?" Renata finally found her voice.

"I'm here, honey."

"Is—is he going to die?" Grandpa wouldn't lie to her. She had to know.

He took a deep breath before he answered, and let it out slowly, but she could still hear the uncertainty in his voice. "We don't know, Renata. There's no way to know. The doctors are doing everything they can for him, so it's up to God to decide. And John. John has to choose to continue to fight the way he has been. He's fighting, honey. He's waiting for you. You just focus on getting here, okay? John is in good hands."

The rest of the drive passed in silence. There were no more phone calls, no more updates, just the unsettling stillness in the car, and the roaring thoughts inside her head. *Don't die, John. I'm sorry I didn't call you. Don't die, John. I love you. I need you. I'm sorry. Don't die.*

They made it in record time, for once, no one making any bones about Phoebe's lead foot. She let Juliette and Renata out at the front entrance of the hospital while she parked the car. The two hurried inside the doors and stopped, looking around them at the immense lobby with its water fountain and gift shop and vast waiting area. Fortunately, the information desk was right in front, like a concierge desk, and a smiling woman caught their attention.

"Can I help you find your way?"

She directed them down the corridors to the trauma center, and once again, Renata was glad she was not doing this alone. She would have been lost in a matter of moments. Juliette seemed to have no trouble with the directions the woman gave her and pulled Renata along until they stood just outside a set of double doors, waiting for them to swing open after pushing the large, square release lever on the wall.

Juliette squeezed her around the shoulders one last time, then they hurried through to the busy counter where a harried-looking attendant in scrubs was trying to explain to a woman that it was not a case of first come, first served in the emergency room, that they prioritized patients based on the severity of their conditions. The poor woman was obviously feeling terrible; she looked feverish and pale, but her belligerence was evidence that she was not yet near her death bed.

Just as the woman stepped away from the window, Grandpa came through the doors from a hallway opposite them. "There you are! Phoebe called and said you'd be here." He embraced both girls quickly, then turned and gestured toward a man who'd come in behind him.

It took Renata a moment to understand that he was with her grandfather, but when she saw his bleary eyes and red nose, she could see he'd been crying.

"This is Scott McCain, Renata. He was with John this morning and has been here waiting for you. Scott, will you take Renata and her sister, Juliette, into John's room? I'll wait for Phoebe."

Scott nodded mutely, then turned his watery eyes on Renata. "I'm so sorry, Mrs. Dixon. I'm terribly sorry. I couldn't leave until I'd talked to you." Then, as though remembering what he was supposed to be doing, he turned and motioned them back toward the hall from where he came. "I'll show you to John."

They followed behind his burly figure; Renata uncertain of her feelings at the moment. He seemed so sincere in his remorse and she was having a hard time holding on to her anger toward him. She tried to put herself in his shoes and realized that regardless of how she was or was not getting along with someone, watching them fall and sustain such terrible injuries must be truly devastating. *Poor guy*, she acknowledged, shaking her head.

"Mrs. Dixon," Scott pulled up short outside a set of double doors with a small square window in each one. "John looks really awful." He paused and drew in a long, stuttering breath. "I just feel like I should warn you."

"Thank you, Mr. McCain. My grandfather already warned me, too." Her hands were shaking again, half in fear of what she'd see, half in need to see her husband, to touch him, to assure herself that he was still alive, still here, still hers.

Scott pushed open the door and stepped back to let her and Juliette in. "He's behind the curtain on the left."

Renata had a moment of hysteria where she imagined they were contestants in a terrible, macabre game show. Juliette squeezed her shoulder comfortingly, but Renata could feel the tremor in her sister's touch.

"I'm okay, Juliette. I'm good. It's going to be okay." She didn't know who she was trying to convince more. Her sister, or herself.

Renata reached around Juliette and pulled back the curtain a little, enough to make eye-contact with a tall young nurse who was holding a set of forceps for a doctor working near John's head.

"Hello," he spoke calmly, as though she'd just entered his storefront. "May I help you?"

"I'm Renata Dixon. John Dixon's wife."

"Oh good. You're here. Come in and say 'hi' to him. He's been waiting to see you."

• • • • • • • • • • •

"It's going to be okay." Her voice pierced the fog of pain and uncertainty. Renata was here. He knew he wasn't supposed to move, but he had to find her, to see her.

"Ren?" He tried to speak, but nothing came out. He clutched at the blanket across his chest; it felt so heavy, pushing him down into the bed he was on.

"Please don't move your head, John." The voice seemed to come from far above him, and he tried to open his eyes to see who was speaking to him. So much pressure on his face, like he was being held in a vise. Everything hurt, but it was as though he felt it from outside his body.

He had to open his eyes.

He had to find Renata.

He had to let her know he was okay.

That had been his thought the moment he came to, faces circling over him, voices careening around the echoing room. "I need to call my wife," he'd spluttered around a mouthful of blood, pushing at the hands that were holding him down. "Renata. I need to tell her—" And then the coughing began, pain punching through his head like a jackhammer. But his throat kept filling with blood, and he couldn't get a breath. He had to roll to his side, or he'd suffocate, but they wouldn't let him.

"Stay still, man!" Someone was shouting at him, a high-pitched voice laced with fear. "Your neck might be broken!"

"He can't breathe," another voice stated, less stridently. "We're going to have to help him turn or he'll choke on his own blood."

The voices faded away, and he opened his eyes to find himself hovering above them all, watching as McCain and Andrews bent over his body, their mouths moving, but no sound coming out. Andrews had his hands on either side of John's face and neck, holding him steady. That younger kid—Logan? Lance? John couldn't recall his name—had his hand on his chest, pinning him to the concrete. McCain. What was that man doing? What was he saying? His face was red from exertion or emotion, but there was no sound. In fact, all around him the air was still, as though he was in a vacuum.

There was so much blood. A pool had formed beneath the head and shoulders of the man on the ground below. He could see McCain's hairy forearms slathered in it. Across the room, some guy was puking in the corner and when John looked back at the broken body being tended to, he felt a wave of compassion wash over him. It was a pretty gruesome sight, to be sure, and he couldn't fault the guy in the corner for being sick. He tipped his head slowly, as though moving through water, and studied the battered face between Andrew's large hands. He didn't recognize it.

"Ah man," he thought. "That poor sucker really took a beating." He was forgetting something, he knew, but it didn't seem to matter so much right now. "I wonder if he has any family."

And suddenly, with a sickening rush, he was back in his body, looking up into the concerned faces of Andrews and McCain, panic strangling him.

"Spit out the blood, Dixon!" McCain was yelling at him. "Spit it out!"

John brought his left hand up to touch his face, unable to accept the fact that the bloody mess he'd looked down on a moment ago was actually him.

But Logan grabbed his wrist and held it firmly. "Don't touch your face, sir."

"John, the paramedics are on their way. Stay still, okay? Gotta protect your spine." Andrew's voice wasn't shrill like McCain's, but John heard something else behind it.

He swallowed a mouthful of blood, his stomach clenching, then gurgled, "My wife. Call my wife." He pulled his hand free from Logan's grip and patted at his belt, where his phone was clipped into its case. "Renata." He didn't know if they knew her name.

Logan pulled the phone out, but McCain grabbed it and started scrolling through it. John took a deep breath and blinked, slowly. Things were getting that dreamy look again, a little fuzzy and misshapen around the edges.

"Stay with us, buddy. Eyes on me, John." Andrew bent low over his face, his voice louder, more commanding. "Stay with us, you hear? Help is on the way."

He could hear sirens, but they sounded like they were coming from above him, and when he tried to open his eyes again, he could only get the left one to comply, and just a slit at that. He was strapped to some kind of a board, his arms pinned to his side, his legs locked in place, something rigid pushing up against his chin, preventing him from looking down to see what was holding him there.

A woman with long black hair pulled back in a ponytail had her back to him, studying a monitor mounted above a bank of metal cabinets.

His wife had come.

"Renata?" he croaked into the oxygen mask over his mouth.

She turned and smiled down at him, but it wasn't his Ren. "Sir, we're almost there. Try to relax, okay?"

"My wife." He needed to call her, to tell her he was okay. She'd be out of her mind with worry right now.

"Yes, sir. She's coming. She'll meet us there."

Another voice cut in, and John could feel a hand on his chest. "Sir, please try to stay calm." Then the two began to speak in low tones, lulling John back into oblivion where there was no pain, no noise, no Renata.

Where was Renata?

TWENTY-THREE

Renata stepped up to the bed. She only glanced at John's face, then averted her eyes quickly, not wanting him to see her distress. They'd covered him with several blankets, but he still trembled noticeably. Probably shock. He'd worked his left hand out from under the covers and it rested on his chest, clenching and unclenching into a fist.

That hand, with its smattering of fine red hair and blunt-tipped fingers, so perfect, so whole, and the wedding band, scratched and dinged by years of wearing it on the job, was medicine to her heart, and she reached out toward it, then paused. "May I touch him?"

"Of course. Please do. The shock is wearing off, and he's beginning to feel things. We're waiting for some more test results before we give him something stronger for pain, so he's going to be a bit uncomfortable. Your presence may help him calm down a little." The nurse smiled kindly at her. "I'm Nate."

Renata thanked him with her eyes before covering her husband's hand with hers.

"John, I'm here." He turned a little toward her voice, but the surgeon who was in the process of cleaning out the splayed tissue on his forehead put a gloved hand against his jaw.

"Mr. Dixon, you need to keep your neck straight, remember? That's why you're wearing the brace." The doctor spoke loudly, as though his patient was hard of hearing. The nurse, however, put a hand on John's shoulder and leaned over him slightly.

"John, your wife is here. You can relax now and let Dr. Hsiung take care of your injuries, okay?"

John squeezed Renata's hand in response and a small spray of blood ejected from between his clenched teeth as he let out a breath, a few tiny droplets landing on the back of her hand.

She straightened her shoulders but didn't let go of John as she studied his battered face. His eyes were both swollen and purple, his right one almost the size of a baseball, his left only open a slit and focused on her face. No matter what she was feeling inside, she could not let her fear and revulsion show. He was gauging her reaction and the trembling in his hands wasn't just from pain.

Her stomach turned as the doctor stapled the wound on his forehead closed.

"That's going to look ugly for now, but when he goes in for surgery, they'll clean it all up," Nate assured her when she stared in horror at the jumbled row of staples that now ran in crooked lines above her husband's eyebrows after the doctor stepped away. "We just need to close him up so he's less susceptible to infection."

John's right arm was strapped to his side beneath the covers, but his shoulder was a terrible mottled black and burgundy where she could see it past the edge of the cervical neck brace they had him in. He pulled his left hand loose and brought it up to his face. Before the nurse could stop him, he started poking at the swollen tissue of his right eye.

"What is that?" he muttered through clenched teeth, his words slightly garbled. "What's on... my eye?"

"John, put your hand down. Hold your wife's hand, please. She needs you to comfort her. She's worried about you." Nate took him by the wrist and directed his hand back into Renata's. "Let her know by squeezing her hand that you're going to be okay."

From behind her, Juliette whispered in her ear. "Rennie, Grandpa and Phoebe are out in the hallway. I'm going to step out and let him come in with you, okay?"

Renata just nodded. She'd forgotten she wasn't alone.

In a few moments, Grandpa's lean frame slipped in beside her and he put one arm around her shoulders and one hand on John's leg. "Hang in there, son. You're looking better already."

Better? He had looked worse than this? John's hair was matted with a blackened crust of dried blood, his nose flattened and pushed slightly to the left side of his face. His lips were swollen and split, and his jaw looked out of alignment. Renata had never seen anything like it in her life. He looked like something from one of the contraband zombie movies the girls used to watch in high school when they were trying to scare themselves silly.

As though hearing her thoughts, Grandpa turned to her and placed a tender kiss over her temple. "He looks better, Renata. He really does. You hang in there, too, okay?"

The curtain drew back again and a man in black pants and a white dress shirt peered into the crowded space. "I'm Luke Simons. Clergy. I just ran into the transfer team out in the hallway. They're coming in shortly, so I won't stay, lest I get in the way." He handed Renata a card. "I'll come visit you in your room in a little while, all right?" His handshake was warm and confident, and Renata noticed how he didn't seem at all disturbed by John's appearance.

"Mr. Dixon?" He leaned close to John's face and spoke quietly. "I'm praying for you, brother. I'll be back when you're settled in your room."

John squeezed Renata's hand in response. She could tell his pain was intensifying just by how still he was.

At that moment, a man in navy scrubs poked his head around the edge of the curtain. "We're here for Dixon, John. Is he ready to transfer?"

Nate turned to Renata. "We're moving him to the Critical Care Unit. Your nurse up there will go over all the test results with you and will advise you on the treatment plan for your husband."

He came around the end of the bed and put both hands on John's ankles, but stood so that he was turned slightly toward Renata. "Mrs. Dixon, your husband is a fighter," he said quietly. "He's strong and healthy, and he's much more settled now that you're here." He indicated the monitor behind him. His voice dropped a little lower. "It's going to get harder before it gets better, but don't let yourself get discouraged. He's a champion."

Then he turned and faced John directly. "You're a champ, John Dixon. Don't you forget that." He pulled the curtain open and directed Renata and Grandpa to stand aside to let the transfer nurse in.

"I'll see you upstairs in your room, honey, okay? I'm not going anywhere. I'll be right behind you." Renata leaned down and pressed a kiss to the back of his hand. "I love you. I'm right here."

When they wheeled him out into the hall, Phoebe and Juliette were standing against the far wall. Phoebe's eyes grew wide and frightened at the sight of John's terrible injuries, but Renata kept on walking. From the corner of her eye, she saw Juliette take Phoebe in her arms, the younger woman's face pressed to her shoulder. Then Renata looked away, hoping they'd follow.

Grandpa stayed right beside her, his hand resting lightly on her shoulder blade. She let him lead her along. When they reached the Critical Care Unit, a new medical crew took over immediately.

The nurse spoke kindly to them. "It can be difficult for family members to watch this part. You're welcome to stay, but it might be easier on everyone if you just step out of the room until we have him comfortable."

They worked remarkably fast. Within what seemed only moments, John was hooked up to monitors and IVs, his face washed, his lips coated in some kind of salve. He looked much better and considerably more comfortable. The nurse dimmed the lights and informed them that he was now hooked up to a good pain medication and that he would probably sleep much of the time.

"That doesn't mean he won't know you're here. There's nothing more helpful to our patients than having loved ones around when they open their eyes, no matter how briefly. We have an ophthalmologist coming in later today after the swelling goes down a little. He'll be checking for any damage to his eyes. The Neurosurgeon team is here right now. They're reviewing his chart at the nurse's station. They'll be in to see him soon, too. Tomorrow morning, Dr. Stanley will be in with his team to assess Mr. Dixon. He's a wonderfully gifted plastic surgeon who specializes in miracles."

She reached over and made a few more notations on a clipboard beside a monitor, then turned back to Renata and held out her hand. "My name is Cheryl. I'll be your nurse until the shift is over, then you'll have Lisa for this evening. If you need anything, don't hesitate to ask."

She was brisk and business-like, but she was also very informative, keeping them clued in to everything she did to John over the next several hours.

Renata's sisters stayed for a while before she told them to go home and fill Granny G in on things and to help out with the boys. Gia was on her way and would be there any time.

"That's what I need most, I think," Renata sighed, relieved that they would take on the responsibility of the kids for at least the next few days. "I need to know that my little guys are taken care of so that I don't have to worry about them, too."

"Victor will help, Ren. Maybe he can pick them up from school in his cruiser. Do you think they'd like that?" Juliette was anxious to get home to the man she loved, Renata could tell, and she couldn't blame her. The absurd notion crossed her mind of how absolutely lovely it would be to go home to find John there, waiting for her, to comfort her, to assure her that everything would be okay.

"That would be wonderful, Juliette. You know they'd love it, even if he didn't show up in the police car. Thank you." She turned to Phoebe, a pale, solemn version of her usual capricious sister. "Give me a hug, Phoebe. Rub off some of your perfume on me. I forgot to put any on."

Phoebe's eyes were bright with tears as she hugged her, her untamed curls tickling Renata's cheeks. "Why are you comforting me?" she whispered.

"Because you look like you're just about ready to come undone, little sister." Renata smiled, leaned back to look at Phoebe, but kept her arms around her as she said, "Thank you for coming to get me. I don't know what I would have done if I'd been alone when I got the news." She stretched out an arm to Juliette, who joined the hug. "I'm so glad you were there. I'm so glad you came for me."

Just then, Gia came scurrying in, looking frightened and alone and terribly young. All three of them chuckled at the sight of her and opened their arms to her, too. After a few more comforting moments, Juliette and Phoebe headed for home an hour away.

Gia and Grandpa stayed by John's bedside, an extra pair of eyes, hands, and ears for Renata. Gia called the secretary at Renata's church requesting prayer, and Pastor Benton surprised her by making the long drive out to visit and pray at the bedside with them. At one point, John squeezed his hand to acknowledge his presence, and the man smiled like he'd been given a shot of hope.

"You've got an army of prayer warriors holding you up, John. You remember that, all right?"

TWENTY-FOUR

THE PASTOR FROM THE hospital, Luke Simons, did come to them as he'd promised. He spoke in such gentle, soothing tones, praying quietly over John, his hand resting on John's head in benediction. Grandpa and Gia had both stepped out to update Granny G and the other sisters, but returned in time to speak to Pastor Simons, too.

"Well, maybe you could remember to add me and my wife to your prayers, too. Renata's John has been a son to us, and I know my wife is heartbroken. She's a praying woman, but she's usually on her knees praying for others, and I don't know how many prayers she gets in return."

"I'd be honored," Pastor Simons said, his kindness toward them like a warm blanket. "Why don't we do that right now. Let's gather around John again so he can join us as we pray over this whole family, shall we? Would you like to join us?" He waved a hand to include Gia.

John had been completely unresponsive the whole time they were there, but they lined up on both sides of his bed, Renata resting a hand on his chest, and they bowed their heads in prayer. Pastor Simons boldly laid out his requests to God, asking Him to not only preserve John's life, but to restore him back to normal, to heal his wounds in miraculous ways, and to leave the doctors so amazed that they'd be unable to deny the existence and power of a loving Creator.

"And Lord, your prayer warriors need prayers, too. So, we cover Mrs. Gustafson. Keep her knees sturdy, her faith strong, and her heart whole, as she carries the burdens of her family to you."

He wrapped his prayer up with words of encouragement and support for Renata. "In Jesus' mighty and powerful name, we ask these things. We all agree by saying, 'Amen!'"

And they did.

The pastor left shortly, then Scott McCain made another appearance.

It had been hours since she'd arrived, and Renata had forgotten all about him.

He stood tentatively in the doorway, as though waiting to be invited in. Renata had seen him coming down the hall; in the CCU, the walls were glass panels so patients could be observed at all times. Privacy was limited to a pulled curtain and bed linens. She turned away as he approached and shot a beseeching look at her grandfather.

Grandpa stood quickly and crossed the room to the man, but he shook his hand and ushered him in, obviously misunderstanding Renata's silent plea. "He's resting peacefully right now, Scott. His nurse says he's on some pretty strong medication, so we may not get much of a response out of him."

The two men stood beside the bed near John's head. Renata sat in her chair, head down.

"Hello, Mrs. Dixon." Scott's voice sounded gruff, broken.

"Mr. McCain." She glanced up at him briefly, just quickly enough to be polite, then turned back to look at John's face.

"If there's anything I can do...." McCain's voice trailed off.

"No. But thank you. And thank you for staying with my husband today. I appreciate that. I know he does, too." Why was he here? What had prompted the pompous idiot to come back? Why did she have to be kind to him? He hadn't spared John a day of peace since starting the job with him, and now he wanted to share in her dark hour?

"Scott, could I ask you a huge favor?" Grandpa spoke up.

"Of course! Please. If there's anything I can do. I meant what I said." McCain was clearly anxious to help.

"I haven't had my afternoon coffee today, thanks to John here, and I know the girls haven't either. Would you and Gia go down to the cafeteria and pick us up a couple?" Grandpa took out his wallet and started to pull out some cash.

"Coffee's on me, sir," McCain insisted, then turned to the curious Gia and waited while she slipped her feet into a pair of UGG boots.

When they'd left, Grandpa spoke softly, but firmly. "Renata, that man is braver than I would be in his shoes. He's here, isn't he?"

"Of course, he's here, Grandpa. Because he's riddled with guilt. My husband is here because of that man." She didn't raise her voice either, but her finger jabbing the air in McCain's direction was just as effective as a yell. "Is there anything he can do for us? Yes. Leave, and never come back. Hasn't he done enough?"

"He didn't push John off the ladder." Grandpa's voice remained calm.

"Maybe not, but he sure pushed him in every other way. McCain has been nothing but a thorn in John's side from the very first day they started this project. John's safety was jeopardized on a regular basis on that job site because McCain doesn't know jack about electrical stuff. McCain, himself, said John was up rewiring something that had been done badly. You can bet he was fixing McCain's mistakes, not his own. If John hadn't fallen off a ladder, it would have been something else. Or someone else."

"Renata, sometimes accidents happen. Sometimes there's no one to blame, no matter how badly you may want to point fingers. Sometimes, you have to look a man in the eye and respect him—and yourself—enough to give him grace, *because* he doesn't deserve it." He came around the bed and sat on the edge of it, a few feet from her chair. "You harbor resentment too easily, little Ren."

He sighed, straightened his spine, and cleared his throat before continuing, his voice firm. "Scott McCain will be returning shortly, and he will probably be carrying your coffee. You will do the right thing; do you hear me? You will thank him, not just for the coffee, but for thinking on his feet when John fell. Your husband is alive because of that man, no matter what you believe his motivation was. He called emergency services. He stayed with him, talking to him, making phone calls for him. He was the first person to give me any information about John. He stayed at his bedside until I arrived, then he insisted on staying close until you arrived, so he could tell us exactly what happened in case the story got muddled along the way. He stayed to make sure you were going to be able to keep it together." He rested his palms on his thighs and crossed his ankles. "You come from good stock, Renata Gustafson Dixon. Don't embarrass yourself."

Renata sat in stunned silence. She hadn't thought it through that way until now, McCain's part in the whole ordeal, what his decision to stay said about the man. But even more shocking was the number of words and sentences her grandfather had just strung together to put her in her place. Oh, he loved to talk. He loved to tell stories. But he didn't do long lectures, especially when it came to discipline. Usually, he just dealt swiftly and justly, and it was over.

And that's exactly what he was doing. Disciplining her.

He was right. McCain, as blustering a buffoon as he was, had stayed the course today. He had to have sensed her animosity, yet he came back anyway. She owed him much more than a cold shoulder.

"What's wrong with me, Grandpa? Why am I so awful to people? It's like my automatic response these days." She voiced the question quietly, but she knew he wouldn't judge her for admitting it.

"These days? Honey, you've always been quick to judge. But." He held up a hand when she opened her mouth to deny it. "But it's because you've always been a black and white kind of girl. Just like your Simon. There's nothing between the extremes with you, and in most cases, that's fine. But it doesn't leave you with much room for human error, does it?"

Renata shook her head and finished his thought for him. "And it doesn't leave anyone else with much room for error, either."

"Good girl." He grinned at her a little shyly. "I'm not claiming to be God, but I have a feeling you're almost as surprised as I am about how much I've just said. I had planned to just tell you to grow up." He chuckled and reached out to ruffle her hair. "I like your haircut, Little Ren. It reminds me of you when you were a little thing. Your hair stuck up all over your head. Just like Simon's does now."

"Thanks, Grandpa." She reached up and grabbed the hand that rested on her head. She held it between her own, her thumbs tracing the prominent veins and ridged knuckles. "I love you. I'm glad you're here."

When McCain and Gia returned bearing coffee, cake pops, and several bagels with packets of cream cheese, Renata graciously thanked him for the refreshments.

Then she pulled him aside and quietly and sincerely thanked him for saving John's life.

Scott McCain rubbed his already reddened eyes, told her again how terrible he felt, how if there was anything at all he could do, just to call him. He gave her his private number, his work number, and his email address, then hurried from the room, looking like he was ready to cry again, but obviously greatly relieved.

Awash in the glow of grace, Renata thought. That's how he looked to her. And that's how she felt.

That evening, she called and spoke to each one of the boys for several minutes, assuring them that their daddy was okay, that he was sleeping, and to make sure and pray for him with Granny G.

"I'm glad you came home, Mom." Reuben didn't say it with any condemnation, but Renata felt the weight of guilt settle back on her shoulders.

"Oh, honey. I came straight away. Of course, I came home."

"I know. I didn't mean that I was afraid you wouldn't. I just meant that I'm glad you're home. I like Aunt Gia, but I missed you."

"I missed you, too, son. I'm glad I'm home, too."

Simon wasn't so sweet. "See what happens when you take a vacation from us?"

Renata could think of nothing to say back to him.

"Don't go away anymore, Mommy." Suddenly his tough little shell cracked, and his voice squeaked as he began to sniffle. "I didn't like not knowing where you were."

"Simon, my precious boy. I love you. I'm home. I'm going to stay here at the hospital with Daddy, but I'm home."

"Can we come see you guys?"

"Not right away. Not until we know better how he's doing. We're in a part of the hospital where kids aren't allowed to visit, probably because kids carry gross germs with them." She wanted him to feel better.

"Not me. I wash my hands."

"I know. You're about as germ-free as they come. But the rules are the rules. As soon as they move Daddy, I'll be sure and ask if you and your brothers can come visit, okay? In the meantime, I'll call every morning and every night."

"What about after school?"

Her heart strings tightened at the vulnerability in his usually churlish tone.

"You call me after school, okay? You call me on Daddy's phone. Mine broke."

"Is that why you didn't call us last night? Because your phone broke?"

Renata sighed. "Yes," she said, wishing that everything was different, that the last few days hadn't happened.

"Okay. I'll talk to you in the morning. Granny G said we get to sleep on your old bed tonight."

"All four of you?"

"Yeah. I don't know how that's going to work. I'll probably end up on the floor."

Levi was his normal sweet self, telling her how much he loved her and to be sure and tell Daddy he loved him, too.

Judah got distracted by something his brothers were doing, and forgetting that he was talking to her, he set the phone down. She finally hung up, hoping Granny G would find the phone before morning. She'd try calling her back in an hour or so, after the kids were in bed.

It was eight o'clock, and the room was still except for the ticking and beeping of the machines surrounding the patient, the lights dimmed. Renata sat in a chair beside John's sleeping form, his hand in hers, her head resting on the mattress near his thigh. To her surprise, Phoebe had returned to stay with her through the night. She and Gia and Grandpa took off to find the cafeteria and something to eat before Grandpa and Gia headed home. Renata didn't want anything; she was curiously not hungry at all, even though she'd eaten only a half a bagel all day, and she was glad for the sudden reprieve from visitors.

"Renata?" A hushed male voice called her name, and she lifted her head to see the shadowy large form in the doorway.

Tim Larsen. He'd finally come. She stood up, and he quickly crossed the room to her side, enveloping her in a solid embrace.

TWENTY-FIVE

It occurred to her in an abstract way that this was the first time she'd ever been so thoroughly hugged by the man, but in the absence of John's arms around her, Tim's felt pretty good at that moment.

And then she was crying. Sobbing.

"I'm so sorry, Renata. I'm sorry I wasn't here." He kept himself straight, solid, letting her lean into his strength, but she could tell he was feeling a little out of his element.

Poor guy, she thought, as she started to pull away. Reaching into her pocket, she retrieved the packet of tissues she'd kept on hand but had only pulled out to offer her sisters up until now.

"I—I wasn't here either, Tim." She drew the edges of her cardigan together, tucking the tissue into her sleeve, and turned back toward the bed where John lay in a heavily drugged state. "I'm sorry I just unloaded on you."

"I'm not." His confident response surprised her a little. "I should have been here for you earlier."

"So where have you been, then?" Even though her words were straight-forward, her tone was gentle. If she knew her husband's best friend at all, she knew he would have been here if there had been any way possible. He would have a very good reason for his delay.

"I took the week off to go visit my folks up north. It was their anniversary yesterday. I came as soon as your sister called." That meant the man had gotten in his truck and driven more than six hours to be there.

He cautiously approached the bed and peered down at John. Renata heard his intake of breath, but didn't turn to look at him. She knew all too well what must be going through his mind.

She'd been staring at John's face all afternoon, still in a bit of shock over the damage that had been done. He looked nothing like her husband. His eyes were no longer quite so swollen, but the pooling blood beneath his skin was seeping across the rest of his face. He looked like he had puffy jowls and his nose was just a purple blob sitting slightly to the left of center, crusted blood filling his nostrils. His breaths came short and shallow through his parted lips.

It must be a terrible thing for Tim to see him like this. Renata had been shocked, but there was something about being a mother that prepared a woman for suffering, she was certain. Men seemed to find it very difficult to handle their loved ones' pain.

They stood side by side in silence for a long time. She wondered if he had questions, if he even wanted answers. She wondered if she should offer information; if his reticence was because he didn't know what to ask. She crossed her arms and hugged herself, suddenly feeling like an ill-equipped liaison. What does one say to a man's best friend?

"Can he hear me?" Tim's voice was so low, Renata had to look up at him to make sure he'd spoken.

"Yes." She reached out and put a hand on John's chest, just over his heart. "John, honey? Tim is here. He came all the way from his parents' house to see you."

John worked his mouth a little in awareness, as though trying to speak. His eyes were still horribly swollen, but she thought she saw his left eye crack open just a hairline.

"John? Brother, it's me, Tim. You look like roadkill, man."

Renata rolled her eyes and covered her mouth, not sure whether she should laugh or cry. But Tim had somehow come to grips with what he was dealing with, and he started talking about how his parents were doing, how beautiful the snow was right now, how he'd gone out to the cabin to check on it for his folks and had discovered a family of raccoons living under the porch.

Renata watched as Tim began to relax a little, how the shock of John's condition was beginning to recede, how even John's slightest response seemed to encourage the normally strong-and-silent-type Tim to keep talking. She brought a chair around for him to sit in and saw his hand reaching for the worn Bible tucked into his back pocket.

"Excuse me, Tim," she interrupted, her voice gentle. "I haven't been out of the room for more than a few minutes to use the restroom. Would you be willing to stay here with John while I take a little breather?" She didn't really need one, but she somehow felt like Tim might be more comfortable if he was given some time with John to sort through things. He was the one man she felt completely at ease leaving alone with her husband. If he awoke, Tim's face would comfort him.

If Tim had come from his folks' house in Sutter Creek, then he must have started driving as soon as he got word. She knew the men were close and she was overwhelmed by Tim's efforts to come to John's bedside today. It gave her pause to realize that she didn't have any friends in her life like Tim. Other than Granny G, the only women's names on their emergency list on the fridge at home were her sisters.

Her sisters. And they would drop whatever they were doing and come, just like Tim had done for John. Just like they'd done for her only yesterday. Was it only yesterday?

The three of them had put their own lives on hold to come to her rescue, even though she didn't want to be rescued. They'd dropped everything, taken on her family, driven more than two hours just to let her know they cared enough to be worried about her.

"Not Phoebe, though. She was practically dragged, kicking and screaming."

No, Phoebe may not have been thrilled about the idea, but she had come, nonetheless. And Phoebe had cried real tears over Renata's miscarriages, her lost babies.

Maybe, just maybe, Renata wasn't being fair to Phoebe. Maybe it was time to bury the hatchet and love Phoebe for who she was.

She made her way down the hall and out of the unit after first assuring the nurse she would only be gone for a few minutes. Maybe she'd try to find Phoebe and Gia; Grandpa had probably already left for home by now. As she waited for the elevator that would take her down to the main floor, her mind drifted to Phoebe again.

Renata would never forget the first time she brought John home for dinner. The seventeen-year-old Phoebe had sized him up with her kohl-lined cow eyes, her features soft with youthful sensuality. Renata had warned her conservative boyfriend about the girl. He'd clearly been uncomfortable by Phoebe's open admiration, and he'd kept her at arm's length the whole night.

As though sensing blood, Phoebe had relentlessly teased and flirted with him, right up until Renata and he were married, getting some kind of thrill from watching Renata fume and bluster. John took it all in stride, reminding her that it was her reaction that kept Phoebe going, not any unrequited interest in him. Renata wasn't so sure.

The day of their wedding, Phoebe had hugged them both ferociously. "Don't worry, Rennie. He's all yours." Turning to John, she winked and said, "And I do like you, John Dixon, but you can stop looking at me like you're afraid I'm going to gobble you up. I don't mess with married men." Then she'd flitted off to harass some other poor guy.

If John had ever shown so much as a hint of a response to the girl, Renata might not have handled things so well, but he'd gone over and above the call of duty to make it clear with whom his affections lay. Even so, because of Phoebe's treachery with Brad, it had taken Renata a long time to stop being so wary of Phoebe when she was around John.

As Renata stepped off the elevator, she saw them, and her eyes narrowed at the way her sister was hanging on the police officer.

Juliette's police officer, Victor Jarrett.

He grinned down at Phoebe, patted the hand she'd tucked into the corner of his arm, and said something to her that made her giggle. Where was Juliette? Was she really so naïve that she would leave her hunky man alone with Phoebe?

Just then, Phoebe glanced up and saw her, and her face instantly fell. She pulled away from Victor and hurried over to Renata. "Is everything okay? What are you doing? Why are you down here?"

Her shrill questions echoed in the cavernous hallway where the elevators released their riders, and Renata put one hand up over her ear at the sound. She eyed Victor over Phoebe's head; his own expression became grim as he approached her a little more slowly.

"I'm so sorry about John, Renata," he said when he was close. He put out a hand, but she didn't take it, fending off Phoebe's hug as well. "We were just coming up to see you."

Renata looked at the two of them with raised eyebrows. "You and Phoebe? How sweet."

Victor seemed confused by her response, but she didn't miss the guilty look that was quickly replaced by a mocking smirk on Phoebe's face. "Jules is in the little girls' room, Ren."

"Well, she should be more careful about where she leaves her valuables lying around. And with whom." She eyed Victor pointedly, then added, "Tim Larsen is upstairs with John right now, so I'm going for a walk. I need to breathe some nontoxic air." She turned and headed down the hall away from them.

TWENTY-SIX

Something was weighing down his eyelids. When John tried to raise his hand to push it away, he found it wedged against his ribs, and a sharp pain seized his whole right side. He caught his breath at the agony of it. *In through the nose, out through the mouth. In through the nose, out through the mouth.* He'd done Lamaze classes with Renata enough times to know how to work his way through pain... but as soon as he closed his mouth to breathe in, his throat filled with the metallic taste of blood and no air. He coughed in reaction, but his jaw was stiff and swollen, and he felt the wetness dribble from the corners of his mouth.

Something was holding him down, pinning him to the bed. Panic began to build in his chest, and with his left hand, he clawed at the bands around his neck and shoulders, but there was no strength in his fingers. He couldn't get a grip, he couldn't see. What were they doing to him? Where was he?

Coughing again, his mouth filled with the contents of his throat, and he tried to spit it out, his stomach bucking in response to the blood he'd already swallowed. What if he needed to throw up? He'd suffocate on his own vomit.

Someone wiped at his face with a cool, wet cloth.

He could hear a keening sound, like a teakettle that was just beginning to whistle, and it took him a minute to realize that it was the sound of his own voice seeping out between his clenched teeth. There was a buzzing in his right ear; static, like a bad connection.

John tried to move his legs, but they were weighed down, draped in lead, like at the dentist's office.

Oh God, help me. Help me. Please help me.

"John. Calm down. Brother, you gotta calm down."

He recognized that voice... Tim? Tim was holding him prisoner? Why? He flung his left arm out, his fist coming in contact with something.

"Hey," Tim grunted. "John, stop. You're going to hurt yourself." He felt Tim's rough fingers wrap around his wrist and guide it down to his side again.

"What's going on in here?" Another voice, familiar too, but this one he couldn't quite place. "Mr. Dixon, I need you to calm down, please. We can't have any temper tantrums now, you hear?" Her voice was full, and he envisioned his heavily jowled third grade teacher in her orthopedic shoes, Mrs. Hartley. What was she doing here?

What was over his eyes? A cloth? A bandage? It occurred to him that his head hurt terribly, too. He pulled his hand free of Tim's grip and reached up to feel the bandage, but his fingers only touched something mushy, like a water balloon.

"Wuz thiz?" His voice bubbled out of him, making the static in his ear crackle sharply.

"Stop poking, John. Put your hand down, please." Mrs. Hartley was talking very firmly to him; he'd recognize that tone anywhere. *What* was she doing here?

"Wher'm I?" Where was Renata? *Renata! Oh, God, where is Renata? I have to tell her I'm okay.* "Ren. Tell... tell...."

"John. John, it's Tim. You're in the hospital, man. You fell. Renata will be right back. She just stepped out for a minute." Tim's assurance made him breathe easier. Renata would be right back, he'd said.

John tried to relax, but he was in too much pain. Everything hurt. His head, his eyes, his nose... he couldn't feel his nose. Was there really a water balloon on his face? His jaws ached, his chest hurt when he breathed, his right shoulder was on fire.

What had happened?

Pinpricks of light began pinging behind his eyelids, and he watched them, trying to focus on anything but his pain. Soon the lights dimmed, Tim's steady voice faded, and Mrs. Hartley's chesty hum drifted away into nothing.

Soft, deep nothing.

• • • • • • • • • • •

RENATA STOOD IN THE little courtyard off of the cafeteria watching the reflection of lights flicker off the damp sidewalk. It had rained sometime this afternoon, and she'd been completely unaware. It was freezing outside, but it felt good on her flushed skin.

Just when she'd considered making peace with Phoebe, she'd seen her for who she really was. Nothing had changed in the last fifteen years, Phoebe still had to sink her claws into every man she met, especially those already belonging to someone else. The flirting, grasping girl had become a wanton, grasping woman, always reaching for things that didn't belong to her. Had she ever stopped reaching for John? Just because Renata trusted John didn't mean that Phoebe could be trusted.

Renata's feelings were in such an uproar. A part of her knew she was trying to lash out at someone, something, and Phoebe was just so...so *available*! But seriously, couldn't her sister restrain herself, at least while she was here at the hospital? John was lying in critical condition upstairs, and Phoebe was down here, putting the moves on her sister's boyfriend. She was trouble; that was all there was to it.

"You've always been a black and white kind of girl. There's nothing between the extremes with you." Grandpa's words popped into her head and she frowned.

"I know!" she whispered to the lamppost beside her. "But some people only live in the middle somewhere and that can't be right, either."

Did Phoebe feel strongly about anything? About anyone? As far as Renata knew, her younger sister hadn't had a serious boyfriend since, well, since high school. In fact, she couldn't remember her dating anyone long-term back then, either. Was there a lost love in her life? Was there someone she was pining away for? Someone she couldn't move beyond?

Was it John?

John. Momentarily lightheaded, Renata reached for the post to steady herself, the chilled steel beneath her hands startlingly cold. *I can't live without him, God. Please don't take him from me.*

She pressed her chilled palms to her cheeks. "Stop it, Renata. Don't think like that," she berated herself out loud. But she was suddenly afraid, afraid he might slip away from her in the moments she was not at his side. Her heart began to race, and she turned to go back inside, her footsteps quickening as she hurried down the hall toward the elevator.

John. John. John. His name flashed in her mind as the number flashed on the panel over the elevator. *Stay with me. Stay with me. Stay with me.*

TWENTY-SEVEN

The room was so peaceful when she made it back, in complete contrast to the panic that had spurred her on through the unfamiliar corridors and stations. She paused in the open doorway, her heart racing at the sight of the dimmed lights, at first concerned it meant the worst. But her eyes adjusted quickly, noting the whirring and beeping of machines, the monitor on its tray flashing zigzag signs of life. Now that John's spine was stable, the head of his bed had to stay slightly elevated, and Tim sat close, facing John, leaning forward in his seat a little like they were deep in conversation. His brown curls were lit up by the low-watt light above him, and he read aloud from a Bible open on the bed beside John's rising and falling chest.

Renata stayed where she was, watching the man her husband loved like a brother. He reached up to adjust the blanket across John's shoulder, then murmured something too quiet for her to hear. She knew she should make a noise, do something to let him know she was there, but the atmosphere in the room felt holy, and she was loathed to break the spell.

Finally, Tim leaned back in his chair and caught sight of her standing there. He rose immediately, always the gentleman, and stepped aside to offer the chair to her.

"He woke up for a few minutes and asked about you," he said as she lowered herself into the seat, still warm from Tim's body heat. He drew up another chair and sat next to her. "Told him you'd be right back."

Tim was one of those guys who didn't say much. He wasn't exactly shy, Renata had decided long ago. Just reserved, treading carefully around women in particular. She didn't really get it. He was quite handsome in that rugged hunter, flannel and jeans way, respectful and old-fashioned, and he was an incredibly skilled carpenter, specializing in custom cabinetry. He and John had met years ago on a job, had discovered they had more in common than just work, and had become fast friends. John always said that if it ever came down to it, he'd want Tim at his back.

For whatever reason, Tim had always seemed at ease around her, most likely because she was John's wife and had no expectations of him, except to respect their marriage, which he did to a fault. He was great with the boys, always up for a game of Tackle the Tim, or football, or Frisbee. He was as proud of the boys as any favorite uncle when they came home with a stringer full of fish, a good grade on a report card, a black eye from a fly-ball. And it was Tim's family's cabin the JFFs went to on their hunting trips. Tim Larsen, Renata was happy to say, was the ultimate Jesus Freak in Flannel.

So, sitting here tonight, John lying battered and bruised before them, it only seemed natural for her to reach out to Tim. He took her hand between his big, callused palms and held it tightly, saying only, "Cold fingers."

It could have been minutes, it could have been hours, when quiet voices from down the hall heralded the arrival of her sisters and Victor. Renata took a deep breath and closed her eyes, not wanting to see Phoebe right now, or Victor, either, for that matter. When she opened them again, Tim was studying her, his brows lowered in concern.

"You alright?"

She paused, wondering what this gentle giant would do if she asked him to deal with Phoebe for her, and the thought made her smile. "I'm fine, Tim. Thank you. It's just my sisters."

He squeezed her hand, then released it, taking up his Bible from the bed. Like a security blanket, she thought, not unkindly. She could think of worse things to find security in.

"Rennie?" Juliette's soft voice beckoned from the doorway, Victor looming behind her, Phoebe still at his side. Renata waved them in but didn't get up. Tim did, of course, and introduced himself to Victor. To Renata's surprise, he greeted Juliette warmly, too, shaking her hand and telling her it was nice to see her again.

Then he turned to Phoebe. Renata held her breath and waited for her sister's inappropriate response to the man.

But if she'd been surprised at Tim's reaction to Juliette, she was shocked when Phoebe, in a hushed voice, greeted him politely, barely even sparing the man a second look. Instead, she turned her gaze to John, her large eyes drifting up his supine form to his battered face, spotlighted under the reading light still on over his bed.

"How is he, Rennie?" Her voice, still hushed, wobbled a little, and she stepped closer to the other side of the bed across from where Renata sat. As she came into the circle of light, Renata saw evidence that she'd been crying, the tip of her nose red, her cheeks bright.

She sighed, guilt washing over her at her ugly thoughts toward Phoebe. "No changes. The drugs are helping him sleep. Tim said he woke up briefly while I was downstairs, but other than that...." She shrugged and reached out to place a hand on John's chest, her fingertips brushing along the ridge of his left collarbone.

They'd removed the neck brace after they'd transferred John, the doctor having cleared his spine, but his right collarbone was broken, a few ribs were cracked, and his shoulder had been partially dislocated, so they'd immobilized that whole side by strapping his arm to his abdomen using elastic bandages around his torso and neck. His left arm hosted a forked IV, a cuff that automatically took his blood pressure every hour, and an oxygen monitor on his finger. Wires ran from the machine by the bed to electrodes on his chest and an oxygen mask sat low over his mouth, his nose completely non-functioning.

Phoebe still didn't meet Renata's eyes, her own glued to John's face. Her arms were crossed over her stomach and she was shaking her head ever so slightly as she studied him. Victor approached the bed behind her, calm and collected, his face showing no sign of shock or discomfort over the sight before him. He put a hand on Phoebe's shoulder, and she reached up to pat it with her own.

Renata watched the interaction with raised eyebrows. Had they just come to gawk at her husband and comfort each other? She didn't need this. And where did Juliette fit into this cozy little picture? Renata glanced over at her oldest sister, who was speaking in low tones to Tim close to the door.

"How are you holding up, Renata?" Victor asked, removing his hand from Phoebe's shoulder and turning to face her.

She shrugged. How did he think she was?

"Thanks for letting me help out with the boys. I'm working the early shift the rest of the week, so it actually works out perfectly for me to pick them up from school." A note of steel seeped into his voice. "Is there anything else I can do? Do you need me to... well, to look into things? At John's work?"

Renata's head snapped up. "What do you mean?" But she knew exactly what he was getting at. It had been no secret that John was struggling at this job. It had been no secret, either, that he'd been concerned about things being done not quite above board, corners being cut.

The room grew silent, and Juliette came to stand beside Victor, slipping her arms around his waist. Victor's arm settled around her shoulders and drew her close to him.

Renata didn't hear him approach, but suddenly Tim was standing behind her, his hand on the back of her chair, making her long to lean into him the way Juliette was leaning into Victor.

"No." Renata shook her head. "No. I can't even think that way right now. I—no." She remembered McCain's face when he'd left, and if ever there was a guilty man, that was one. But like Grandpa had so clearly pointed out, the man had stayed and faced her, had gone above and beyond the call of duty, had made phone calls and stayed past his welcome, just to be sure she was going to be okay.

Renata wondered what McCain was doing right now, who he had at home to comfort him. What if he was alone? What if he had to carry the burden of today, fault or none, alone in the dark night? She silently whispered a prayer that McCain had a sweet wife who would speak softly to him.

"No. It was an accident. I know it was." It had to be. She couldn't accept anything else.

"Renata," John muttered, the sound muffled behind the oxygen mask. His left hand slowly came up to cover hers where it still rested on his chest.

TWENTY-EIGHT

John tried to open his eyes, but he was so tired, and his eyelids so heavy. He could hear people talking around him in quiet words, but it was Renata's voice he listened for, the others coming into focus one at a time. Victor, Phoebe. Who else?

A shadow loomed over him, blocking the light, making it easier to crack open his left eyelid. "Tim," he grunted.

"Hey, brother. I'm here." Tim was smiling; John could see his teeth.

"Stay with Ren for me, Tim. Renata needs you." His words came out slowly and slurred, taking every ounce of effort he had in him. "Ren?" He turned his head in the direction he'd heard her voice.

"I'm here, honey. Right here. I'm not going anywhere." And there were her eyes, her straight narrow nose, her sweet lips—

"Hair?" He reached up, his hand moving through water, and touched the chopped ends behind her ear. "Your hair?"

She grabbed his fingers and held them to her cheek. "Oh, honey. It'll grow back, I promise." And then she was crying. He could feel her beginning to shake, but his arm was so heavy, so weak, he couldn't hold it up any longer. If she hadn't been holding onto it so tightly, it would have fallen to the mattress at his side.

John closed his eyes, trying to comprehend the picture of his wife he'd just seen. Her long, beautiful hair was gone. Was that why she was crying? Her hair? "Renata," he muttered. "You are so beautiful to me." The song he often whisper-sang to her when they danced together in the darkened house after the boys were in bed. "So beautiful... to me."

"I love you, John-boy," she whispered, her mouth close to his ear. "I love you."

He sighed deeply, sinking back into the cloud on which he was resting, his wife's tender voice carrying him gently away from the pain piercing his skull behind his eyes, the band around his ribcage that made it difficult to breathe. He almost thought he could smell her, like she'd just walked through a rose garden. But then there was nothing.

· · · · · ● · ● · · · ·

RENATA KEPT HER FACE pressed to John's cheek long after she knew he'd drifted off again. She couldn't bear the thought that her missing hair had unsettled him so much. *Oh Renata, why did you chop your hair off?*

Finally, she straightened, wiped at her tears, and sat back in her chair, not letting go of her husband's hand, and not looking away from his face. She spoke softly, trying to keep her voice from breaking. "I need some time, guys."

Without a word, Juliette circled the bed, grabbed Phoebe's hand and drew her along with her. She pulled Renata up out of the chair and put her arms around both girls. They held to each other tightly, the three of them huddled together, before Juliette pulled back.

"Would you like us to stay? Phoebe and I can spend the night. Vic has to work early, so he has to go back soon, but you know we're here for you."

Renata shook her head. "No, I'm okay, really. I don't expect anything to change tonight. Go home and get some rest. I may think of something I need tomorrow, but for now, I'm fine."

"I'm staying." Tim spoke from behind her, his voice low and gruff but firm. "I'll make sure she's okay."

The room fell silent again, but only for a few brief moments. Then Victor nodded and said, "Sounds good."

Renata wanted to argue, to demand they all leave her alone, Tim, too, but the terrible thought flashed across her mind of John waking up to no one while she was in the bathroom, or asleep in the lounge chair in the corner. If Tim stayed, they could take turns keeping watch. At least the quiet man wouldn't expect her to converse with him.

She hugged her sisters again, reassuring them repeatedly that she'd be all right, then even hugged Victor.

And fifteen minutes later, the room was still once more, she and Tim sitting side-by-side in the chairs next to the bed, but this time, not touching. Tim's Bible lay open in his lap and he silently read to himself.

"Thanks for staying," she whispered, knowing she was interrupting, but needing to let him know she appreciated it.

"Yep."

"Will you—will you read out loud again?" She smiled weakly at him when he glanced up, his brows arched in surprise. "You have a nice voice, Tim. Very soothing. And I could use a little soothing right now. As I'm sure John could, too."

A moment of silence passed, then Tim flipped a few pages to a new passage and began to read.

He who dwells in the shelter of the Most High
Will abide in the shadow of the Almighty.
I will say to the Lord, "My refuge and my fortress,
My God, in whom I trust!"

Renata lay her head down on the bed beside John's hand and closed her eyes, Tim's voice and the powerful words of comfort from Psalm 91 washing over her, quieting her spirit.

He will cover you with His feathers,
And under His wings you may seek refuge;
His faithfulness is a shield and bulwark.
You will not be afraid of the terror by night...

She awoke to the harsh sound of her alarm clock, the angry beeps jarring her from turbulent dreams she couldn't recall.

Suddenly, the room filled with stampeding feet and voices, strident and demanding.

Not her alarm clock, she realized in sudden clarity.

Tim hauled her to her feet, dragging her back away from John's bed. As he did, he kicked her chair clear so the emergency staff could get to John, whose body was rigid and jerking, his heels hammering the mattress, his head twisting too far to the right side and pressing back into his pillows. He let out a harsh, gurgling sound from between his clenched teeth, and trails of blood and saliva dribbled from the corners of his mouth. His clawed left hand pummeled his stomach, and Renata couldn't swallow the sob that tore from her.

Tim held her tightly to him, one hand pressing her head to his chest as the two of them stood trembling together in the corner of the room, watching the terrible scene unfold. She only caught glimpses of John between the nurses and doctors who had converged on her husband, but the seizure seemed to go on and on and on. More staff hurried in, and finally, someone noticed them, a woman in giraffe scrubs, a nurse Renata didn't recognize.

"Why don't we go out to the waiting area, shall we?" She spoke patiently, gently, a hand on Renata's back. "This might take a while."

"No, please." Renata's voice trembled, fear and shock threatening to overwhelm her, but as long as Tim would hold her up, she wasn't going anywhere. "I won't get in the way, I promise. I can't—I can't leave him."

The woman studied them both for a moment, glanced back over her shoulder at the patient and staff, then up at Tim. Renata couldn't see his expression; she wouldn't take her eyes off John's feet. The movements were slowing now, but she could tell it was still uncontrolled motion.

"I'll take her out if it's too much," Tim said, his voice loud against her ear still pressed to his chest.

The nurse nodded, then joined a group near the monitors, murmuring something to them before heading back out to the nurse's station.

Although John's movements ceased, the activity around his bed did not diminish. Voices rose, calling out short commands, monitors beeped and whined, more staff hurried in and out, and Renata watched the controlled frenzy in horror, knowing in her heart that nothing would ever be the same again.

· · · • · • · • · · ·

JOHN LOOKED UP AT the faces coming in and out of focus above him, calling his name, shining bright lights in his eyes. He blinked slowly, then realized both his eyes opened and closed just fine. There was no pain, no pressure on his chest, no vise clamped around his head. He took a slow deep breath, in through his nose... and there was that delicious aroma of rose petals and citrus, filling his senses, surrounding him with peace and comfort.

Easing out of the center of the chaos, he paused to watch the activity around his bed, his battered and broken body seized up in one last rebellion against the abuse it had taken, and then he turned to look for his wife.

He smiled when his eyes found her, held in the protective arms of the man who was Jonathan to his David, closer than a brother.

Stay with Ren for me, man. She'll need you more than ever now.

Then he turned away.

All would be well.

TWENTY-NINE

The sun streamed in the window, ignoring Renata's angry demands for it to go away. She rolled away from the brightness pressing against her eyelids, but she refused to open her eyes, knowing what she'd find if she did.

John's empty side of the bed.

She found it anyway, her hands, of their own accord, reaching for him blindly, fingers clutching at his pillow and drawing it to her face and breathing in the scent of him.

Sounds of the kids up and about, getting ready for school, came muffled through her closed bedroom door, and she wondered which of her sisters was in the kitchen, or if it was Granny G, making sure the boys were dressed and fed and delivered to the right schools.

"My babies," she whimpered, knowing she needed to go to them, knowing they needed her to be strong, to assure them that they would get through these dark days, but she was immobilized by her own grief and had no will to feed them empty promises.

She couldn't even face today; how on earth was she supposed to think about tomorrow? And the next day. And the next. Just thinking about a future without John made her stomach heave.

There was a light tap on the door. She didn't answer, but she didn't have to. She knew whomever it was would come in, regardless of whether she bid them enter or not. They'd bring a fresh tray of food that would grow cold on her dresser, a hot cup of tea or coffee that would remain untouched on the nightstand, an offer to help out in any way they could, an offer she'd ignore. Renata didn't even bother pretending to be asleep anymore; she wasn't fooling anyone, anyway.

"Mom?" It was Reuben. "Mommy?" Her heart hitched at the misery in his voice, a sob catching in her throat, but she swallowed it down and kept her face buried in John's pillow. Reuben was quiet for so long, she thought maybe he'd left the room, but a moment later, she felt the mattress dip behind her.

"I miss you, Mom." He rested his hand on the back of her head, his fingers absentmindedly toying with her chopped hair. "We're going to school now. I just wanted to say 'goodbye' and let you know we're going with Tim to the dog park this afternoon. He's going to pick us up from school and we'll come back here for Harry and Sally." He paused, withdrew his hand, his voice dropping to almost a whisper. "You could come, if you wanted."

Renata ached to reach out to him, to hug his sturdy young frame to her, but she was afraid to touch him, afraid she might break, and her eleven-year-old would have to hold her together. She had to say something, but what?

She felt the mattress shift again and a wave of panic welled up inside her, forcing her into action. She turned to find him sitting with his back to her, his elbows on his knees, a posture she often found John in when he had something on his mind. Reuben's young, wiry frame was already beginning to have the look of John's, and it made her chest hurt to see. She placed her hand gently on his back.

"Not today, honey. But tell Tim 'thank you' for me, okay? I'm glad you're going with him."

Reuben didn't look at her, but his shoulders sagged, and he nodded, then stood. Renata rolled away from him, unable to bear seeing the disappointment on his face. The door closed softly. She was alone.

Alone.

A few minutes later, Gia poked her head in to let her know they were leaving, and Judah shimmied past. He surprised both sisters by coming around the bed and putting his not-quite-clean hands on either side of Renata's face and planting a bubblegum toothpaste scented kiss on her nose.

"That's from Daddy in heaven," he explained, his eyes wide and serious. "He told me to kiss your nose." Then he bounded out of the room, leaving the two women speechless.

Gia followed him shortly, pulling the door closed without another word.

Renata curled in on herself, pressing her face into John's pillow as her grief threatened to overwhelm her.

• • • • • • • • • •

SLEEP DID NOT RESCUE her from the day, no matter how long she lay there. Renata pulled herself up to sitting, sliding her legs over the edge of the bed. Her head felt like it weighed a hundred pounds, and she braced her hands on her knees lest she topple face first to the floor.

"Renata, you need a shower," she grumbled, catching a whiff of herself. She stood up slowly, a little lightheaded, her empty stomach balking. "Food first."

It was chilly, so she slipped into John's robe that hung on the back of their bedroom door, tying it loosely around her waist, taking comfort in the sensation of being enveloped by him. She picked up the tray Gia had left her—a piece of toast with peanut butter, a cup of cold coffee, and half a ruby grapefruit in a bowl—and carried it to the kitchen where she dumped the food in the trash, poured the coffee down the drain, then washed her dishes.

Harry and Sally wandered in behind her, greeted her with subdued expressions and slow tail wags, then returned to their pillows, both staring balefully at the front door, as though expecting John to come through it at any moment.

Renata found a can of ready to serve chicken noodle soup in the cupboard and heated it up in a bowl in the microwave, then stood at the sink and ate it.

"At least I'm not eating it out of the can today," she muttered aloud. She stared out at the wet March morning, wondering when the weather was going to change. It had rained on and off for weeks, and even though it was spring, usually by the middle of March in Southern California, the sunshine days started outnumbering the glum-weather days.

Maybe the whole earth was in mourning with her.

Just as she finished washing the bowl and spoon, she heard the garage door go up. Renata wasn't expecting anyone, not until the boys came home from school. She stood still, waiting for whomever it was to come inside, but no one did. She glanced over at the dogs, and although both of them were flopping their tails a little and their ears had perked up, they didn't seem at all concerned.

Finally, curiosity got the best of her. She drew the lapels of John's robe together, and she opened the door from the kitchen into the garage.

Tim.

She hadn't seen him since the funeral almost two weeks ago. He'd been by the house almost every day since that terrible night in the hospital; not to see her, but to make sure there wasn't anything that needed to be done around the place.

Tim had taken it upon himself to arrange with McCain to have John's truck and tools delivered to the house. He'd contacted the clients on John's schedules, and he'd organized their hunting buddies to be pallbearers alongside Victor, Reuben, and Simon, who had both insisted on helping to carry their father's casket. On the one dry day last week, she'd peered out the window to find him mowing her lawn, and just a few days ago, he'd come to Gia's rescue, unbeknownst to Renata, when Judah had flushed a Hot Wheels car down the toilet.

He froze when he saw her standing in the doorway.

"What are you doing here, Tim?" She wasn't interested in niceties and instead of looking at him directly, she stared at the cab of John's truck, parked on the far side of the two-car garage. If she squinted, she could almost picture him sitting there, listening to the last few minutes of a song or message on one of his favorite radio stations before coming in. She balled her hands into fists inside the deep pockets of his robe.

"Renata." Tim was standing near John's workbench, his hand resting on one of her husband's toolboxes. "Sorry to have bothered you."

"What are you doing here?" she asked again. It was cold in the garage, especially with the big door up, and she shivered. "And why is it okay that you just walked in without knocking?"

"I didn't want to disturb you, that's all. I thought I could get in here, take care of business, and get out. Again, my apologies." He held up both hands in surrender. "The mower was running a little rough last week. Needs a tune-up. And the trimmer was out of line." He snatched up a spool of thick plastic line from the workbench and held it up for her.

She stared at her toes for a few moments, the socks she wore stretched out and twisted upside down on her feet. She knew she should thank him for his efforts, but she felt weird about taking favors from him. He was John's friend, not hers, and she didn't want or need his pity right now. In fact, she didn't really want to see him at all. His face, his very presence, brought back the events and the emotions of that night like a kick in the gut.

"You shouldn't be here," she finally ground out, lifting her eyes to his face for the first time.

He didn't say anything. He didn't leave, either. He slowly set the line back on the workbench, but didn't look away from her. His eyes beneath his broad brow seemed deeper than usual, but she didn't want to think about his grief. Hers was more than she could handle already, and she had her children to think about, too, once she could manage to take on a little more. In the meantime, the kids were leaning heavily on Gia and Granny G, and Juliette and Victor continued to help out as much as their schedules would allow after school. Even Phoebe had been by a few times, poking her head into the bedroom to whisper a gentle 'hi' to Renata.

But that's what family did.

Tim had his own family. Tim had a brother who lived close by, a whole group of friends that John had been a part of, and his own parents, alive and well, who thought the world of John. Why did he have to come here and burden Renata with his grief? Why couldn't he go somewhere else for solace? His presence was more than she could bear.

She turned and went back inside, closing the door softly behind her. Maybe after her shower he'd be gone, and she wouldn't have to think about him anymore.

THIRTY

Renata glanced at the clock on the wall. It was Friday, and the kids would be here any minute, dropping off backpacks and lunch boxes before changing into play clothes. They'd greet her with hurried hugs, then bolt back out through the garage to the truck parked in the driveway, Tim waiting patiently at the wheel. He never set foot in the house when he came, not even to use the bathroom, and Renata knew it was out of respect for her obvious aversion to his presence.

She also knew she should be ashamed by that knowledge, and part of her truly was, but the longer she avoided him, the more difficult it became to broach the subject, even in her own mind.

She got up, straightened the throw on the sofa, and refilled her glass of soda water. She could handle her sisters when they came, greeting them politely, if a little distantly. They'd each picked a day to help her: Gia on Mondays, Phoebe on Wednesdays, and Juliette on Thursdays with Victor. Renata tolerated Victor because the boys were always so thrilled when he picked them up from school in his cruiser.

Her favorite days were Tuesdays when Grandpa and Granny G came early to help her get the boys ready for school. Grandpa would drop the kids off, then return, and the three of them would putter around the house together, cleaning bedrooms and washing sheets, even walking the dogs up to the end of the block and back. For whatever reason, Renata could talk freely about John with her grandparents, crying inconsolably or not at all. Perhaps it was because they'd never once uttered the words, 'It will be okay,' to her.

Tim had insisted on picking up the boys from school on Fridays, and because Simon, especially, seemed to respond well to Tim's stoic personality, she didn't make a stink about it. But that didn't mean she needed to greet him when he arrived. Just because her boys liked being around him didn't mean she had to.

Two months, three weeks, one day, and almost eight hours had crawled by since John left them. Their lives had taken on a new version of reality, one encased in a house of glass. During the week, except for on Tuesdays when her grandparents spent the day with her, they all got up and ready for the day, including Renata, then she delivered them to their respective places, even Judah, who now attended daycare every weekday. Then she drove home to await their return.

Some days, John's absence came at her from the most unexpected places, and it was all she could do to breathe, no less be productive. When that happened, she usually ended up crawling back into bed, crying until she fell asleep or threw up, her stomach roiling with her grief. Before the boys and whichever of her family showed up with their eyes full of concern, she'd wash her face, freshen up her makeup, and head to the kitchen to cook.

Except for Tuesdays when her grandparents came, and Sundays when they all went to the grandparents for a family dinner, on the days she wasn't catatonic in bed, Renata cooked. Over the length of her thirteen-year marriage, she'd collected a box full of recipes she'd had every intention of cooking one day, and now, she was determined to try every single one of them. Mondays she cooked with chicken. Chicken cacciatore, chicken and vegetable kebabs, chicken and dumplings, roast chicken, barbecue chicken, Kung Pao chicken, coconut curry chicken.

On Wednesdays, she cooked with seafood. Fish tacos, grilled salmon with dill sauce, crab salad, seafood chowder, shrimp linguine, tuna pot pie.

On Thursdays, it was beef or pork. Spaghetti and meatballs, pork tenderloin, pork chops and gravy, beef stew, beef stroganoff, beef wellington, French dip sandwiches, sweet and sour Pork, beef and broccoli, hamburgers and fries.

Fridays she tried her hand at desserts, knowing Tim would most likely feed the boys, and they'd come home in the evening, worn out from an afternoon at the park or wherever else he took them. Lemon meringue pie, melt in your mouth brownies, chocolate Daquois cake, molasses crinkle cookies, mixed berry tarts, apple cobbler, orange upside-down cake, French silk pie. They'd be thrilled for another dose of dessert, and she always had Simon run out through the garage to the driveway to give Tim a sampling of whatever she'd made. Again, he wouldn't come in, but he wouldn't leave, either, until she'd come to the door and given him a wave of assurance that the boys were safe inside and all was well.

Saturdays were a free for all. Whatever she felt like cooking. Quiche, baked potatoes, eggplant Parmesan, French onion soup.

No one complained, especially not her sisters, who either stayed to eat with them, or took meals home. Sure, sometimes the boys didn't care for her more exotic experiments, but Renata didn't take it personally. If the recipe was a winner, she kept it. If it didn't fly, it ended up in the trash, along with whatever leftovers there were.

She was standing at the counter, reading over the recipe for a layered strawberry Napoleon dessert, when the troop surged through the door to drop off backpacks and change their clothes. She turned to greet them, but her smile faded when Tim filed inside behind them.

Her hand flew to her hair, and she felt a hot flush creep up her chest and neck.

Renata knew she looked fine; that wasn't it. She no longer hung around her house in her flannel pajamas and John's bathrobe. She made a point to get up each morning and get dressed, partly so the boys wouldn't worry so much, and partly because, even though everything else had changed in her life, Renata was still a creature of habit and order.

But ever since John had died, her chopped hair had been like a mark of shame. It was absurd, she knew, but she'd become obsessed with it, worrying it with her fingers while she lay in bed at night, wondering in the dark if John's shock over it in the hospital had somehow contributed to his demise. Then she'd berate herself for being so silly, so self-focused, but every time she caught a glimpse of herself in the mirror, she grimaced, hating it. How long before it grew back, she wondered.

Seeing her sisters almost every day, Juliette and Phoebe, with their sleek black waves so like hers had once been, Gia's copper curls tumbling down her back, was a constant reminder of what now felt like an inadequacy in her. Like she was somehow less of a woman without her hair. *A woman's hair is her crown of beauty,* the Bible said. She couldn't agree more, and without it, without John there to assure her she was beautiful to him, she felt a little like Rapunzel, no longer knowing her place in the world.

So, she stayed home. Except to take her boys to school, and to her grandparents' house for Sunday dinner down the block, she stayed home and cooked and cleaned. She didn't know if she'd ever leave the house again.

"Renata," Tim said, pausing just inside the open door. The sight of him taking up too much space in her home made her want to flee down the hall to the sanctuary of her room, slamming the door behind her.

"Come in, please," she said instead. "And close the door. The air conditioner is on." She hugged the boys as they blew past, and then turned back to her recipe, prepared to ignore Tim. Whatever he'd come inside to do, he could just do it and be on his way.

"Renata, I'd like to talk to you." He'd closed the door behind him, but he hadn't moved any closer. The boys had all disappeared to their bedrooms. "Before the boys get back, if possible."

She nodded, not wanting to look at him.

"I'd like to plan a fishing trip next month after school gets out, maybe take Reuben and Simon hunting small game. A couple weeks up at my folks' place," he said without preamble. There was something to be said about a guy like Tim. He didn't beat around the bush or play games. Because he used so few words, he made the ones he did speak count.

But the idea of the boys being gone for a week or more was more than she wanted to think about. During the day, while they were in school, and even in the hours they were out with her family and Tim, those hours were tolerable because she had things to do, new recipes to try, laundry and dishes and bathrooms to clean. At night, however, when the house was too quiet, she took comfort in getting up to check on them, laying a hand on their young chests, feeling the rise and fall beneath her palms, the butterfly tremor of hearts in motion beneath thin-skinned rib cages.

"No. They can't go."

He didn't respond, so she expounded. "I don't care if you all take them from me during the day, but you can't have them at night, too." She closed her eyes, hating the way her voice sounded, how it squeezed out from her tight throat in a flattened, pinched quality. She took a deep breath. "I'm sorry, Tim. I know they'd like it. But I—I'm not ready for that yet."

"Renata, I'd like you to come with us. My parents would love to have you."

If he'd said anything else, Renata would have just shaken her head and stuck with her answer. But Tim's words shook her to the core. Not only was he asking her to accompany him on a trip doing an activity she'd never enjoyed with her husband, but he wanted her to leave her home, leave John behind. Leave his bed, his pillow, his clothes. His presence.

"Are you crazy?" She turned around and glared at him. "Look at me, Tim. Look at me!" She stood with her hands out to the side, her ruffled apron hanging limply from her too-thin frame. "Do I look like a woman who wants to go fishing? Hunting?"

A movement down the hall caught her eye; the boys were listening. She lowered her voice. "Listen to me, Tim. Do not, I repeat, do not put any notions into those boys' heads, you understand?" She raised a finger and pointed at him. "We're not leaving this house this summer, and that's final."

Tim, to his credit, stood his ground. He didn't cross his arms or shake his head. He didn't roll his eyes or even grunt. His short beard didn't hide the clenching of his jaw, though, and she got some satisfaction out of that. Until he spoke.

In a voice steady and sure, like he was talking to a spooked horse, he said, "That's what I'm afraid of, Renata."

• • • • • • • • •

NO ONE SPOKE TO her that evening. Reuben and Simon muttered quietly back and forth, giving her the evil eye every time she looked their way.

Judah refused to eat at the table with her, instead opting to eat *under* the table, crying loudly the whole time because she wouldn't let him eat in his room.

After banishing Tim without her boys and without his weekly portion of dessert, she'd opened up a couple of cans of ravioli, steamed some broccoli, which the boys all really liked, and found a box of Goldfish at the back of the pantry.

Levi didn't say anything, but he wasn't smiling over his dinner, or the dessert that had turned out so deliciously with the fresh strawberries and real whipped cream.

No one was. Even though they practically licked their plates clean, when she asked if they liked the strawberry Napoleon dessert, Reuben raised an eyebrow in an expression so like John's it hurt to look at him.

But his words hit even harder. "Wasn't Napoleon a traitor?"

The offer of a big bowl of popcorn and a Netflix movie didn't help matters.

"Tim was going to take us to a movie tonight. He always lets us have our own popcorn." That was Levi, his voice not unkind, but the disappointment obvious. Judah finally agreed, climbing onto the couch beside Renata and proceeding to wipe his snotty nose on her sleeve.

Reuben and Simon disappeared to their room, Levi waffled back and forth for a few minutes, trying to decide whether to watch Tarzan for the hundredth time, per Judah's request, or join the other boys who were probably plotting their revenge. He finally drifted down the hall.

Renata was surprised to find that she was relieved. Then she grimaced, her stomach churning a little in shame. And indigestion.

She'd been a mess ever since she'd come home from the hospital, taking antacids with every meal. She wasn't ever hungry and hardly ate anything in spite of all the cooking she did because eating made her nauseated. And she slept terribly, although she was tired all the time—

She suddenly stiffened, her heart racing. Nausea. Fatigue. Food cravings. Heartburn. She used the bathroom a lot, too, but that was because she drank so much soda water to soothe her stomach.

Wasn't it?

But no. No, no, no. Chills swept down her body from the roots of her cropped hair to the tips of her toes inside her slippers. She hadn't had a period since John's accident. In fact, she hadn't had a period since the first week of February, two weeks before his fall, and now it was May.

"I'll be right back, Judah. Lay your head on the armrest, okay?" Judah had calmed down considerably and turned to curl his little body around the bowl of popcorn she handed him, his eyes never leaving the television screen where the young Tarzan teased his ape mother.

Renata walked as calmly as she could down the hall, past the boys' room, not wanting to alarm anyone. Their door was closed anyway, but she was pretty sure they'd be listening for her footsteps.

In her bathroom, she rooted around in the cupboard under the sink, afraid to hope, afraid to think what this might mean, afraid to know what her heart already told her was true.

"Happy Mother's Day," she whispered giddily to herself in the mirror a few minutes later. She had no one else to tell, no one else she wanted to tell right now.

THIRTY-ONE

For the next three weeks, Renata waited to tell anyone lest it not be real. Lest she lose this one, too. It had always been between the second and third month before. If she was still pregnant by the end of May, she'd be four months along.

It was like her little secret spring of joy in the dark valley she traversed. She knew she should go to the doctor, but she didn't want to hear that her home tests weren't accurate, that her body was lying, that she had fooled herself into believing it was possible. She'd wait until the end of May, then go.

Much to Harry and Sally's delight, she started walking the dogs twice a day while the boys were at school. It was only two loops around the block, but it was enough to get out and get some fresh air, a little exercise.

Her recipes changed dramatically. She cleaned out her pantry, tossing most of the stockpile of processed foods that were easy to prepare and yet so bad for everyone, and although she didn't flip out and go health nut crazy, she made certain that the meals she prepared were nutritious and vitamin rich. Even her Friday desserts were lighter, more fresh fruit and less white sugar and flour.

She forced herself to eat what she cooked, and to eat more regularly. She went to bed at a decent hour instead of staying up until she couldn't hold her head up. No longer hating bedtime, with great anticipation, she climbed in on John's side so she could talk to him, so she could acknowledge their baby growing inside of her. Feeling enveloped by him, his scent, his presence, her hands cupping her still flat abdomen, she whispered her words of hope only to him. "Do you know about this one,

John? Is this our baby girl? Will she have red hair like yours? Pale skin like mine? Freckles?"

She wept still, but the tears of grief now mingled with a rising courage in her.

And she prayed. For the first time in a long time, she just talked to God. All day long, she carried on a conversation with him in her head, as though He was right there with her, standing over her shoulder, walking through the day with her. She knew He was; she'd always believed it in her head before, but for the first time in her life, she started to believe it in her heart; to *live* as though it were true. There were times when she would pause, hold her breath, and listen quietly, certain she'd heard a still small voice whisper her name. It was the most comforting sensation she could imagine.

The boys had forgiven her by that Sunday, which was a relief, because it was Mother's Day. Thanks to the rest of the family making sure they were armed to the gills with gifts, both store-bought and home-made for her, she was showered with love by the whole family, and she received it all with much gratitude.

Tim must have forgiven her, too, because he texted her that following Friday, as usual, and said he'd be picking the boys up, unless she had other plans for them. He continued to come by at least once a week and do odd jobs around the outside of the house. Mowing the lawns, picking up after the dogs, replacing a section of the fencing between her house and the neighbor's where one of the boys had practiced his batting skills.

Things were slowly going back to normal, or at least, their new version of normal.

During the last week of May, Renata climbed behind the wheel of her Pilot, and backed the car out of the driveway and out onto the street. Other than taking the boys to school in the mornings, she'd driven it only three other times since the accident. She'd gone to the grocery store by herself once, but she broke down in the freezer section in front of John's favorite Moose Tracks ice cream and had to abandon her half-full cart in the aisle. She'd picked Judah up early once; he'd come down with a fever. And a week ago, she'd dropped off Reuben's science project report for him because he'd left it sitting on the kitchen counter. She had no idea what it was even about; something he'd worked on with Tim.

Others had used the car, though—Gia and Phoebe often picked up the boys with it because they both had tiny cars. She noticed there was a new sticker in the upper left corner of her windshield; someone had even taken it in for an oil change a few weeks ago. She'd have to find out who and thank them.

Her doctor, a sixty-something year old man who'd delivered all four of her boys, and who'd also delivered the confirmation of each miscarriage, beamed at her as he strode back into the exam room where she waited.

"Renata, this is wonderful. Wonderful! I'm not even going to reprimand you for not coming to see me sooner. Congratulations, my dear." It was the first time she'd seen Dr. Flynn since John's death, but she'd informed the nurse of the accident when she made the appointment, so their visit wouldn't be any more awkward than absolutely necessary. He'd embraced her warmly as soon as he saw her, told her how terribly sorry he was for her loss, then got on with business. She loved him all the more for not making her cry.

"What kind of support system do you have, my dear?" His question caught her off guard, mainly because she'd been expecting to have to give him information about diet and exercise and sleeping habits instead.

"Oh. Well, my sisters. My grandparents live just down the block from me."

"But no one could come with you today?"

Renata frowned at his question. He seemed overly concerned about this. "I haven't told anyone yet. I wanted to get past...."

"Of course, of course." He nodded. "But you will tell them now?"

She hesitated, suddenly overwhelmed with the desire to keep this her secret a little longer. It was her direct link to John, and she wasn't ready to share it with anyone.

"Renata, listen. I'm going to speak to you now as a friend who happens to be your doctor, not the other way around."

She sighed, not wanting a lecture, but out of respect, she nodded.

"This is not the time for you to withdraw. Every new baby is a precious gift, and in your case, your circumstances add a unique element to this particular gift. This is a time for celebration, for people to gather around you and help you prepare to welcome a new life into your family. I know you well enough to know that you're a strong, independent woman, and even though John's passing is a tragedy beyond measure, if you had to face tomorrow alone, you could and you would. But you don't have to. You have a family who loves you, four boys who depend on you, and a new baby coming who will only benefit from you asking for help." He crossed his arms and continued, not giving her a chance for rebuttal.

"How are you doing financially? I know it's a personal question, but are you going to have to go back to work soon?"

Renata shook her head, relieved all over again at John's foresight. "No. John had good life insurance. I'm set for several years, if I'm careful. Eventually, I'll have to think about it, but probably not until this one is in school, maybe even junior high."

Dr. Flynn nodded sagely. "Excellent. Excellent. Good man, that John. I can't tell you how much that sets my mind at ease." He reached out and patted her knee. "Okay. So, as your doctor, I'm writing you a few prescriptions for prenatal vitamins and an ultrasound for next month before your next visit. As your friend, I'm writing you a prescription requiring you to tell your family about this baby before your next visit. That gives you almost a whole month. Got it?"

Renata nodded. Fine. But for the next month, she would be like Mary, the mother of Jesus, keeping this secret in her heart and treasuring it for as long as she was able.

• • • • • • • • • •

WHEN RENATA PULLED BACK into her driveway before noon, she grimaced to find Tim's truck parked out front. She didn't see him, though, so she got out, locked up her car, and made for the front door rather than going through the garage past John's truck.

Just as she was sliding her key into the lock, Tim stepped out from around the side of the house and walked toward her, a ladder in one hand, a tool of some kind in the other. He was dressed in an old pair of jeans and a white t-shirt, flakes of paint sprinkling his shoulders and caught in his shaggy hair.

He grinned when he saw her, a slow smile of surprise mingled with satisfaction, and she was shocked at the thoughts that went through her mind.

About Tim.

About how attractive he was.

About how tight his shirt was.

About how good it was to see him.

"Renata. Good to see you."

She stared at his chest, warmth flooding her face, unable to meet his eyes. Had she said that out loud, or had he read her mind? "Hey, Tim." Her hands fumbled a little with the key, but she got the door unlocked and pushed it open, slipping inside before he could read any more of her other thoughts.

"Get a grip, girl," she muttered, angry at herself for letting her mind wander.

Angry at Tim for being here.

Angry at John for not being here.

Suddenly, a thought occurred to her. She tore open the door and stepped out into the bright sunshine again.

Tim was up on the ladder in the driveway, scraping paint from the eaves, his arms overhead, one hand gripping the framework for balance, the other wielding the scraper.

Her heart skipped a beat at the sight of him, an uncontrolled fear for his safety rising up in her. She studied his tan work boots braced on the rungs of the ladder. "Did you take my car in for an oil change?" she asked, her tone harsh, abrupt.

Tim turned around to look down at her, still holding onto the eave overhead, his other hand resting on the top of the ladder now. She stole a quick glance up at his face but didn't like the way his posture enhanced his muscular frame. So she turned her gaze to her car, pointing at the sticker in the window.

"I did."

"When? Why?"

"Last week. Because it needed it."

"Who told you it needed it?" she asked, unable to argue that fact.

"The old sticker in the window. It was supposed to be done in February."

"Yes, well, I was a little busy in February," she snarled. *Oh Renata, stop. Just stop and go back inside.* What had happened to her buoyant mood of moments ago, and why was she lashing out at Tim again?

Tim came down the ladder, slowly, carefully, then turned to face her, feet planted wide in challenge. He crossed his arms over his chest, putting his rather impressive biceps on display, making Renata think of the Mr. Clean guy.

Except that Tim had lots of hair and a neatly trimmed beard.

She took an involuntary step backward, her hand waving behind her in search of the doorknob.

Tim seemed to realize how intimidating he looked. He uncrossed his arms, reached out to grip the ladder, and propped one foot on the bottom rung. He turned so he no longer faced her, but he tipped his head to look at her sideways.

"I lost him, too, Renata."

Hot tears welled up and over, tracking silently down her cheeks. She stood there, one hand on the door, one hand curved protectively across her belly, hating herself. Missing John. Wondering why she felt so much rage toward this man who had been nothing but a rock to her and her boys for three and a half long months now, whom she had spurned and spewed at time and time again, but who had remained steadfast and present. Her emotions toward him rankled her, made her want to lash out at him even more, send him running so she wouldn't have to deal with any of it.

"Why are you here, Tim?" she finally asked, his name coming out more of a sob.

"I'm prepping your eaves to paint them."

"No, not *what* are you doing here? Why? *Why* do you keep coming back here? Why are you helping me?" It was her turn to cross her arms tightly over her chest, trying desperately to hold the pieces of her world together. Wasn't this supposed to get easier in time?

"Because I want to." His voice cracked a little on the word 'want' but he didn't seem to notice.

Renata did. She kept doggedly after him, anyway. "But why? What makes you think we need you around here, huh?" She bit her lip hard, the pain goading her. "I don't need your charity, Tim. You don't owe us—or John, for that matter—anything."

"Owe you?" Tim gripped the ladder so tightly it rattled against the driveway. "Charity? What in the world do you think I am, Renata?" He lifted the ladder off the ground a few inches and slammed it back down. Not hard, but enough to make some noise.

Enough to make her flinch.

"Did it ever once occur to you that I'm here because I love your family? John's family? He was my best friend, Renata. My best friend." He angrily swiped at his eyes with the back of his hand. "This isn't about owing anyone anything. It's what friends do for each other. What men do for their fallen brothers." She'd forgotten Tim had spent some time in Afghanistan. Because of exemplary performance and conduct, he'd been honorably discharged after his term of service was up. He'd even been injured at one point, and sent home for medical treatment, but he'd returned afterward to complete his term.

He turned and took a step toward her, then another. He didn't raise his voice, but it got more and more intense the closer he got.

Renata pressed her back to the door behind her.

"If it had been me, if I was gone and he was here in my shoes, John would do the same thing for me. This is what he'd be doing for my fam—"

"You don't have a family!" She pointed a finger at him, her voice rising with each word. "I wish it *had* been you! I wish it was him here with me right now, not you!"

Tim was so close now she had to look up to meet his eyes. She jammed her finger into his chest as she cried out. "I need John, not you! I need my husband, not his best buddy. I need—" Her voice broke, and she brought her hands up to cover her face, sobs tearing from deep down inside. "Oh God, I miss him so much."

Tim's arms came around her, and she leaned into him. He held her like that only for a moment, then gently ushered her inside the house. Closing the door behind them, he pulled her up against him again and she let him.

Eyes closed, she soaked in the comfort his big body offered her as he wrapped himself around her like a shield of protection against the world. For the first time since John's death, she gave in to the need to sob in someone's embrace, not caring what he thought of her, not caring what she thought of herself.

Slowly, she eased her arms around his waist, imaging John holding her, imagining it was his chest she buried her face into, his head resting against the top of hers, his hand stroking her back. If she kept her eyes closed, if they didn't speak, maybe, just maybe, she could believe it for a few moments....

No. She was not going to play those games. This was Tim, offering her whatever comfort he could, and perhaps even asking for a little from her in return. She would honor him and his friendship by not pretending otherwise.

"I'm pregnant, Tim," she whispered, the relief of saying those words out loud making her knees buckle.

THIRTY-TWO

Painting the eaves seemed to take a lot longer than Renata thought it should.

Tim started coming by more often, a couple days a week, right after the boys left for school in the morning. He'd ask her how she was doing, if there was anything he could do for her, then he'd head outside to put in a few hours on the house.

He was usually gone by noon, poking his head inside to let her know he was leaving, except for on Fridays when he'd pick up the boys. He began asking her to join them for the afternoon, or for dinner, at least, but she always turned him down.

She still didn't have any desire to leave the house, not just because of her hair, but because she felt close to John in her home, close to the new baby growing in her belly.

Besides, she knew her kids, especially Simon, loved the undivided attention Tim gave them. School would be out for summer soon, anyway, and she wasn't sure how involved he'd be after that.

Tim, however, began accepting her invitation to join them for dessert at the end of the night, coming in with the boys and sliding unpretentiously into John's empty chair when Simon directed him to it. He didn't apologize to her for sitting there, and she didn't feel that he should. She knew he wasn't trying to take John's place.

They hadn't talked much since that day after her doctor's appointment, but Renata was shocked to realize how much of a relief it was that someone else knew her secret. An exchanged look, a question in his eyes, a new level of attentiveness whenever he was around.

Neither Juliette nor Gia seemed to notice anything different about her, but Phoebe put a hand on her shoulder one Wednesday after dropping the boys off. "Ren, you look good. Your cheeks don't look so sunken in. Your eyes, they're brighter. I'm glad."

"Thanks, Phoebe." Her sister was an artist, a woman whose job it was to study expressions and notice nuances. "I'm beginning to feel like tomorrow may come after all." She chuckled, then rephrased her thoughts. "Rather, I'm less afraid of it than I used to be."

On the Tuesday before her ultrasound, Renata told her grandparents about the baby. They hugged her and wept with her and promised to keep her secret until she'd had a chance to tell her sisters. They also offered to take the boys when she did.

That Thursday, she called a G-FOURce, much to her sisters' surprise. She offered to cook, but Juliette insisted on bringing Chinese food from The Green Dragon to give her a night off. Phoebe showed up with two six-packs of fancy ginger ale in glass bottles, and Gia brought a batch of Granny G's cinnamon chocolate chip cookies.

The house was clean, the lawn freshly mowed, thanks to Tim, and the air-conditioned interior of the home was a refreshing contrast to the early evening heat of June.

Renata hadn't had takeout Chinese food in months. She had to hold her breath when the cartons were popped open on the counter, the overwhelming aromas assaulting her hypersensitive nose. The nausea passed quickly, the way it usually did these days, and she filled her plate without mishap. They sat around chatting, this being the first G-FOURce they'd had since John's fall, at least that she knew about. She supposed it was entirely probable that her sisters had, in fact, met without her.

After dinner, she transferred the cookies to a platter, and set them on the table, along with mugs and spoons and tea bags. While they waited for the teakettle to whistle, Gia officially opened the G-FOURce with the pledge, and when they released hands, fingers fluttering in the air over their heads, Renata giggled.

The others looked at her curiously, but Phoebe's eyes narrowed. "What's up with you, sister? There's something different about you."

"You look amazing," Juliette agreed, now studying her, too.

Renata stood, the teakettle just beginning to sputter. When she'd filled everyone's mugs and sat back down, she opted not to drag it out.

"I'm pregnant," she said, swirling her Earl Grey tea bag in her mug. "Four and a half months."

The room went dead silent, spoons stilling, mouths open, eyes wide. Suddenly, Gia leapt out of her chair, jumped up and down a few times, squealing like a little girl at her birthday party, then circled the table to wrap Renata in a tremendous hug. "Oh Rennie! Rennie! I'm so happy!"

Renata looked across at Juliette, whose eyes glistened, her hands pressed to her smiling mouth, then at Phoebe, clutching her mug tightly, tears beginning to fill her eyes, too, and spilling over. The look on Phoebe's face was mixed with something else, and Renata felt the old twinge of doubt and resentment rearing its ugly head inside her, but she pushed it down. No, this was good news, and Dr. Flynn had been right. She needed her family now in ways she'd never dreamed she would.

They talked for at least another hour, about how she was feeling, how the boys were holding up. Renata hadn't yet told them. She wanted to give them enough time to grieve their father before they had to make room for another Dixon, but she planned to tell them after her ultrasound when she could show them a picture.

"Are you going to find out what you're having?" Gia asked the question on everyone's mind.

"I still don't know," Renata admitted. "I'm hoping for a girl, of course, but this baby is such a miracle already that I almost feel like I should just wait and be surprised, you know?"

"Who's going with you?" Phoebe asked.

Renata shrugged. "Well, I'd planned to go alone, but if one of you—or all of you—want to go, I wouldn't say 'no' to you." She smiled shyly. "It's next Monday at ten."

"I'd love to be there," Phoebe said immediately, much to Renata's surprise. She'd not shown any interest in Renata's other pregnancies.

"I can work a later shift on Monday if someone else can pick the boys up for me," Gia said. "I'd like to be there, too, if I can."

"Will they let us all in?" Juliette asked, ever the least impulsive of the bunch. "If they will, then I'll be there. Sharon will cover me at work. She keeps offering to help out in any way she can." Sharon Scoville was Juliette's best friend and coworker at the University.

And so it was on Monday, that all four girls piled into Renata's Pilot and headed off to see the first photo of Renata and John's baby, the newest member-to-be of the G-FOURce.

Because they asked, and the ultrasound tech confirmed that the baby was most certainly a girl.

• • • • ● • ● • • •

THEY STOPPED FOR LUNCH, and Renata called an impromptu G-FOURce over their iced teas and shredded chicken tostada salads.

"Because I want you to know that I'm okay, and if we need to talk about Angela, I'm ready," Renata explained in response to the curious looks.

Juliette laid down her fork, wiped her mouth, and took a hearty gulp of tea before speaking. "Well, just so you know, I have heard from her. Her parole hearing has been postponed for six months, which, according to Angela, means it won't happen until after the holidays, most likely not until the end of January next year. In other words," she reached over and laid a hand on Renata's arm. "We don't need to make any decisions about Angela right now, okay? Right now, we have a baby girl to plan for, one who is arriving in less than five months."

Gia sat back in her chair and sighed dreamily. "Oh, you guys! I just realized we're going to have a baby for Christmas!"

"The best Christmas gift ever," Phoebe chimed in with a wide smile, although a little less exuberantly than Gia.

"The best," Renata agreed.

When they arrived back at Renata's house to pick up their cars, Tim was there, up on a ladder, replacing a section of rain gutter at the corner of the house.

"Oh, my," Phoebe purred in admiration. "Now that would make me want to come home more often." In the front passenger seat, she turned with raised eyebrows to Renata.

Tim wore his regular work uniform of tight t-shirt and Levis, and today, he had a tool belt strapped low around his hips. The midday sun was high in the sky and it was hot, his arms glistening with sweat, a damp patch in a V down the middle of his back. On his head he wore a Denver Broncos cap backwards, his almost shoulder-length hair curling below the bill. It was so cliché, Renata couldn't help but smile, and when he turned to wave at them, Gia giggled from the backseat.

"And you passed that up, Jules," Phoebe quipped, turning around to wink at Juliette.

"Yes, I did. For Victor. I think I did all right," Juliette replied, but she was smiling, too. "On the other hand, if he'd shown up looking like that, I might have at least gone to dinner with him."

"Juliette Gustafson!" Renata reprimanded, laughing outright at her sister's comment. When she'd sent Tim Larsen on a blind date with Juliette, she'd had every hope the two of them would find common ground and become friends, if not more. But Juliette had bowed out of the Monday ManDates G-FOURce intervention they'd put into play after Juliette had left her boyfriend of ten years. She had fallen for Officer Victor Jarrett over all the men her sisters had practically gift-wrapped for her, and Juliette was decidedly happy with her choice.

And somehow, over the last several months, the reservations Renata had felt toward Victor had all but evaporated as he had shown his true colors over and over with her boys. They already called him Uncle Vic, and she was just waiting for the announcement that he had popped the question to Juliette. In fact, she was sure it would have come sooner had it not been for John's accident.

They all got out and headed inside with the excuse of one last bathroom stop before they were on their way. But Renata was pretty sure it was to get a little extra eye-candy through the front window, courtesy of Tim Larsen in a tool belt. Phoebe confirmed her suspicions once they were inside. She made a beeline to the window and unabashedly stared out at him.

"Oh yeah," Phoebe hummed, loudly enough for the rest of them to hear. "Lift it higher, honey. That's right. Flex for mama."

Gia and Juliette stayed back a little, but their eyes were glued to the man on the ladder, too.

"Phoebe, step away from the window," Renata scolded, laughing all the while. "If he catches you looking, he'll be mortified." But she, too, was peering over Phoebe's shoulder at the man, appreciating the fact that he was outside on her front lawn... and not Juliette's.

THIRTY-THREE

As a compromise, Renata agreed to let Tim take the boys camping for a couple days the first weekend of August. She worried he'd have his hands full with all four of them, but he assured her he was perfectly capable of keeping track of them, even Judah.

"I've had some practice these last few months," he claimed, the two of them sitting at the table over a cup of coffee for him and herbal tea for her, talking quietly so the boys wouldn't hear them. Reuben, Simon, and Levi were sprawled on the floor watching Spiderman, and Judah was already in bed, having passed out in Tim's truck on the way home from their Friday outing. Today, he'd taken them swimming at the community pool, a place Renata would never in a million years have let them go in the past. Tim had barbecued burgers for the boys back at his place, then they all trooped home to end the evening with vanilla ice cream and some of Renata's plum tarts she'd whipped up while they were out.

"Maybe, but you've not even had them overnight. What if Judah wets the sleeping bag? What are you going to do then?" She hoped he wasn't biting off more than he could chew.

A thought drifted through her mind that this must be what it was like for divorced parents with joint custody, and for some reason, it made her sad for the man across from her.

Without looking at him, she quietly asked, "Tim, don't you have a life of your own? I mean, aren't there other things you'd like to do on Friday night than babysit my boys?" She glanced over at the kids, making certain they couldn't hear her low questions. Levi's eyes were drifting closed in spite of Green Goblin's maniacal laugh. She hoped he wouldn't have nightmares.

More than her concern for Tim, though, was her concern for the boys. Tim wasn't their father, and he was under no obligation to continue these Friday outings. School was out and so far, he still picked them up at three on Fridays, but from home now. Inevitably, though, the day would come when he had his own life, even his own family to tend to.

Tim didn't answer right away, so she prodded harder. "What about a woman? Is there someone you're seeing?" She did look up at him then and smiled when she saw the color in his cheeks. He'd survived six years in the desert, looked the enemy in the face, and come home with honor, but the man blushed at the suggestion he might be getting some romance on with anyone.

It was his turn to look away. His eyes drifted over to the boys, and she marveled at how his expression softened when he did. "I'm not going anywhere, Renata."

For several minutes, they sat in silence, watching the movie over the heads of her children. Finally, Renata reached out and laid a hand on Tim's forearm, feeling the muscles bunch under her touch. He stared down at her fingers for a moment before looking up at her. "Thank you," she said. "For everything. They're doing so well with all of this, and I know so much of that is because of you."

Tim shook his head, but said, "You're welcome. Glad I can be of help to you." And that was Tim to the core. He may or may not agree with her sentiment, but there was no false humility in him, either.

It was true. During those first few weeks after John's funeral, Renata had been completely lost and untethered. If it hadn't been for her family gathering around and being there for her children when Renata wasn't, she didn't know how they would have gotten through things. As it was, although each of the boys mourned their dad in their own way, and still did on many occasions, none of them had lashed out in ways that were dangerous or unhealthy. Levi was still plagued by nightmares a few times a week, and it did surprise her that it was her sweet, go-with-the-flow boy who struggled this way, but otherwise, they all talked openly about John now, about missing him, about all the things they would be doing if he was there.

It was one of the reasons she'd agreed to the camping trip. The boys needed it. And Tim, who had often accompanied them on their boys-only camping trips with John, was the perfect person to take them, proving that there was still a lot of living left to be done for them.

Conversely, Renata wasn't sure how she'd do on her own in the house for three nights. Of course, she'd have Harry and Sally, and the constant companionship of the Holy Spirit was like a tangible presence to her, but maybe she'd see if Gia wanted to keep her company while the boys were gone.

She needed to make a point to thank her family for everything they'd done and were doing to keep the Dixon ship from completely sinking. It wasn't that she'd taken it for granted, their willingness to step up; she simply had not been capable of it herself. But it had not gone unnoticed. None of it had.

John's parents had come for the funeral and left shortly after. Although they were delightful people, John was an only child, and a rather well-adjusted and independent one at that, and a few years after he and Renata married, his parents had moved to Florida on the other side of the continent, his father retiring early after some jackpot investment he'd cashed in on. They were the perfect long-distance grandparents, always sending wonderful gifts to the boys, never forgetting any birthdays, anniversaries, or any other special events, but they didn't know how to behave around the kids, so they rarely visited. Renata thought she might be seeing even less of them in the future, in spite of promises made while they'd been here.

Suddenly, she realized what she was doing. Her fingers were brushing back and forth, ever so slowly, over the coarse hairs on Tim's forearms. She quickly withdrew her hand and took a sip of her tea, then she blurted out in a rushed whisper before she could lose her courage, "Tim, I'd like to tell the boys about the baby with you here. Can you come for breakfast tomorrow?"

His eyes grew wide, and he swallowed hard, making his Adam's apple bob up and down visibly. "Why?" he asked, when he finally found his voice.

"I mean, at the same time that we tell them about the camping trip. I just think it might be a little easier for them to deal with. A new baby is always tough—you should have seen Simon's reaction when we told him about Judah—but a sister?" She winced and cocked her head to look up at him, putting as much appeal in her gaze as she could muster. "If we buffer it with news of a camping trip, then maybe they'll handle it better."

Tim only nodded, but she knew that didn't necessarily mean he agreed with her. She lowered her voice even more, not looking away.

"I'm also a little worried about telling them by myself. They might need you—er, a man—around to show them how they're supposed to react. They always looked to John for his reaction to things, and even though they have their own individual ways of processing things, he gave them a starting point, you know? They might be worried, but if you're here and you make it clear that this is a good thing, then I think they'll go that direction, too."

Tim still only nodded again. To an untrained eye, this nod would look exactly like the other, but Renata smiled gratefully, having grown accustomed to reading his face.

And a little over an hour later, when she lay in bed explaining things to John, she sensed another presence sitting in the shadows of her mind: Tim, quiet and steady, nodding understandingly at her side.

THIRTY-FOUR

Tim arrived at eight o'clock the next morning, a box of Krispy Kreme doughnuts in his hand. Renata frowned when she met him at the door, but he grinned and said, "Never go to battle without backup."

He was freshly showered, his hair still damp, and Renata couldn't help noticing how good he smelled when he passed by her into the house. She ducked her head and closed the door slowly, not wanting to follow too closely behind him. She wasn't sure how to handle the not-so-subtle shift in her awareness of him.

Renata had always known Tim Larsen was a good-looking man. She'd always known him to be a godly man, too, and a good friend to John. She'd never felt anything close to what might be inappropriate feelings toward him or coming from him, but she'd dreamed about him last night, and she'd awakened from it, heart pounding, torn between curiosity and guilt.

It was nothing untoward or disrespectful. It was just the fact that it had been Tim in her dreams and not John. It had been Tim standing behind her on the deck of a sailboat, his arms around her, large working-man hands spread protectively over her very pregnant belly. Her hair was long and flowing out behind her as they faced into the wind, and she leaned back against the solid wall of him, perfectly content.

She subconsciously placed her hand over her abdomen, her baby bump suddenly prominent in the last two or three weeks. This was the fifth baby she'd carried this far into pregnancy, and she typically showed early with her petite frame, but she'd lost so much weight right after John's death that it had taken much longer to show this time. Now, at just over five months along, she was amazed none of the boys had noticed. Thankfully, it was summer, and she had a closet full of pretty little sun dresses she was making good use of.

Beneath her hand, the baby fluttered, and she stood stock still, not wanting to miss it. She knew this would be her last pregnancy, and she wanted to savor every moment. This little girl moved a lot at night when Renata lay on her back whispering to John, almost as though she knew she was being talked about, but she was beginning to make her presence known during the day now, too, with little nudges and hiccups.

Renata looked up to see Tim studying her belly where her hand rested, his eyes soft, a look she'd seen on John's face many times before.

Everything inside her tightened, squeezed, even her heart seemed to slow for a beat, then another, then suddenly pick up speed, hammering inside her chest like a battering ram.

He lifted his gaze and found her watching him, and for just a moment, his expression didn't change, the yearning in his eyes palpable. Then he cleared his throat, turned toward the kitchen, and set the doughnuts on the counter.

"What can I do to help?" he asked, his voice steady as ever. "Where are the boys?"

"Actually, Judah is the only one up, and he's out back with the dogs." It had taken her a moment to find her voice, but when she spoke, she was glad to hear only a trace of a tremor in it, something Tim couldn't possibly notice. "Since you're the one who wore them out so completely yesterday, maybe you can go rouse them from their slumber." Sending him out of her kitchen had been a spark of genius. There was no way she'd be able to finish cooking with him so close.

Half an hour later, they sat around the picnic table out back, paper plates loaded with breakfast burritos, fresh fruit, and vanilla flavored Greek Yogurt for Renata. She had it at almost every meal; she couldn't get enough of the stuff.

It was only a little after nine in the morning, and it was already hot. Renata felt a sheen of sweat building up on her forehead and upper lip and fanned herself with a spare plate. Glancing around the table, no one else seemed to feel the heat, and she grimaced, recalling how warm she always felt during her pregnancies. In fact, she was not looking forward to being in her third trimester during the hottest part of the year. Baby D would be born the first week of November, but high temperatures in August and September, and sometimes even in October in Southern California, often hovered around 100 degrees for weeks on end.

She glanced at Tim at the other end of the table. He looked cool as a cucumber, relaxed and fresh in his short-sleeved plaid shirt untucked over jeans. He caught her eye and straightened, an eyebrow raised in question. He was so attentive, it almost hurt.

"Okay, boys. Time to clean up. Reuben, get a paper bag from the broom closet and collect all the trash, please. Simon, grab the forks, Levi the fruit bowl, and Judah, you get the salt and pepper and bring it all inside." In response to the immediate groans, she held up a finger. "*If* you do it all without complaining, I will share with you the special treat Tim brought with him. If not, I will keep it all to myself." She grinned at Tim, who was watching her with an unreadable look. "I might share some with Tim, since he isn't whining."

"What is it?" Judah asked, clearly debating whether it was worth the trade.

"Can't tell you, man," Tim teased. "But I'll help with cleanup and we'll let your mom chill." He winked at her.

She smiled and watched as he and the boys made quick work of clearing the table. A few minutes later they all came swarming back outside, Reuben carrying the box of doughnuts, Simon a tall glass of ice water for her, Levi a stack of napkins, and Tim carrying Judah on his back, bringing up the rear.

"Before you dig in," she said, straightening in her seat and lowering her feet from where she'd propped them up on one of the benches. "We have a few announcements to make."

She noticed Reuben's shoulders stiffen, and he looked from Renata to Tim and back again. She felt heat rise in her cheeks at his obvious assumption and couldn't bring herself to look at Tim.

The boys returned to their seats; Judah unable to resist touching the box of doughnuts. He laid his perpetually grubby fingers on the corner of it and stared balefully at her, trying desperately to be patient.

"Okay. I'll get right to it." Suddenly nervous, she tucked a strand of hair behind her ear. To her delight, it seemed to be growing quickly now that she was on her prenatal vitamins. "So, Reuben, you remember I told you Daddy and I were trying to have a baby before... well, before his accident?"

Reuben nodded slowly, eyes narrowing.

"Well, God has given us a miracle. That little baby we wanted. I'm pregnant. With a baby girl."

In the brief silence that followed, Renata had a chance to imagine all kinds of scenarios unfolding. What actually did happen was not one of them.

THIRTY-FIVE

Reuben shoved back from the table so hard that the bench he and Levi shared fell backwards, sending Levi tumbling to the stone patio so suddenly that it knocked the breath out of him.

Tim scrambled to his feet and raced to the boy's side, one big hand on his chest to keep him from trying to get up too quickly. Levi made a terrible keening sound as he tried to take a breath, then began sobbing when the air finally did fill his lungs.

Simon sat like a stone, unmoving on the bench he shared with Judah, hands braced on the table in front of him.

Judah, taking advantage of the chaos around him, tore into the doughnuts and had three piled up in front of him before Reuben snatched the box from his hands and hurled it at Tim, who still knelt over Levi. The doughnuts flew in every direction.

"You bastard!" Reuben shouted.

Judah reacted in horror, not over the bad word, but over the terrible waste of good doughnuts, his wail rising like a siren.

"Reuben!" Shock shuddered through Renata at her son's language, at the rage that tore out of his mouth, at the color of his face as he glared at Tim.

"Couldn't keep your hands off her, could you! I'm not blind! I see you watching her, your eyes bulging out of your head, practically drooling over her. Do you think I'm stupid? Do you think I don't know how this works? I'm almost twelve, not two!" Reuben picked up his cup, still half full of milk, and hurled it, too. "That's my mother, you—you—" His words broke off as though he couldn't come up with anything foul enough to call the man.

Fortunately, the cup was plastic, but milk splattered the front of Tim's shirt and face quite effectively, the cup bouncing off his chest and hitting Levi in the forehead.

Levi cried harder, now holding both hands to his face.

Renata was on her feet and grabbed Reuben's arm before he could throw Levi's cup, too. "Stop it! Stop, Reuben!"

He turned on her, his eyes filled with angry tears, and between gut-wrenching sobs, his words blasted from his mouth like weapons. "You're the one who's stupid, Mom! Did you really think we'd be happy about this? You let Dad's back-stabbing traitor friend scr—"

"Reuben John Dixon!" Tim roared, effectively cutting off the ugly word. He rose to his full height, and even with his shirt front splattered with milk, and doughnut crumbs in his hair, the man was intimidation personified. "Don't you ever speak to your mother that way again, son."

"I'm not your son!" Reuben yelled, struggling halfheartedly against Renata's hold.

"I'm not finished," Tim said, taking a step toward the boy. "Don't you ever speak to any woman that way; do you hear me? I don't care what she's done—or what you *think* she's done—that is not the kind of language a real man ever uses. Ever." His voice shook with his own fury, the words coming out clear and hard, each one cut out of the air with precision.

At the table, Simon still had not moved.

Renata released Reuben, who suddenly deflated under Tim's reprimand, and she hurried to Levi's side, crouching down next to him. He was trying to sit up, and she stopped him. "Did you hit your head, honey?" Her own voice shook, too, but with the adrenaline rush of shock.

"No," Levi whimpered. "Just my back. I—I couldn't breathe." He let her help him stand, then the two of them stepped back while Tim righted the bench.

Renata glanced over at Judah, who sobbed around huge bites of doughnut.

Reuben turned as though to leave, but Tim stopped him with a gentle command, his voice much calmer now. "Don't you leave, young man. We've got a mess to clean up."

Reuben's eyes scanned the patio. Harry and Sally had discovered the Krispy Kreme manna from heaven and were eagerly doing their part to help with the cleanup.

"I'm not talking about that mess. Sit." Tim pointed at the bench where Levi was already settling back into place, wiping at his nose with the back of his hand. "I'm going to go change my shirt. You boys sit here and get your heads on straight until I get back. Anyone gets up, you'll deal with me." He gave each of them a ferocious glare. "Judah, stop crying. Now."

Judah looked up, eyes wide, a chunk of chewed doughnut falling from his open mouth, but he didn't make another peep.

Renata sat back down in her own seat and did her best not to cry, too, but silent tears leaked from the corners of her eyes. This was all so wrong. She'd seen things going so differently.

Tim returned less than five minutes later, his hair free of crumbs and frosting flakes and combed back from his broad forehead, wearing a red t-shirt that had seen better days, one he must have had stashed in his truck. He surveyed the silent group, then lowered himself slowly into his chair at the end of the table.

Reuben's head hung so low his chin rested on his chest. Simon blinked often, but otherwise, had not changed position. Levi had salvaged a doughnut from somewhere and was pinching off tiny pieces of it and sticking them in his mouth. Judah had devoured all three of the doughnuts he'd scored and now was squirming on his seat in a way that Renata recognized as urgent.

"Excuse us, Tim. Judah and I will be right back." She stood and grabbed Judah's gooey hand, pulling him from the bench. They made it to the bathroom just in time.

After washing Judah's hands and face, she splashed cool water on her own face, then took a few deep cleansing breaths before heading back out to the patio with him.

To her surprise, the doughnut mess was cleaned up, the milk that had splashed on surfaces other than Tim was hosed down, and the boys were sitting quietly in their seats, Tim with his elbows on the table, hands folded together in front of him. She and Judah quickly filed into the thick silence.

"I want to make something absolutely clear." Tim's gentle expression belied the firmness of his tone. "I want you to look at me, all of you." He waited until the boys complied. Renata watched him, too, a little in awe of this authoritative man opposite her. But it was easy to see why he'd done so well in the military.

"Reuben, your accusations and disrespect toward your mother are absolutely inexcusable. I understand your concern, but ask questions first. Never assume. Your language? Unacceptable in any company." He took a deep breath, then turned to face Renata. "Time for a birds and bees talk."

Renata's eyes grew wide, and she opened her mouth to speak, her glance darting around the table at the various-aged boys.

Tim laughed when he saw her face, but he held up his hand to stop her. She closed her mouth with a snap and crossed her arms, hoping against hope she could trust him.

"It usually takes nine months for a baby to grow inside a woman. It's the end of July and your mom has been pregnant for almost six months. Reuben, Simon, you do the math."

When there was no reply, Tim nodded as though he could read their mental calculations. "That's right. Your mom got pregnant in February. *Before* your dad died. I, comrades, had nothing to do with it."

"Well," Renata muttered, eyeing him across the table. "That was candid."

"Nothing wrong with candid, Mrs. Dixon." He put a hand on Reuben's shoulder and gave the boy a gentle shake. "We're dealing with a few young men, here. Not babies."

A weighty silence settled around the table as the adults gave the boys a chance to process the information. Levi was staring at Renata, a funny expression on his face. Judah flopped onto his side on the bench, his head bumping into Simon's elbow. Simon scowled at him, but didn't retaliate. Reuben's eyes were glued to his lap again.

"I thought you were getting fat," Levi finally said. "But you're just growing a baby, right?"

Tim made a big show of coughing, and Renata gave him the evil eye. "Yes, Levi. I'm growing a baby." She stood up, smoothed her dress over her belly and turned sideways. Five sets of male eyes, including Judah's from his position on his back, widened in an array of expressions: surprise, dismay, guilt, curiosity, and in Tim's eyes, that same look of yearning she'd seen when he'd first arrived that morning. She sat quickly.

"Did you swallow a baby?" Judah asked, sitting up, one of his hands going subconsciously to his own rounded belly.

"Does it move?" Levi wondered.

"When will it be here?" Simon finally spoke, but his expression didn't change.

Reuben said nothing.

"I did not swallow a baby, Judah. There's a baby growing inside me and in a few months, it will come out and live with us." She could see the wheels turning in his little red-haired head, but she moved on before he could ask anything else that she wasn't prepared to answer. "Levi, yes. *She* does move. This baby is a she, not an it. I can feel her moving sometimes from the inside, but it might not be very easy for any of you on the outside. In another month, though, you'll definitely be able to feel her kick and punch."

"Is that how she's going to get out? Pow! Kablam!" Judah threw a double punch out in front of him, and Tim snatched his water glass away moments before the little fists made contact.

"And Simon, she's due November 7th. A few weeks before Thanksgiving." She turned to her oldest son. "Reuben, what about you? Do you have any questions?"

It took him a while, but she could tell he had something on his mind. Finally, he lifted his head. "Did Dad know about her?"

Renata brought a hand up to her mouth. His question, heavy with all the mixed emotions of the morning, hit her in the middle of her chest. "Oh, honey. I didn't even know until the beginning of May, and even then, I didn't want to say anything until I saw Dr. Flynn a few weeks later, so he could tell me everything was all right. But the moment I found out, I told Daddy. I lie in bed every night talking to him about her. He knows, Reuben. He knows."

Her oldest son nodded and lowered his gaze again, swiping the back of his hand across his eyes.

"Why didn't you tell us then?" Simon's eyes were bright, but he still kept a stoic face.

"Well, I've had a hard time getting pregnant lately." Renata hadn't planned on the conversation going in this direction, and she didn't know if Tim was aware of her past miscarriages or not, but he was already invested, whether he liked it or not. So she took a deep breath and dove in. "In the last year and a half, I've been pregnant with three other babies, but each time, something went wrong, and those babies went back to heaven before they were born. I wanted to make sure we'd get to keep this one before I said anything, that's all."

Simon took a deep breath in, held it for a second, then blew it out slowly. A tiny smile curled one corner of his mouth. "Maybe God took them back so they could help Daddy not be so lonely for us."

"Pow! Kapow-pow!" Judah muttered after a few moments, scooting off the bench so he could air box without interference.

THIRTY-SIX

"Just so you know, Reuben apologized to me. And to his brothers," Tim said after climbing into his truck and rolling down the window so he could talk to her. Even from where she stood a couple feet away, she could feel the heat emanating from the cab, the summer sun beating down on the black vehicle.

The boys were busy out back going through the camping stuff Tim had brought down from the attic for them. They'd all worked together to set up the tent in the backyard to make sure all the parts were present and accounted for, and they'd left it up for the boys to play in over the weekend. Tim would stop by on Wednesday after work and have them help him dismantle it and load their gear in his truck. They'd head out Thursday morning early and come back some time on Sunday.

"I'm glad. Oh Tim," she put both hands to her cheeks. "I'm so sorry about how that went down. I just didn't think—I had no idea he would think—that Reuben...." Her voice trailed off, fading into her embarrassment. She shouldn't have said anything.

"You shouldn't be sorry, Renata. I'm proud of Reuben. He might have handled it wrong, but his reaction was justified." Tim squinted at her in the bright sun, then leaned forward to turn the key in the ignition. "He is the man of the house now, and it's his job to defend the castle."

The truck came to life, rumbling quietly beneath him. He waited a minute or two before switching on the air conditioning. "Maybe it's time to rethink these Friday nights, Renata. Maybe it's time to move on, you know?" His expression was odd as he studied her; she kind of thought he was hoping she'd contradict him. But she'd been pondering much of the same thing all morning. If the boys jumped to those conclusions about her and Tim, what would other people think?

On the other hand, Renata had only been *thinking* those things. Now to have Tim voice them made her feel a little hollow. She looked forward to Friday nights with him and the boys all week, she realized, even more than Tuesdays with her grandparents.

Suddenly, she realized that her fear of him moving on, of Tim getting a life of his own and no longer spending time with the boys, was also because she was afraid that he'd leave her, too. She stared at his big, solid chest, then realized she was doing so and looked away. "Oh. Okay," she said, her voice coming out a little shaky. "You might be right."

Tim grimaced at her response, but nodded, his hands gripping the steering wheel so hard it made his knuckles go white against his tan skin. He peered out at the garage door, obviously seeing something else in his mind, the corners of his mouth pulling down in thought. Finally, he said, "Hey. It's hot. You should head back inside and put your feet up. Let's just think about it, okay? I'll be back on Wednesday."

Renata stepped back, feeling dismissed, and crossed her arms. He waited, as though expecting her to say something more, but what was there to add? She didn't like it, but she knew he was right. They'd gotten pretty comfortable playing little family over the last month, and maybe, just maybe, they were losing their perspective on things. It wasn't about what she wanted, but about what was best for the boys now, for this new baby.

A little voice cried out inside her, however, as Tim backed down the driveway and pulled slowly out into the street, lifting a hand for one last wave. Maybe, just maybe, Tim might be the best thing for the boys, for this new baby.

Maybe, just maybe, he might be the best thing for her.

"But we're not the best thing for him," she argued as she turned and headed back inside, her footsteps dragging. It was too much to ask of any man.

She had just settled into the corner of the couch with a glass of lemonade when the boys came charging inside, hot and sweaty from work and play, but apparently all getting along for once. As an amoebic unit, they swarmed the kitchen, filled short tumblers with lemonade for themselves, then sat at the table with their juice, knowing better than to bring the sticky stuff into the living room where one or more would inevitably spill.

Things got really quiet, and Renata wondered what was going on in their little heads.

"Mom?" It was Reuben, the go-to spokesperson. Judah knocked over his glass, but it was already empty.

Renata got up and came to sit at the table with them, grabbing the pitcher on the way over and refilling everyone's cups. "What's up?"

"I'm sorry I said those things to you outside. That I thought those things about you and Tim." He swallowed hard, but courageously kept his eyes locked with hers. "And I'm sorry I used bad words, too, especially in front of Judah, who doesn't know better."

Renata smiled at him and nodded, her heart melting over how mature he sounded, how hard he was trying to make things right.

"I'm going to help do dishes every night until we go camping." His expression made it seem like he was signing up for latrine duty. "And I'm going to work for Tim for a few hours after we get back from camping to pay him back for the doughnuts, if that's okay with you."

"Of course," Renata agreed, relieved that Tim had covered the consequences of Reuben's behavior so effectively.

"We also want to tell you we're glad you're having a baby. It's like a present from Dad, right?"

"Even if she is a girl," Simon added.

"I like girls," Judah chimed in, his youthful lisp making it sound like 'ghouls'. "They have pretty pantsies."

"Judah!" Renata stared wide-eyed at him. "What on earth are you talking about?"

"Tina at school always wears fancy pantsies," he explained. "They have dots and flowers and butterflies on them. I like them."

"So, you want to wear girl panties?" Simon poked Judah in the side of the head.

"No! Don't poke me!" Judah tried to retaliate, but Renata grabbed his arm and kept him firmly in his seat.

"Simon, cut it out. Judah, yes, girls often have pretty things. But just so you know, some girls like Spiderman and Batman underwear, too, okay?"

"Yeah, there's a girl in my class who wears boxers," Reuben chimed in.

Renata turned to him with raised eyebrows. "And how do you know that?"

"Because they hang out over the top of her jeans, Mom. She's not dropping her drawers to show us." Reuben rolled his eyes at her, then stopped, realizing what he was doing.

"Is she going to sleep in our room?" Levi asked, his eyes suddenly wide.

"No, honey," Renata chuckled. "My room will be the girls' room, okay? She'll sleep in there with me." There were sighs of relief from three of the boys.

"She can sleep wiff me sometimes," Judah said, shrugging his shoulders in a gesture that reminded Renata of Reuben. "I could tell her stories."

"That's very nice of you, Judah. Maybe when she's a little older, she'd like that."

THIRTY-SEVEN

Late Wednesday afternoon, Phoebe came for dinner at Renata's request. She was grinning broadly when she let herself in the front door.

Renata looked up from the granola bars she was making for the boys to take camping. "Hey, Phoebe."

"Hey, yourself. So, I see Mr. Tool Belt is back. That's his truck out front, right?" Phoebe sashayed into the kitchen, set down her huge handbag, then hugged Renata from behind, splaying her hands over the baby bump.

Renata smiled, but kept working. "They're all out back if you want to say 'hi' to everyone. Getting camping gear organized."

"Well, I might just do that. How do I look?" She fluffed her hair and pursed her lips, striking a super model pose.

"You're beautiful," Renata said. She meant it, too. Phoebe looked like Monica Bellucci, with her shiny black hair and full, pouty lips painted red. She was the epitome of sultry, and although Renata knew Tim wasn't really Phoebe's type, she also knew her sister had eyes in her head, and Tim was definitely easy on anyone's eyes, tool belt or no.

Phoebe swept through the living room and out the back door, her melodic voice calling out a greeting to the guys. Renata sighed. Her type or not, Tim might be good for Phoebe. Just what her wayward sister might need to settle down and grow up a little. He was a solid, godly man, so different than the fly-by-night younger men Phoebe always had on her arm. And as a skilled carpenter, he was an artist in his own right. Not only would he be a good thing in Phoebe's life, but if the two of them got together, it would keep Tim in the boys' lives, too.

Could she handle seeing Phoebe and Tim together? The thought of it made her chest hurt. Bracing both hands on the counter, she dropped her chin to her chest, closed her eyes, and took a few deep breaths in through the nose and out through the mouth.

Lamaze. She hadn't even thought about that yet. She remembered all the techniques, but a brush-up wouldn't be a bad thing. She'd have a new partner this time, and she'd have to choose someone soon so they could do the classes together, but how to choose one sister over the other without hurting feelings was impossible.

"Who's going to help us, sweetie pie?" It was almost a moan. "Who will be there for us?"

"Renata? You alright?"

Her eyes flew open, her hand going to her chest in surprise. "Oh! Tim! Sorry, I didn't hear you come in."

He crossed the room quickly and peered down at her, reaching out to put a hand on her arm, then withdrawing it immediately. "Do you need to sit down?"

"I'm fine. Just taking a breather. You know, in through the nose, out through the mouth," she replied, smirking at her terrible joke. Tim was clearly concerned.

"You look a little pale. Maybe you should sit. Do you need a glass of water?"

"I'm fine, Tim. Really." She shrugged and picked up the spoon she'd been using to stir her ingredients. "I was just thinking about the future, that's all. I know it's going to be hard for a while. Maybe for a long while. But we're going to be okay. I know that, too." Glancing up at him, she gave him a wry smile. "I just get a little overwhelmed sometimes."

A look of such compassion crossed his features that it brought tears to her eyes. He did touch her then, his hand on her bicep, stroking her arm from shoulder to elbow, his work-hardened hands rough against her skin. "I'm not going anywhere, Renata."

"I know," she murmured, taking a step back, so he was no longer touching her. "You already said that. But you should. I mean, you need your own life, Tim." She turned her gaze to the sliding glass door that led out back. She could see Phoebe pushing Judah on the swing, laughing at something one of the boys said. "What about Phoebe? Maybe you should ask her out."

Tim laughed, low and gentle. "What is it with you trying to set me up with your sisters?"

It was her turn to chuckle. "Yeah, that last one didn't work out so well, did it?" She turned to face him then, arms crossed over her chest, emphasizing the baby bump she now sported proudly in a snug knit tunic with a pair of leggings. His eyes went to her belly and lingered there, that same look of longing on his face. Baby D kicked in reaction to Renata's pulse speeding up.

Suddenly, she reached for his hand where it rested on the counter, and without looking at him for fear she'd lose her nerve, with both her hands over his, she pressed his palm to the curve of her belly just under her rib cage. She could feel every muscle in his forearm bunch in resistance, but she said, "Sh. It's okay." The words didn't make sense, really, but her tone was soothing, the same one she used when trying to calm one of her boys. "She's a busy girl right now. Just wait."

They stood that way for several moments, neither moving, not even breathing. Just waiting. And then there it was. A series of quick bumps against his hand. His fingers tightened reflexively over her stomach, and she heard his sharp intake of breath. She lifted her eyes to his, smiling proudly over her baby's performance.

His expression of pure wonder made her a little dizzy. She glanced away, unable to bear whatever it was she saw in his eyes. She turned to look out at the backyard.

Phoebe stood at the sliding glass door, her fingers wrapped around the handle, preparing to slide it open. Her eyes were wide, one eyebrow arched, her perfect mouth slightly open in question.

Renata lifted both hands from Tim's, but his stayed there, curved around the slope of her stomach. She took a tiny step back and his hand slid away, his fingers closing around empty air into a clenched fist between them, as though holding tight to the miracle he'd just experienced.

"It's Phoebe." She whispered a warning just as the door opened. Why did this feel so reminiscent of the day Phoebe caught Renata and Brad kissing all those years ago?

"Hey, you two. Is Baby D kicking? Can I feel?" Phoebe crossed the living room to where they stood, her hands extended toward Renata's belly. "Hello, little girl! It's your Auntie Phebes. Kick twice if you love me," she cooed as she rested both hands where Tim's large one had been only moments before.

Renata sighed, the intimacy of the moment evaporating, and pressed down on Phoebe's hand to nudge the baby, who was still quite active inside her.

"Ooh! I felt her!" Phoebe voiced her excitement, but when she lifted her eyes to Renata's, they were filled with questions clearly not about the baby.

Tim headed out through the garage without another word, Phoebe's eyes following him. Then she turned back to Renata.

"So, did I interrupt something?"

"He was feeling the baby move, Phoebe. Just like you are." Renata rolled her eyes and pulled away from Phoebe's hands.

"Um, no. Not just like I was," Phoebe contradicted. "I saw his face. I don't believe I've ever looked at you that way. That'd be sick and wrong." She crossed her arms and leaned against the counter. "He's been spending a lot of time here, according to the boys. You two getting a little... friendly?"

Renata ever so carefully lay down the spoon she'd picked up and narrowed her eyes at Phoebe. "No." Then she turned and stalked to her bedroom, slamming the door behind her.

When she came out about an hour later, the house was curiously quiet. There was a note on her counter from Phoebe. *Took the boys to the grandparents for dinner. Told them you weren't feeling well. We'll be back by 8. Sorry for being a jerk. Love you. P*

There was also a text on her phone from Tim. *Boys with Phoebe for dinner. See you in the morning at 7. Sorry for bailing—still lots to do tonight. Tim.*

THIRTY-EIGHT

Tim pulled in at seven o'clock a.m. on the button, his truck bed loaded and tarped for the road. The boys were just sitting down for a breakfast of scrambled eggs, homemade hash browns, and turkey bacon, and Renata insisted he join them.

She didn't eat much before ten o'clock. Even though she rarely suffered from full-on morning sickness anymore, her tummy still felt a little unsettled in the mornings. She had a cup of Greek yogurt topped with a handful of blueberries and some leftover granola from the bars she'd made yesterday.

Tim said nothing about the way things ended last night, so Renata didn't either, but both of them were much more reserved than usual.

They all used the bathroom one more time, gathered in a circle and prayed for safety and fun for the boys and lots of peace and quiet for Renata, and then they were gone.

Instead of asking for company, Renata decided this was going to be her weekend to find her courage. If things got too tough, she could always call someone or go to Granny G's place for the night. But it was time to rearrange her bedroom to accommodate a baby and all the paraphernalia that came with one.

She might even work up the courage to go through John's side of the closet and get rid of some of his things. The boys had already gone in and pulled out a few of their favorite items, including a pair of dress shoes Judah insisted he wanted. She had no idea what he planned to do with them, but he had hugged them tightly to his chest, demanding she let him have them forever and ever.

Maybe she'd go to church on Sunday. She hadn't been since the funeral, and even though her freezer still held remnants of the meals that the prayer group had so faithfully delivered for that first month, she hadn't been able to bring herself to go without John. Her grandparents took the boys with them but never pressured her to go, and for that, she was grateful. But with no one to worry about getting ready but herself, it seemed like the timing was right. She could show up late, sit near the back, and slip out early if she felt the need.

When the troops got home Sunday night, she'd have Tim pull the crib down from the attic for her before he went back to his place.

Renata did great all day Thursday. When Juliette called to check on her, Renata beamed as she told her sister about the progress she'd made. After a cool shower, she watched a Jane Austen movie, one she'd never get away with if the boys were home, then went to bed, too exhausted to feel sorry for herself being alone. She fell asleep singing to Baby D.

Renata did great all day Friday. She mourned her way through John's side of the closet, boxing most of his clothes up and carting the stuff out to the garage. She wasn't quite ready to take everything to the Goodwill yet, but she organized the boxes neatly in the back of John's truck where no one would stumble across them and ask questions.

But when dinner rolled around, and she sat in front of the television with a chicken salad sandwich and her yogurt and fruit, she felt such a longing for companionship that she could hardly eat.

In a fit of despair, she slipped out to the garage, opened one of the boxes, and dug around until she found John's shirt from Phoebe. She pulled it out, brought it to her face, and breathed him in before slipping it on over the tank top she had on. He'd worn it the night before his fall—she'd found it and his pajama pants in a neatly folded pile on his side of the bed—and she hadn't been able to bring herself to wash it.

She had tossed her own shirt from Phoebe in with his when she'd packed the box, and it now mocked her cruelly from the jumbled contents, almost as though it had been a portent of things to come. Hunting Widow. She closed the flaps with a sob and left the garage.

She resisted the urge to call Tim and check on the boys, and rather than a romcom or drama that would make her ache for John, she pulled out *Tomb*

Raider, a favorite movie of his. He had a not-so-secret thing for Angelina Jolie, but Renata didn't mind. The woman made a perfect Lara Croft, and these movies had motivated Renata to get back in shape after every pregnancy.

She went to bed crying anyway, missing her husband desperately, missing her boys just as desperately.

Missing Tim and their Friday night desserts.

She knew the Holy Spirit was there with her, but she had a difficult time finding any peace.

Renata did all right on Saturday, but every car that drove by had her lifting her head to see if it was them, hoping they'd come home a day early. Harry and Sally seemed to sense her disquiet and stayed close on her heels all morning. She finally banished them to the backyard, lest she trip over one of them and hurt herself.

By three o'clock, she had a headache that wouldn't let up, so she lay down with one of the romance novels she'd found in a shoe box while organizing her side of the closet today.

After John's death, she had rounded up all her novels and sent them with Gia to the thrift store. She'd determined there was no such thing as a happily-ever-after for her, and she didn't want to read about anyone else's, either.

Somehow, she'd missed this box, though, and now, as she poured over the books, she started to see them the way John did.

He laughed about them, but his words rang with truth now that she wasn't busy defending her addiction. On every cover was a man with an open shirt, an undershirt, or no shirt at all, and every woman seemed to be wearing dresses that were difficult to keep on. Even the covers where everyone was fully clothed, the models were disproportionately endowed, leaving little to the imagination, and looking inordinately uncomfortable in the awkward, clandestine poses. In all the years Renata had been married to John, they'd never once pressed together in the positions the models did on these covers, not even in the most passionate, intimate of moments.

For whatever reason, Ella Robbins couldn't hold her attention tonight. She sighed, tucked the books back inside the shoe box and set it on the floor. It would go out to the truck with the rest of the boxes.

Instead, she picked up John's Bible from his nightstand and turned to Psalm 91, the passage Tim had read aloud in the hospital. She'd read it over so many times, she had it memorized, but somehow seeing the words on the page made them feel more authentic, as though they were a direct connection to God, to her husband, to those last minutes she'd spent with him. She was so glad their last words to each other had been of love.

"Thank you, Lord, for letting me get there in time to say goodbye. And for letting Tim get there in time, too." She felt a small fissure of guilt creeping in as she thought about Tim.

At first, she tried to ignore it. Then she tried to embrace it so she could feel ashamed for thinking of him. But as she lay there in the stillness of this room that had been her sanctuary for so much of her life, she began to unwrap her feelings about him honestly. Who was here to judge her but herself? And it wasn't as though God didn't already know the struggle she was going through.

She'd known Tim almost as long as John had. The two men had met on a job and become fast friends. She trusted him more than any other man she knew, other than Grandpa. Good grief, she'd sent her boys off camping with him, something she wouldn't even feel comfortable doing with Juliette's police boyfriend yet. She knew he was a committed believer—he and John studied the Bible together faithfully.

As a skilled carpenter, Tim had a reputation in the business for doing beautiful cabinetry, and his clients loved and respected him. He often turned away work because he was so busy. He also did custom projects on the side, mostly furniture; his favorite pieces were dining room sets, and the few she'd seen before he delivered them to their happy owners were stunning.

She knew very little about his years in the war; he simply didn't talk about it, ever. She'd asked John once if he knew. Her husband had told her he did, but that Tim had trusted him not to tell her unless she insisted on knowing. "He doesn't want to be the reason I keep secrets from you," John had explained. "So, he's okay if I do tell you. But it is his business, and I'd like to respect his wishes if you're okay with it." She'd agreed, even though she'd been riddled with curiosity. Over time, however, it had stopped mattering.

Tim had a close family stemming from up in the Sacramento region. Both his parents were still alive and well, and fairly well-off, to boot. His younger sister lived with her husband and children close to the parents, but Tim ended up in Midtown after his service term was up. He'd somehow made connections in the area and had chosen to make it his home away from home. He had an older brother who traveled a lot with his job, but he was based out of the Los Angeles area, so Tim saw him several times a year. He was a recruiter for one of the L. A. sports teams, and although Renata had never met him, if he was built anything like Tim, he was probably an athlete himself, too.

Tim was respectful, thoughtful, and honest. He treated everyone with dignity, even her boys. He had been the best of friends to John while he was alive, like brothers, and now, in her husband's absence, Tim was doing his best to continue being the same kind of friend to John by looking after John's widow and unborn child and covering the gaping holes left by the loss of a father in the boys' lives.

If Renata was being honest with herself, she was beginning to lean on Tim to cover the gaping holes left by the loss of a husband, too.

But what did she have to offer Tim? Another man's ready-made family? Her heart that would always belong in a small way to John? No money to speak of, except for what they'd live on for the next few years, if she was careful. A woman quick to pass judgment and even quicker to worry about the judgment of others. And a new baby on the way.

It was too much to ask of him. Too much to expect him to consider.

She would have to talk to him when they got back, and soon. This needed to stop. She couldn't let it go on any longer or the boys would be devastated when he got tired of playing surrogate dad and moved on.

Who was she kidding? *She* would be devastated when Tim got tired of them and moved on.

But she couldn't see past him to a life without him in it. She didn't want to see her life without him.

"Oh John. Why did you have to leave me all alone?"

• • • • • • • •

Renata did attend church on Sunday, but she went to the early morning service where she'd see few people she knew, if any.

She didn't sleep well Saturday night. The house was too quiet, too still. Even Baby D seemed to want to take the night off from keeping Renata company, and no amount of poking and nudging her belly would garner so much as a push back.

So when Renata woke up with the morning sun, she didn't even bother trying to get back to sleep, but instead, got up and went to church.

Baby D got all excited about the music, and by the time Renata left the service, she was in better spirits and looking forward to whipping up something fun for the boys to eat when they got home. They were probably tired of camping food by now, so she'd have to think of something special. Maybe just her crock pot spaghetti and gigantic meatballs. The boys loved the meal, and she was pretty sure it would be a winner with Tim, too.

Would he stay for dinner?

She got things started, took the dogs for a walk around the block, then headed over to her grandparents' home for the family meal.

As she sat in her place at the table, Juliette and Victor across from her, Gia and her best friend, Ricky, who joined them for many a family meal, Phoebe, Granny G and Grandpa, she listened to the ebb and flow of life around her. She realized that although being without John beside her felt awfully unbalanced in so many ways, a new rhythm was beginning to envelop her, one she thought she might be able to move with. It would take some getting used to, but she wasn't a quitter. And once she freed Tim to go live his own life, she and the kids would need this bunch more than ever.

"You guys," she said, interrupting a few conversations going on around her, suddenly anxious to let them know what was in her heart. "I just want you to know how grateful I am for each one of you. For everything you've done for me and the boys and Baby D over these last several months." She began to tear up a little, her emotions rising to the surface. "I have the best family in the whole world. I don't want another day to go by without telling you that I know how fortunate I am to be a part of this motley crew. Thank you for not giving up on me."

Juliette reached across the table and squeezed her hand. Granny G got up from her seat and circled the table to hug her. Phoebe leaned over and kissed her on the cheek, then laughed at the red lip marks she left behind. Gia smiled, dewy-eyed herself, and the three guys just nodded and looked a little awkward in the face of all the female emotions.

John wouldn't want her to wallow. He'd be happy knowing she was here, letting her family carry her along in his absence.

He'd be happy she'd gone to church this morning.

He'd be happy to know that Tim was watching out for her and his sons. And his daughter.

But would he be happy that his wife was beginning to dream about Tim? To miss him when he wasn't there? Would John be happy to know that she was going to push him away before her heart—and their boys' hearts—could be broken?

At two o'clock, her phone rang. Tim's number showed up on the screen, and her traitorous heart skipped a beat. She excused herself from the living room where they were lounging, letting their food digest before they all went their separate ways. Granny G had gone to her room to rest for a bit. Grandpa was asleep in his easy chair ,and Phoebe was sketching him. Juliette and Victor were talking quietly, giving the long-suffering artist pointers on how to improve her portrait.

"Hello," Renata said into the phone as she stepped out onto the front porch.

"Hi, Mom." It was Reuben, and as much as her heart filled with love to hear his voice after so many days apart, she couldn't ignore the little jolt of disappointment that it hadn't been Tim's deep voice greeting her on the other end.

"Hey, honey. You guys heading home soon?" She was suddenly anxious to see them all.

"Actually, Tim told me to call you because we're already in the car and we'll probably be home in an hour, if that's okay. He said if you're busy, he can take us to his house first, then bring us home at five or six like we'd planned." He spoke carefully, as though he'd rehearsed what he was supposed to say to her.

"Oh goodness, honey. Come home! I'm over at Granny G's right now, but we're just watching Aunt Phoebe draw pictures of Grandpa while he's sleeping, so I can leave any time." She leaned against the door frame, the heat making her feel limp. "Did you have a good time?"

"Oh, yeah!" His voice grew animated as he began to regale her with some anecdote about fishing, then she heard the sounds of an argument breaking out in the background. Tim's voice rumbled over the top of things, and she giggled when she heard the impatient tone of it. He must be exhausted.

"Reuben?" She had to say his name three times before she got his attention. "Why don't you wait to tell me about it when you get here? We'll get you boys cleaned up, then we'll eat dinner together and everyone can be a part of it, okay?"

"Okay. That's what Tim just said, too."

Of course. "Good. Then I think that's a good plan." She paused just a moment, then added, "And tell Tim he's invited to stay for dinner, too."

Reuben immediately relayed the message, to Renata's chagrin, but a moment later he said, "Tim's cool with that. What are we having?"

"Spaghetti and Mama meatballs."

"Yes!" He hooted out the plan to the rest of them and the celebratory shrieks coming through the phone were deafening. She was pretty sure Tim was making just as much noise as the rest of them.

They said their goodbyes, then she went back inside her grandparents' house to let the family know she was heading out.

THIRTY-NINE

BY THE TIME TIM arrived, Renata already had the garage door up so they could unload the camping gear easily and stash it where it needed to go. The boys piled out of the cab and charged her, each of them greeting her with great enthusiasm, even Simon.

"Did you miss us, Mommy?" Judah asked, his face smudged and dirty, his red hair standing on end.

"Oh Judah, I missed you like crazy!" she exclaimed, crouching down to hug him so she wouldn't have to lift him up. He was still small and wiry, and if she hadn't been pregnant, she wouldn't have hesitated, but she wasn't taking any chances with stuff like that. She'd already done enough straining over the last few days with carrying boxes and moving some of the lighter pieces of furniture around in her room, and she felt it in her back and shoulders.

The boys all hurried inside to use the bathroom and get something to drink. Tim climbed out from behind the wheel a little slower than usual, and she laughed when she saw him. He looked absolutely wiped out. He was almost as grungy as Judah, and his hair looked ratty and dirty. He struck a pose, obviously well aware of what a sight he was.

"Renata, I never imagined how much work they could be," he muttered. "You, Mrs. Dixon, are a saint. That's all I have to say in my defense."

"Hey, give yourself some credit," she exclaimed. "You brought all four of them home in one piece. No one is crying, no one is bleeding, and none of them have any new pets, do they? No lizards or freaky insects?" She couldn't keep the smile off her face.

"I checked their pockets before I let them in the truck. Judah tried to bring home a dead—"

Renata held up a hand to stop him. "I don't want to know."

Tim laughed heartily and agreed that she probably didn't. He sighed, then eyed the cargo strapped down under the tarp in the truck bed. She took pity on him.

"Hey. It's early. Why don't you just dump everything on the floor in the garage, go home and get cleaned up? Take a nap if you want. Then come back for spaghetti in a couple of hours, okay?"

He didn't seem convinced, so she poked him in the chest. "I won't let you in my house smelling like this. You want to eat my famous spaghetti, you shower first."

He grinned then, and all the dirt in the world couldn't hide how lovely that smile was. "Aye, aye, Captain," he said, snapping his heels together and saluting her. "Send out the troops and we'll make short work of this first."

She turned to head inside, but he stopped her with a hand on her arm. She looked up at him, her eyes meeting his. He was awfully close to her, and he really didn't smell so bad after all.

"They're great. Your boys. You should be proud of them."

Renata beamed. They *were* great; she knew that, and she *was* very proud of them. "I know," she said quietly. "Thank you, Tim. You have no idea how important this trip will be to them for years to come."

He nodded. "And you? How did you do?" he asked. "How's the baby?" His eyes dropped to her stomach and stayed there for several moments, almost as though watching for movement. Baby D was completely still at the moment, though, having worn herself out dancing in church.

"We did all right," she said, choosing to be honest. "Had a couple rough moments, but God stuck around all weekend." She patted her belly. "This one is already good company, too."

"Good. We prayed for you every night, Renata. We—the boys missed you," he amended. His voice was husky, low, and she needed to get back on solid ground.

"Oh right," she quipped, rolling her eyes. "I'm sure they did. In between catching fish, hiking, roasting hot dogs and marshmallows, drinking coffee, telling ghost stories around the campfire... I 'm sure they missed me terribly."

Tim laughed again and nodded. "You certainly know your men folk. Well, they are glad to be home, I can assure you of that."

"Not such a good cook, are you?" she teased, turning back toward the house. She had to get away from him. It was too easy, too good. Too much.

"Actually," he called out after her. "I'm pretty good in the kitchen. One of these days, I'm going to cook for you, Mrs. Dixon."

She kept walking, her pulse racing.

After Tim had gone, she put Judah in the bathtub in her room and the three older boys took turns in the shower in the other one. She had to send Simon back in when she caught a whiff of his wet, unwashed hair. After Judah got out of the tub, she had him lie down on her bed with a few books while she went to the kitchen to check on the spaghetti sauce. By the time she got back to the bedroom, he was fast asleep, a book clutched to his chest.

"I love you, little man," she said, kissing his forehead. She'd let him sleep for a half hour or so, but not any longer.

She sent the other three to walk the dogs down to Granny G's place to say 'hi' to whoever was still there, and in the ensuing stillness in the house, she thanked God for bringing her children home to her.

Singing a soft lullaby to Baby D, she was putting together a fresh green salad when she heard the door from the garage open. She turned, expecting to see the boys.

It was Tim, come back a little earlier than she'd expected.

Tim, looking like a new man, his hair clean and curling long around his face, his beard neatly trimmed.

She caught a whiff of his cologne, the male fragrance making her nostrils flare slightly in appreciation. Jeans and a plaid shirt over a white t-shirt; did the man have anything else in his wardrobe? Did the man *need* anything else in his wardrobe? She certainly wasn't complaining.

"Oh! Hi. Come in." She washed her hands and dried them on the towel hanging over the handle of the dishwasher, busying herself for a moment while she collected her wayward thoughts. "The boys are down the block at my grandparents. Except Judah. He's napping."

"I see. Um," Tim paused just inside the door. "Do you want me to come back when they're here?"

She smiled, trying to put him at ease. Trying to act like she was at ease. "No, of course not. They'll be back any minute. Come in." Then she remembered the job she had for him.

"Actually, there's something you could help me with. Would you mind?"

"Anything," he exclaimed, apparently relieved to have something to do.

They stepped out into the garage, and she apologized for the heat, glad she'd left the door up all afternoon. Giving him directions, he climbed up into the attic storage John had built several years ago and located the crib they'd dismantled and stored up there. It had been through all four boys and needed a good scrub down and probably a fresh coat of paint, but it was a great crib, complete with an old-fashioned canopy, and she loved it.

Tim insisted on putting it together for her, so she brought a floor fan out to the garage for him. By the time he had it assembled, the boys had returned with the dogs, Levi carrying a plastic container of brownies.

"Perfect," Renata declared. "I have vanilla ice cream, too. Reuben, will you go wake up Judah, please?"

FORTY

The meal turned out perfectly. Judah woke up in a good mood, much to everyone's surprise. No one spilled a drink, no one lost a meatball, and everyone ate until they had no room left for another bite of ice cream.

"Movie time!" Reuben declared, launching himself over the arm of the couch and sprawling on his back on the cushions, arms flung wide. Then he looked back at Renata to gauge her reaction, his eyes pleading permission.

She nodded, a sense of well-being washing over her at the sight of the four heads congregated in their living room. It was good to have her family home again.

She glanced over at Tim who still sat at the table with her, his big hand wrapped loosely around his half-empty coffee cup. He, too, was watching the boys with the kind of look she used to see on John's face. Suddenly he turned his gaze to her and caught her watching him. A slow grin lifted the corners of his mouth.

Renata ducked her head and stared down into her peppermint tea. She had to get this over with before she lost her nerve. The sun had just disappeared beyond the horizon, and the stars were beginning to blink into existence. It wasn't by any means chilly outside, but there was a breeze blowing; she could see leaves skittering across the patio in the glow from the porch light. "Tim?"

The expression on his face softened noticeably when she said his name. It didn't matter how much she'd practiced what she would say to him. This was going to be harder than she could have imagined.

The boys were hunkering down for the long haul. They had settled on *The Incredibles*, a favorite of their father's, and it occurred to Renata that John must have been on their minds—and in much of their conversation—a lot during the camping trip. She stood up and raised her voice to be heard over the previews. "Guys, Tim and I are going to go out back for some fresh air. We'll be right outside if you need us, okay?" She didn't look at Tim, but from the corner of her eye, she could see him straighten in his seat.

Reuben waved a hand over his shoulder and Judah hollered, "Okay, Mommy! Bye!"

She rose and refilled Tim's coffee. "I need to talk to you," she murmured by way of explanation.

He nodded and followed her past the boys and out the sliding glass door. She didn't want to sit under the porch light because she thought she might cry, and she didn't want the boys to worry if they happened to look out at them. Instead, she made her way across the yard to a bench that sat beneath the huge sycamore tree where Judah's swing hung. The bench had been a birthday gift to her from John and the boys. It had an elegant 'R' emblazoned on the scrolled backrest.

Tim followed without a word. Renata waved at the bench, indicating he sit, then remembered after he did that Tim had actually made the bench, commissioned by John. She sighed at the irony of the situation and lowered herself carefully onto the wooden seat of Judah's swing, unable to be still. She kicked off her sandals, and using her bare toes, she set herself in motion just enough that she wouldn't have to look at Tim, even though his face was in shadows, and she couldn't really see his eyes very well, anyway.

Before she could say another word, he spoke first. She could hear a smile in his voice. "I was hoping to talk to you, too. I was going to wait until after dinner, but I couldn't sit still at home. That's why I came back early this afternoon."

"Oh." She gave herself another little push. "Why didn't you say so? The crib could have waited."

He shrugged, his big shoulders moving slowly up and back down. "Honestly, I lost my nerve," he said.

When he didn't expound, she prodded him along. "So, what did you want to talk about?" Maybe this was good. Maybe he could do the talking.

Either way, her heart was going to break, but at least if he said that he thought it was the best thing for them, then she wouldn't have to lie about how she felt.

Tim sipped his coffee but didn't speak. He twisted a little on the bench and ran his thumb over the prominent R, as though examining his handiwork.

"It's so beautiful, Tim," she acknowledged. "Your work is remarkable. That bench is very special to me."

"I'm glad," he responded, his voice gentle, matter of fact. The breeze kicked up again, sending some of his long curls across his face. He didn't seem to notice. Renata waited, wishing paradoxically that John was there to give her courage.

Finally, Tim set his cup down on the bench beside him and sat forward, elbows on his knees. "Renata, it's been almost six months since John's accident." He released a puff of air, the sound almost a snort. "Something I'm sure you, of all people, already know."

Renata smiled sadly. Yes, she knew almost down to the hour, but at least she was no longer counting the minutes.

"I've wanted to talk to you about this for some time now, but I didn't want to put you in a difficult position." He reached down and picked up a twig, spinning it between his thumb and forefinger.

Renata chewed on her lip, impatient now to get things out on the table, but wanting him to be the one to do it.

He continued slowly, weighing out his words. "You're already carrying so much on your shoulders. Your grief, the boys having to adjust to their dad being gone. And with this new baby, I just felt like I needed to wait a little longer. To be sure she was... that you weren't going to... lose her, too."

Renata clenched her teeth, tired of feeling tied up in knots about her feelings toward him. Why did he have to be so nice about it? They needed to get this over with. "Listen, Tim. I'm a big girl. And I have an even bigger God who I've been learning to lean on in a whole new way. I'll be the first to admit that I'm a basket case sometimes. I get overwhelmed at the thought of doing life alone, of being both mom and dad to those boys, to this new little one." She rested a hand on her stomach. "But I've got a wonderful support system with my family. They're the best, you know?"

She met his gaze, wanting him to see how sincere she was. "We're much better now, Tim. You don't need to keep coming anymore. You've been a great friend. Better than any man could ask for. But talk about burdens! I know how much of a burden my little troop can be. I saw your face today when you got home. I know how completely worn out you felt. It's a lot, isn't it?"

Tim had straightened up in the seat, and even in the shadows, she could see he was frowning.

"It's all right, really. I know you've said we're not an obligation to you, but if it hadn't been for your friendship with John, you'd feel differently, I know. I release you of any duty you feel you may have toward us. We're doing so much better now, and a lot of the thanks goes to you. I can't tell you how grateful I am for—"

"You release me? From my duty?" Tim cut her off, his words low, but sharp. Renata caught her breath, surprised by the brisk tone. "As in, 'Job well done, soldier. Here's your honorary discharge papers?'"

Renata let her breath out in a whoosh and pushed the swing into motion again, suddenly more nervous than ever. Obviously, she'd said something wrong. "Well, yes, I guess if you want to put it that way." How could she tell him that she had to make him leave before she fell in love with him?

Who was she kidding? How could she tell him that he had to leave before she started building her life around him? Because she already loved him, and it wasn't right, and it was too soon, and no one would understand, and they would all assume the worst and—and she didn't even understand how it had happened, herself. She shook her head at how pitiful the truth really was. She couldn't tell him any of it, because knowing him, he would try to take responsibility for her own misguided feelings, and that would be even more embarrassing.

"Tim, the boys still need you to be their friend, but I don't want them to count on you to be at their beck and call from now until eternity. That's not fair to either of you."

Tim rose to his feet, shoving his hands in his pockets. "And what about you?"

"What about me?" she asked. What was he getting at?

"Do you still need me as a friend? Or are you tired of having me at your beck and call, too?"

"What? No. That's not what I said. I'm not tired of it, of you. But I can't bear the thought of counting on you, only to have you gone one day. Just like John." The truth flung itself out there, and in her dismay, she tried to stop the swing, but her foot bumped the ground oddly and spun her around in a slow circle.

Before she'd made a complete revolution, Tim was beside her, one hand on the rope above her head, the other sliding around her waist and hauling her up off the plank seat. He set her on her feet and ground out, "Can't you just be still when you're talking to me?"

And with that comment, she found her spine. "Okay. You don't have to manhandle me. All you had to do was ask, you know." She crossed her arms over her chest and stood facing him, the beginnings of a temper tantrum stroking her nerve endings.

"Fine. Let me ask you this. Are you asking me to stop spending time with the boys? With you?" He was angry, too. Why? Hadn't she just helped him get past the worst of things? Or maybe he was one of those guys who did the leaving. Maybe that was why he didn't have a girlfriend, wasn't married after all these years.

"Yes." She didn't say more, not trusting her voice. At least she wasn't crying.

"Just like that, huh? Take them camping, show them a good time, thank you very much, now get the heck out of Dodge?" He waved a beefy arm toward the sliding glass door where she could see Levi and Judah lying side-by-side on the floor, the flickering action on the television screen reflecting off their faces. She thought Levi might be asleep.

Turning back to him, she said, "Why are you acting like this? What did I say to make you so mad? It's time to move on, Tim, don't you think? John is dead. He's not coming back. You're free to go."

He just stood there, staring at her.

She opened her arms to her sides and thrust out her belly. "For Pete's sake, Tim. You're hanging out with a widow who has four kids and another on the way. Look at me! Don't you see anything wrong with this picture?"

FORTY-ONE

Tim did look at her. He looked at her for so long that she finally dropped her arms, slipped on her shoes, and started to walk away, frustration and defeat in her voice. "Fine. Don't talk. What a surprise. I need to go check on the boys."

In three long strides, Tim had stepped in front of her, effectively blocking her way. "Oh, no you don't. Is this where Reuben gets it? That boy is the king of walking away when the going gets uncomfortable."

"Excuse me? Are you going to prevent me from going inside my house?" Renata took a step back and glared up at him, fists clenched at her sides.

"Yes, Mrs. Dixon. If you think you're going to walk away from me before we resolve this, then I'm going to prevent you from doing so." He crossed his arms and thrust out his chest. "We've got a mess to clean up before you go anywhere."

"I am not a child, Tim. Don't treat me like one." Renata was so angry now she could barely speak. How dare he! He'd used those exact same words with Reuben just a week ago.

"Then don't act like one."

"And what do you know about children, Bachelor Tim?" She lifted both hands and shoved hard against his crossed arms. "Out of my way."

Tim didn't move. He didn't even rock backward from her effort. Towering a foot over her petite frame, he grinned down at her, taunting her. "Name calling now, huh? I told you, I'm not going anywhere, little girl."

Something inside her snapped when he called her 'little girl', Brad Haley's sneering voice reverberating in her head. That temper tantrum, that ugly little she-devil that hadn't made an appearance in months, rose inside her, consuming her with frustration and bitterness toward this man who wouldn't just leave her to the misery of a future without him. As though watching from outside her body, she saw her hand come up, fingers open, then crack against Tim's cheek, the sound of her palm against his skin loud in the electric silence between them.

Tim snatched her hand so quickly, she didn't even have time to feel the stinging of her palm before he'd spun her around like a choreographed dance move, effectively immobilizing her as he yanked her up against him. Her back was pressed to the solid wall of him, and her head thumped against his sternum. Her slender fingers clenched inside his big hand; her arm folded tight to her chest in front of her. His other arm circled her waist loosely, his free hand spread out over her abdomen in a gesture that could only be construed as protective.

It reminded her so acutely of the dream she'd had, standing almost exactly the way they were now. But in her dream, she'd been there by choice, not held captive by him. She tried to pull free, clawing at him with her free hand.

"Let me go," she hissed, angry tears spilling from her eyes. "I'm going to scream so loud your eardrums will bleed."

"Stop, Renata," he ground out, his mouth close to her ear as he bent his head to speak to her. "Stop it, okay? Just stop. I'm not going to hurt you, but I'm not going to let you haul off and hit me like that, either."

He waited until she quit squirming, stopped straining to get free. "It's okay, it's okay." He spoke gently near her ear, sending an involuntary shiver up her spine. "We'll get through this. Stop pushing me away."

They stood like that for several minutes, Tim murmuring quietly to her, his hand holding hers loosening, lacing his fingers together with hers over her pounding heart. His arm encircling her belly was as gentle as a cradle, his cheek pressed to her hair.

He still held her captive, but as the flame of fury fizzled under the onslaught of his tender rebuke, she realized she was right where she wanted to be.

"I'm sorry," she whispered when she could find her voice. "I'm sorry, Tim."

"I forgive you," he whispered back, his breath warm on her cheek. "But I'm not going anywhere."

She stiffened again, but he didn't let go.

"I'm not going anywhere," he repeated. "Got it?"

"Stop. Stop saying that." She couldn't bear to hear those words, not when she was trying to send him away.

"Now, you're going to listen to me because I have a few things I need to say to you."

She couldn't stay like this, pressed tightly to him. She had to put some space between them lest she melt into him and do or say something she'd regret. But oh, how lovely it felt to be cradled against him. "Let me go." It came out a hoarse moan. "Please."

"No. If I let you go, I'll chicken out again."

She was sure he could feel her heart pounding beneath their clasped hands. "With you here, in my arms like this, in the dark, I can be brave enough to say what I need to say."

Renata's blood raced through her veins. This couldn't be happening. This was all wrong. "Please, Tim. I can't do this. You don't know what you're saying."

"Stay still, little girl." This time when he said it, the words were a caress, an endearment that made her go weak at the knees. "Instead of putting words in my mouth, ask me what I came to say."

Was he serious?

"Ask me." His fingers entwined with hers tightened.

"What—what did you come to say?" she whispered, barely getting the question out.

He smiled. She could feel the muscle of his jaw line move against her cheek. "I love you, Renata Dixon. I love Reuben, Simon, Levi, and Judah. And this little one, too." His fingers moved ever so slightly over her stomach where his hand still rested. "And I know exactly what I'm saying. I know you better than I know any other woman besides my sister and my mother. I knew you first as the wife of my best friend, a woman he loved more than his own life. I would never, ever, ever have allowed myself to love you while he was still alive, Renata, but the night he passed away, you became mine to cover, to care for, and to love."

The words he spoke were like something out of one of her romance novels. Was this the same stoic Tim who barely strung two sentences together unless he was talking about a new gun or a freshly sharpened planer?

"He asked me to stay with you, Renata. Do you know that? John asked me to be here for you."

She squirmed in his arms. She'd heard John say the words. Of course, Tim would stay with her to the bitter end, because it was John's last dying wish, proclamations of love be hanged.

As though reading her mind, he continued. "Know this. I would have stayed even if he hadn't. But he gave me his blessing to love you."

Baby D chose that moment to begin praising the Lord. Tiny limbs flailed inside her womb, bumping against Tim's hand still spread over her abdomen, and the man at her back chuckled with deep satisfaction. They stood as still as statues, both of them connecting with the life growing inside her.

"Renata?" Tim's voice rumbled softly in her ear.

"Hm?"

He loosened his grip on her and turned her so that she was facing him. Then he slid his hands up her arms to cup her face, lifting it so he could see her eyes. The light from the patio made his glisten as he looked down at her. "Tell me you love me, too."

"But—"

"Please."

"Tim, you don't understa—"

He shook her ever so gently, his brow furrowed, but one side of his mouth hitched up in a wry grin. "Why do you always have to have a rebuttal, Renata? You're killing me."

Even as she argued, she leaned into him. "But how will we—"

This time, he cut her off with his mouth on hers, a kiss so sweet, so tender, she whimpered. She brought her hands up to his chest and clung to his shirt. "Tell me you love me," he whispered against her lips.

She wanted to, but she was having a hard time catching her breath.

"Say, "I love you, Tim Larsen,'" he prompted, sliding his arms around her, making her feel small and fragile against his large frame. He swayed slightly side-to-side, the motion soothing, calming. "I need to hear you say it, Renata."

Finally, she rested her head against his chest, listening to his heart thudding beneath her ear. And in a trembling voice, she spoke the words he asked of her. "I love you, Tim Larsen."

FORTY-TWO

Tim led her to the bench, moved his coffee cup to the ground, and sat beside her. Instead of wrapping an arm around her and drawing her close, though, he turned so he was half-facing her and took her hands in his.

"Renata, there's more I need to tell you." He paused, and in the silence, she spoke first.

"Why aren't you married, Tim?" It wasn't an illogical question. The guy was in his mid-thirties and she couldn't find anything wrong with him. Maybe he got a little tongue-tied now and then, or just opted to use fewer words than most, but other than that, he seemed like quite a catch. But in all the years she'd known him, she couldn't remember him having a serious relationship.

"Well, that's part of the more." He turned his face away from her, his eyes on the sliding glass door, but his thoughts clearly somewhere else. She waited, rubbing a thumb over his knuckles encouragingly.

Then he chuckled, surprising her. "I don't know how to tell you this without it sounding like a pitiful war story."

"I promise not to pity you." She smiled gently.

"Okay. Here goes." He took a deep breath and let it out with a whoosh. "I was injured in Afghanistan. You knew that, right?"

"Yes."

"I was also engaged at the time."

"Oh." This was the first time she'd ever heard that.

"My injuries were pretty significant—I took a round to the gut—and it was touch-and-go for a while there. But several surgeries later, they told me I was good to go. My initial tour was up, so I planned to head home and get married. But I kept having these pains low in my gut and groin and thought they must have missed a piece of shrapnel or left a tool inside, or something crazy." He grinned. "You hear stories, you know?"

Renata nodded, but her heart was racing. She didn't know what was coming, but she thought it might not be easy to hear. Or for him to tell.

"So, I went back to my doc, demanding they check things over again." Tim straightened and turned away from her, releasing one of her hands and running his fingers through his hair, pushing it back away from his face. Even through his short beard, she could see the muscles of his jaw working.

"What'd they find?" she asked, not wanting to hurry him, but worried he might lose heart and change his mind about telling her.

"Testicular cancer," he said, his eyes closing briefly. "So I went back under the knife. Came out the other side with one less body part." He made a low sound that might have been a chuckle, except it sounded sad to Renata's ears. "And after we found out the life-saving surgery came with the gift of infertility and possible recurrence, one less fiancée, too."

Renata held her breath, for once at a complete loss for words. She squeezed his hand, letting him know she was still there.

"So, once oncology gave me a clean bill of health, I signed up for another tour, then another. I figured if I was going to die, I'd rather go down fighting. But I couldn't get hit again, no matter how hard I tried. So when my dad got sick and my mom needed help, I hung up my gun and came home."

She still said nothing. Platitudes seemed insensitive.

"Dad got well, and there was no reason for me to stay. My brother hooked me up to apprentice with a guy in Orange County, so I moved out here." He sighed and turned to look at her finally.

Renata met his gaze, wanting to be brave for him, even though her heart raced at the implication of what he was saying.

"You asked why I never married? Well, any offer of marriage from me would come with the promise of no children and the possibility of more cancer."

"I see," she said, nodding slowly in direct opposition to the speed in which her thoughts were whirling around inside her head. She pulled her hand from his grip and turned on the bench so that she was looking out over the yard, toward her house, toward the boys. Her other hand still rested on her belly where Baby D was doing a soft shoe.

She didn't care about the infertility—she came with a wealth of children already, including another on the way.

But the cancer? What if it came back? Could the boys handle losing another man in their lives to death? She knew all too well what losing parents did to a kid. What about this little girl? If Tim stepped in and became a daddy to her, what would happen to her tender heart if the cancer came back? *And what about me?* Renata's heart whimpered. Could she bear it?

After a long silence, Tim murmured, "Come here." He slid an arm around her shoulders and drew her close to his side, pressing a gentle kiss to her temple. "While you were sitting here at home plotting what you would say to me to send me away, I was spending time with your boys trying to figure out what to say to make you change your mind." He brought his free hand up and cupped her cheek. She rested her head into the crook of his shoulder. "You clearly misunderstood what I was saying about moving on, Renata. I meant, maybe it's time to move to the next level. To make it official. To turn what we were playing at into the real thing."

She frowned but didn't lift her head. "Um, moving on usually means, you know, moving on. As in, away from each other."

He chuckled, the sound a percussive rumble under her ear. "Guess I'd better brush up on my relationship terminology, hm?"

"That might be good. Spare us a few fights in the future." She relaxed into him, scooting closer to him on the seat, tucking her legs up beside her.

"Look, Renata. I still can't have children."

"Not a problem for me," she snorted. "I've got a few to spare."

"I've been cancer-free for ten years come November, and that's really good, as far as the statistics go. But I can't promise you it won't come back."

"I know. You can't promise me you won't fall off a ladder tomorrow, either," she said, not joking at all. Because suddenly, it was all very clear to her, the beautiful life the two of them—the *seven* of them—could share. What a waste it would be for them to walk away from today because of fear of tomorrow.

"I know things aren't going to be easy for us. I know people will talk, especially with this new baby. And as much as those guys in there may like me, I'm not John, and I know there will be a few battles waged over that."

"They love you, Tim," she whispered. "They don't need you to be John." She rubbed her cheek against the curve of his collarbone. "And neither do I. Just be you."

Tim grunted in acknowledgment, his hand still on her face, his arm tight around her. His fingers drifted into the hair at the nape of her neck, toying with the short ends. It had grown out significantly, what with all the pregnancy hormones and prenatal vitamins coursing through her system, but still....

Renata lifted her head, flinching away from his touch.

"What's wrong?" he asked, leaning back a little to look at her.

"Nothing." She shook her head and rested it against his shoulder again, not wanting to talk about her hair.

"Renata. I've been pretty up front with you tonight. Don't you think you owe me the same courtesy?" Once again, his rebuke was gentle, but a rebuke, nonetheless.

"Fine. I hate my haircut. Just don't touch it, okay? Then I don't have to think about it." She hid her face against his chest, praying he wouldn't laugh at her. As silly as it sounded, it really bothered her.

Tim didn't laugh. Instead, he disentangled his arm from around her and stood, pulling her up to stand in front of him, holding both her hands in his. Ever so slowly, he lowered himself to one knee in front of her.

Gently, carefully, he turned her hands so that her palms were resting against either side of her protruding stomach, then he covered them with his own.

"Renata Charise Dixon, I want to be the father of your children. All five of them. What do you say to that?"

"But—but your hair is longer than mine." Oh, she wanted it more than anything, but did he really know what he was asking? What he was getting himself into?

He surged to his feet, grabbed her hand, and dragged her back to the house, sliding the glass door open in a dramatic flourish.

"Up and at 'em, comrades!"

Reuben and Simon were still awake, Judah was dozing, but Levi was sound asleep, curled on his side, his back against the skirt of the sofa.

"What are you doing?" Renata asked, trying to decide if she should be upset at him for getting the boys all riled up now that they were settling down for the night.

"Guys, where does your mom keep the hair buzzer?"

Reuben stared up at him, a look of horror on his face.

"Are you going to buzz Mommy's head?" Judah asked blearily, smoothing his hand across his own overgrown crew cut.

"Her hair is too short already," Simon grumbled.

Levi sat up from the floor, rubbing his eyes.

"Nope," Tim assured them with a grin. "Your mom's going to cut mine for me."

"I'm what?" Renata pulled up short, jerking her hand from his. "No, I'm not."

"Well, boys, she won't marry me because my hair is longer than hers is." He shrugged, then crossed his arms over his chest. "So if she won't cut it, I guess that means one of you will have to."

Reuben leapt to his feet, a huge grin on his face, his eyes suddenly bright with what almost looked like malicious intent. "I'll do it! I know where the buzzers are."

Judah jumped up and launched himself at Tim, looping his hands over the man's forearm and hanging there like a little monkey. "Me! Me! Let me!"

"Not happening, guys," Renata called above the melee.

"Are you saying you won't love me if I cut off my hair?" Tim asked, ducking his head to look her in the eye. "Afraid I'll lose all my manly strength?" Then he lifted Judah clear off the ground with one arm, his bicep bunching and bulging under the tight sleeve of his t-shirt, earning whoops of appreciation from the boys... and a snort of appreciation from Renata.

"Of course not. It's just hair. But—"

"That's right. It's just hair." He winked at her and reached out to ruffle the top of her cropped head with his unencumbered hand. "I think she needs proof, guys. Who's with me?"

Judah finally released Tim's arm and jumped up and down, chortling with excitement.

Levi smiled and rubbed his hands together gleefully. "Can we make you bald?"

"As long as it's shorter than your mom's hair, buddy."

"Are you going to be our new dad?" Simon asked, rising slowly from his corner of the sofa.

And suddenly the room went still, four sets of eyes, wide with questions, with curiosity, with… hope? traveled back and forth between Tim and Renata.

Then Tim turned to look at her, too, the hope in his own eyes mirroring the boys'.

She stood stock still, completely at a loss for words for the second time that night.

Then Simon crossed the room to stand beside Tim. He reached out and slipped his hand into the man's large one. "Please say 'yes,' Mom," he said.

Reuben went to Tim's other side, and even though he didn't take Tim's hand, he stood close enough that his shoulder touched Tim's bicep. "We're cool with it. He already asked us."

Levi nodded vigorously, still rubbing his hands together with delight, but now for a different reason.

Judah charged Renata, grabbing her hand and tugging her back toward Tim. "Kiss him, Mommy! Kiss him!"

And she did. To a chorus of "Ew! Gross! Woo-hoo!" and a few other choice expressions only preteen boys could produce.

"You owe us twenty bucks," Reuben directed at Tim a few moments later.

Renata gasped and glared up at the man who still held her shockingly close in front of her boys. "You paid them for this?"

"Just kidding, Mom." Reuben rolled his eyes at her. "Wow. Lovesick much?"

Tim guffawed and held up a hand to him. Reuben slapped his palm, smirking in a rather pleased-with-himself manner.

"Nice one, Reuben," Renata admitted, wondering when her little boys had gotten so clever.

"So, are you going to say 'yes' to me, Renata Dixon?"

"What am I saying 'yes' about?" she teased, reaching up to run her fingers through his shoulder-length hair. "To a haircut?"

"If that's what it takes to get a 'yes' out of you."

"Come on, Mom. You're making us miss our movie," Simon urged.

"Yeah. Come on, Mom," Tim cajoled. "Say you'll have me as the father of your children.'"

Baby D kicked hard, adding her vote of approval to the scoreboard. Renata burst out laughing, a sound that had grown almost foreign to her own ears.

"Yes, Tim Larsen. I'll have you as the father of my children."

EPILOGUE

Tim PULLED INTO THE driveway, relieved to find it empty. He pushed the button on the garage door opener, dipping his head in respect as John's truck came into view, the bed of it still packed with his boxed-up things. They'd get rid of the stuff when Renata was ready, but for now, it was tarped and securely tied down.

Since shortly after John died, Tim had taken the truck out at least once a week to keep the engine running smoothly. Nowadays, the four boys piled into the truck with him, usually before their Friday outings, with Renata's blessing, of course. The tentative plan was to hang on to it for now, Reuben insisting he wanted it for his own when he was old enough to drive.

The boys had spent the night at their grandparents' last night, giving Tim and Renata a chance to finalize their plans for a private wedding ceremony they were having the second weekend in September, shortly after school started. They'd take a week-long honeymoon up to Carmel by the Sea, a wedding gift from Tim's brother, who had a timeshare there. They'd leave the kids with Renata's more than capable family.

Tim didn't care that his bride would be seven months pregnant with another man's child. In fact, he was honored and humbled that she'd agreed to marry him before the baby was born; he wanted to give the little girl he'd already grown to love his name, too.

Charise Olivia Dixon Larsen. It was quite a mouthful, to be sure, but he figured, being Renata's daughter, she could handle it. Her names meant hope and peace. The little one had brought both into their lives.

Every day, he rested his hand on Renata's growing stomach, praying over his soon-to-be wife, his soon-to-be daughter, and his soon-to-be sons, thanking God for the miracle of this little family he loved and needed, who loved and needed him in return.

He'd never blamed his first fiancée for leaving him all those years ago. He'd wanted kids just as badly as she had, and he had grieved his loss to the point of hoping for death on the front lines.

Now here he was, not only gaining a family he already knew so well and loved with all his heart, but he was also getting to experience the miracle of pregnancy and birth and all that went into preparing for a new baby.

It was Saturday, and Renata would soon be back from her morning spent with her sisters at one of their G-FOURce meetings. She had filled him in on the evolving situation with Angela Clinton and her pending parole, and he thought it was wonderful the girls had each other to process through some of this.

He knew how hard it was for Renata to let go of the past, but he'd watched her release so many things in the last several months, mainly her tight hold on the controls in her life. He was so proud of her, of her strength, her beauty, of how she seemed to be blossoming before his eyes. He took great satisfaction in knowing that his presence in her life played a large part in the changes in her.

Lowering the tailgate of his own truck, he pulled the blanketed piece of furniture toward him, the cardboard underneath it helping the runners slide easily across the truck bed. It was bulky, although not very heavy, but hours of labor and an immeasurable amount of love had gone into its construction, and he wasn't taking any chances with it as he carefully hoisted it out of the truck.

"I miss you, brother." Tim said the words under his breath as he passed John's truck, carrying Renata's gift. "We all miss you." He took a deep breath and headed inside the house, maneuvering the tight fit of the door into the kitchen, then down the hall and into the master bedroom.

They'd radically rearranged things in the room, more to accommodate the baby than because of their pending nuptials, but Tim was thankful for the changes. Determining it was best for everyone for now to stay in this home, Renata had bought new bedding and curtains, and they'd painted the room a pale sea blue that reminded him of Renata's eyes when she talked about baby Charise.

It no longer felt like John and Renata's room, at least not to him. He'd only been in it twice before while John was alive, that he could remember, anyway. Both times had been to use the bathroom because the one in the hallway was occupied, but both times, he'd felt like an intruder in a sanctuary where he had no business being.

Now, to him, it was simply Renata's room, a place in which he'd be taking up residence in less than a month from now. He knew it was a little more difficult for her, but he was looking forward to the challenge of claiming it for theirs after they married.

He set the piece of furniture down in the corner next to the bay window, positioning it so it wouldn't bump the walls. A few minutes later, he heard the door from the garage open. He'd made it just in time.

"Tim? Are you here?" Renata's voice was music to his ears, especially when she said his name that way, like she couldn't wait to see him.

"Back here," he called. "In your room."

Her footsteps in the hallway slowed noticeably. They'd made the necessary decision to spend as little time as possible in the house alone together before they were married, and definitely not in the bedroom that would be theirs in a few short weeks. He grinned at her caution; the woman was as anxious to share his bed as he was.

"It's all right. You can come in. I won't touch you." He lowered himself into the bay window seat, his hands braced on the padded bench on either side of him, and he crossed his ankles out in front.

She pushed the door open slowly. "Are you naked?" she asked, her question in jest, but he heard the slight tremor of desire he'd come to recognize in her voice.

Tim guffawed. "Nope. But if you'd rather—"

"Stop. Stop. Sorry." Renata was grinning and shaking her head as she came in and dropped her purse on her dainty Queen Anne style chair just inside the door. Her eyes found him in the window, and she smiled in guileless pleasure, an expression that made his pulse race. Then she noticed the oddly shaped blanketed form in the corner of the room.

"What—what is that?"

He nodded at it and said, "Take a look."

Renata crossed to it and lifted one corner of the cover, letting out a hushed exclamation. Then she whipped the whole blanket off and dropped it on the floor, both hands coming up to cover her mouth.

"Oh, Tim, it's beautiful." She turned shining eyes to him, then back to the piece of furniture. Complete with dove-tailed joints, hand-turned spindles, and wooden pins instead of metal hardware, it was a combination rocker and cradle he'd been working on since the day in May when she'd told him she was having a baby. He'd seen one in a Sam Maloof gallery a few years back and had always thought he'd like to try his hand at one if the right occasion ever arose. As far as he was concerned, this was the perfect occasion for such a project.

"Sit in it. Try it out," he encouraged, confident that he'd made it to her exact specifications. He'd had Phoebe come by his place to test it, as she was the closest of the sisters in size to Renata's normal physique, and Phoebe had assured him that it was just right. He'd had a seat cushion and a little mattress custom-made for it, but he'd set them aside for after the unveiling. The stain he'd used on the cherry wood brought out the gorgeous pattern of the grain, and he wanted her to see how beautiful it was.

Renata sat down and nudged the chair into motion, reminding Tim of her on Judah's swing the night they'd professed their love for each other. She laid one hand on her belly, the other in the cradle section, and smiled dreamily, resting her head against the tall chair back, turning to look at him from half-closed eyes.

"Thank you. We couldn't ask for anything more perfect. You spoil us."

"Something I mean to keep doing for a very long time. All six of you."

"Come over here and kiss me, Mr. Larsen."

Tim grinned and shook his head, his heart almost bursting at the look of contentment on her face. "Nope. I promised I wouldn't touch you."

"Fine." She pushed up out of the chair and crossed to the window seat. "I, on the other hand, made no such promise." Taking his face in her hands, she bent down and kissed him, her mouth soft and warm, her lips opening in a sigh against his.

Several moments later, he stood, turning her slowly so he could pull her to him, her back against his chest. He wrapped his arms around her, their hands joined over her protruding belly.

"Three weeks, three hours and twenty-eight minutes," he whispered in her ear. "Then you'll be mine to have and to hold. But who's counting?" He breathed in the delicious rose and citrus scent that emanated off her skin, her hair. She'd asked him if he wanted her to change her perfume since it had been John who first gave it to her, but he'd objected fiercely. This was the fragrance of Renata to him, one he'd recognize in a crowded room, in the darkest of nights.

"Mmm." She made that sweet sound she always did when she was happy. She leaned her head back against his shoulder. "I love you, Tim."

He was almost shaking with desire for her, this woman so ripe with need, with love, with a child he would call his own. But he would wait, just as he had promised. He would do this right, for her, for him, for the boys, for Charise.

For John.

For God, who had entrusted the heart of this woman and her children into his care.

Tim laced his fingers through Renata's and led her out of the room, closing the door gently behind them. But he made another promise to her as he did so. "Renata Charise Dixon, the next time I come down this hallway with you, you'll be my bride, and I'll be carrying you *into* the room, not leading you *out* of it." He lifted her hand to his lips and eyed her over the top of her knuckles. "And I won't be closing that door quite so gently."

"Hopefully," she added shyly, "you'll be calling me Renata Charise Larsen, too."

Tim laughed out loud. "That I will, my beautiful bride-to-be. That I will." He kissed her on the mouth once more and with great gusto, then led her down the hall toward the front door. "Let's go bring our boys home."

"[He will] comfort all who mourn and provide for those who grieve... to bestow on them a crown of beauty instead of ashes, the oil of joy instead of mourning, and a garment of praise instead of a spirit of despair. They will be called oaks of righteousness...."
Isaiah 61:2-4 NIV

• • • • • • • • • •

Having weathered the worst kind of storm together, Renata and Tim have discovered that they make a pretty good team, and they're ready to face the challenges a shared future might bring.

Renata's profound grief has also helped smooth her sharp edges and given her a new perspective on the lives of those around her.

In particular, the lives of her sisters.

And more specifically, Phoebe's.

Something is terribly wrong there, and Renata is beginning to wonder if she might hold the key to unlock Phoebe's secrets. When someone wears such a perfect mask, it is almost always to cover up the most broken parts of them.

Are you ready for Phoebe's story?
Fair warning: keep your tissue box close!
About **Phoebe & the Rock of Ages**

A wild child. A Jesus freak. A past that is going to set of all kinds of fireworks when their futures collide.

Phoebe has been running wild for most of her life. A gifted and passionate artist, she portrays life the way she sees it. But her jaded perspective is borne out of disillusionment, betrayal, and heartbreaking loss.

Rather than face the past and deal with all the reasons she keeps running, Phoebe charges full throttle into the future, never investing in anything—or anyone—for longer than it takes to finish a job.

When Trevor, a charming, talented musician, causes a roadblock she can't find a way around, Phoebe's fast-paced life comes to a screeching halt.

Just when she thinks she's getting back on track, a family emergency stirs up painful memories long ago laid to rest, and Phoebe suddenly has nowhere left to run.

Will she find the courage to remove her discolored filters so she can truly see herself—her past, her future—the way things really are?

~ ~ ~

Keep reading for an excerpt from **Phoebe and the Rock of Ages.**

From the Author

Dear Reader,

I have a special place in my heart for sisters. I grew up with a sister only eight months younger than I am. Yep, there are only eight months between us. But before you send those side-eyes at my poor parents, one of us is adopted. It was a case of...

"You can't get pregnant."

"Let's adopt."

"Yay! Your baby is ready to pick up at the adoption store!"

"Oh, and double yay... You're also pregnant! Surprise!"

"Wow! Let's keep them both."

"Sure. Why not?"

Or something like that.

In many ways, my sister and I are as close as twins, seeking security and support from each other in ways no one else can possibly provide. And in many ways, we are like oil and water... a beautiful mess. We now live in two different countries, and there is always far too much time that passes between phone calls and visits. But she is in my heart every single day, and I can't imagine my life without her in it.

I have another sister who arrived on the scene many years later, and with a beautiful adoption story of her own. She is the age of my children, so our sister relationship has a precious nature all its own. And again, I can't imagine my life without her in it.

You'll find "sisters" in most of my books: some by birth, some by adoption, and some in name only—friends who have become sisters.

If you're looking for fiction with realistic romance and redemptive story lines, I invite you to check out some of my other books and series.

You may meet your next BFF (Best Fiction Friend)! Or visit me online: **BeckyDoughty.com**.

I write heartfelt and wholesome Contemporary Romance and Women's Fiction. I write fiction because nonfiction is hard! Yes, I've tried. Let's just say I like to color outside the lines when it comes to facts. But emotions and feelings and the roller coaster ride that comes with all relationships? Oh yeah. That's where you'll find me.

Where hope lives and love prevails,
~ Becky Doughty

Let's stay in touch! Head over to BeckyDoughty.com and **sign up for my newsletter** for book and audiobook news (and deals!), and for fun subscriber-exclusive stuff.

An Excerpt: Phoebe & the Rock of Ages

Chapter 1

"Put your clothes on, Brandon," Phoebe ordered. "We're done here."

The man strutted across the room—yes, *strutted*—and scooped up the white bathrobe he'd draped over the back of one of the throne-like chairs they'd used as a prop earlier. He didn't bother slipping into the robe, just hooked it on a finger, flung it over his shoulder, and headed toward the dressing room.

If Phoebe was a betting woman, she'd put money on his clothes being neatly folded and stacked in his designer man-purse, Italian leather shoes on the bottom, wallet, watch, and jewelry tucked inside one of them, then his pants, shirt, socks. He wore his underwear during each shoot, but only at her insistence.

Phoebe grimaced. Why did men feel so at home in their own skin? She knew times were changing, that around the globe, men were becoming increasingly body-conscious, investing in beauty products and cosmetic surgery almost on par with women. But as a whole, they just seemed to be less inhibited than her female clients.

It was jobs like this that made Phoebe question her sanity. It was jobs like this one that tainted every other aspect of her career choice. It was jobs like this that made her want to throw in the towel and go back to work for Maurice "Creepo" Salazar at *Gossamer Magazine*. He kept calling, kept offering her more bait in the form of money, convenient hours, and a clientele list that made her bank account sit up and beg, but she was holding her ground. She wasn't interested in working on any more adult-themed photo shoots, no matter how good the pay.

"Because I'm following my dream," she muttered, her voice flattened by sarcasm as she considered the fact that she'd just spent an hour photographing a nearly naked man in her home studio.

Glamour photo shoots and professional portfolios were an easy way for her to pay the bills, thanks to digital photography and her natural talent for capturing her models' best poses. But bodice ripper covers? It was her shameful little secret... she hoped. She'd seen a few of her covers on books in Renata's collection, and even though her sister was most likely more interested in the words between the covers than in the covers themselves, there was always the possibility she would read the credits one day and discover the truth.

Phoebe shuddered involuntarily.

She glanced around the large studio, her eyes landing first on her easel, then pausing on the potter's wheel. She waited for the familiar tug, for the tingle in her fingertips, the racing pulse. But it didn't come. In fact, there were many days when the urge to pick up a lump of clay no longer consumed her. She sighed deeply, then turned her attention back to the images of the nearly naked man on her monitor.

Brandon really was exceptionally handsome. There wasn't a bad pose in the whole series. Even the shots with his eyes closed worked for the dreamy time-travel feel she was trying to capture. She'd have three cover options ready before the end of the week.

And honestly, she'd much rather take trashy pictures in secret for Rosemary Ramsey at Vineland Publishing than do Creepo's dirty work for him over at *Gossamer*.

· · · · · · · · · ·

By the time Phoebe closed down her design program, she was running late.

As usual.

She touched up her scarlet lipstick, tied a colorful scarf around her head, braided her long curls so they wouldn't get any more tangled than they already were, and snatched up her huge shoulder bag. Scrambling up into Xena, her Jeep Wrangler, she tucked her floor-length skirt under her thighs so she wouldn't accidentally flash anyone driving beside her. She grimaced at the way the strap of the seat belt rubbed at her neck; she lifted the chunky chains she wore out of the way. Then she slipped on her blue-tinted, frameless sunglasses, the ones that highlighted the blue-black sheen of her hair.

After backing out of her driveway, she floored it, anxious to be on her way. It wouldn't be dark for hours still, and the afternoon sun felt good on her skin after sitting still for so long in the air-conditioning. One of her favorite things about living in Southern California was how much of the year she got to drive without the cover on her Jeep.

Xena was an older model, her compact shape and big wheels more to Phoebe's liking than the sleeker, larger design Wrangler was putting out these days. The Jeep's age, however, meant more trips to the auto shop, but Phoebe had a friend in the business, Stan Jacobson, who gladly traded mechanical repairs for any cover shoots she could land him. He was one of her favorite male models because he somehow made hard work and grunge look really sexy, and the authors and publishing houses she worked with were beginning to specifically request him. Besides, he was a really decent guy, too. Keeping him clothed was never an issue, and Phoebe didn't believe she'd ever seen him swagger or strut.

She'd made it about halfway to Juliette's place when she felt the slight hiccup beneath her. Then Xena let out a polite cough. Phoebe's eyes landed on the fuel gauge, but she already knew what she'd see.

Below empty.

She'd meant to get gas on her way home yesterday, but there always seemed to be some pressing reason for her to get to the next place she was going. Case in point: right now, she was running late and had hoped she could hit the gas station *after* the G-FOURce today. But she'd been driving on fumes for two days now, and her luck appeared to be running out.

"No! No, no, no, no!" she growled, her be-ringed hand smacking the steering wheel in frustration as the Jeep spluttered again, this time a little more vehemently. "Come on, Xena! Just a little farther. Come on, baby!" There was a gas station around the corner and Juliette's was only a few blocks beyond that. So close....

Another cough, wheeze, and a shudder, and then the warrior princess moaned and passed out beneath her.

Phoebe coasted to the side of the road, grateful she'd opted not to take the cross-town freeway. There was nothing worse than being stranded on the side of the freeway in a billowy skirt and a topless vehicle in rush hour traffic.

"Been there, done that," she muttered, rolling her eyes.

She sat there for a few moments, weighing out her options. She could call Juliette and tell her she'd be later than usual, and then ring up Grandpa and have him bring her a can of gas.

For the second time this month.

She'd have to endure his lecture, along with the look in his eyes that told her he knew she knew better.

She could call Stan, whose shop was only about a mile away. Let him tease her mercilessly, listen to him remind her that her negligence would be the death of Xena, and then bribe him with dinner, maybe. She'd have to bail on the G-FOURce meeting altogether, though, and that wouldn't go over well with her sisters. Her being late again was already going to be a problem.

She'd just suck it up and walk to the gas station and back. She was a big girl. She didn't need a man to rescue her. And she did have three gas cans in the back of the Jeep already, courtesy of Grandpa, Renata, and, well, she couldn't remember where she got the third one. Maybe she'd bought it herself.

Frustrated at her own ineptitude, Phoebe bolted from the vehicle and slung the long strap of her purse up on her shoulder. She reached for one of the gas cans lined up neatly behind the jump seat and gave it a hopeful shake. No luck. It was empty. With a sigh, she set off, thankful she'd worn her Gladiator sandals today, and not the macramé platforms she'd been considering. They would have complimented her Boho flower child look better, but they were far more decorative than functional. The walk to the gas station and back would not have been fun.

All six fuel pumps were in use. Of course. Phoebe couldn't remember the last time she'd seen the place so busy.

She tried to appear nonchalant as she stood behind a car, waiting for the line to move forward. She dug her phone from her shoulder bag and sent off a text to Juliette.

Be there soon. She started to key in an explanation but ended up just erasing the excuses and sent it with only those three words. She didn't even bother apologizing.

Renata would roll her eyes, Gia would enjoy the extra minutes she could spend playing with Juliette's dog, Bob, and Juliette would make excuses for Phoebe, anyway.

It was the first G-FOURce meeting they'd had since Renata had returned from her honeymoon last month, and truth be told, Phoebe knew there was more to her tardiness than just bad habits. The larger Renata's belly grew, the less Phoebe wanted to be around her. For some reason, this pregnancy jabbed at places in her heart that none of Renata's other ones had.

In fact, it was Phoebe's fault they hadn't met two weeks ago. She had canceled at the last minute, hoping to get out of it completely. They'd simply gone and rescheduled, though, and she wasn't about to bail again. It was just putting off the inevitable. The G-FOURce would go on, come hell or high water.

Her phone beeped.

That's fine. Victor is still here anyway. He picked up some of Mona's pastries for us—I'll make sure no one licks your scone before you get here.

Juliette had an uncharacteristically perverse thing about licking stuff to mark her territory. Phoebe had a sudden—and slightly unsettling—visual of her oldest sister licking Victor, claiming him the same way. The idea made her laugh out loud, partly because she could almost see Juliette going for it and then bursting into tears over how inappropriate it was. And poor, ultra-conservative Officer Vic Jarrett, with his bullet-proof vest and freshly pressed uniform all tucked in and battened down, his storm cloud eyes, naturally bronzed forearms, and long-fingered hands....

She noticed that kind of thing. It was her job to notice people's assets.

Would he blush? Let fly that slow misty morning smile of his?

"I wouldn't mind licking you myself, big guy," she murmured with due appreciation, stepping up and slipping her credit card into the payment center on the pump.

A low chuckle emanated from the other side of the dock, bringing her up short, the gas can still clutched in one hand. She whispered a word she never said around her sisters.

Moving ever so slowly, she leaned slightly to the left and peered around the pump, her eyes widening at the shiny black Harley propped up on its double kickstand, its rider standing with his back to her, one hand cupping his neck just below his damp hairline. A denim jacket was draped over the wide bike seat, a black helmet resting on top of it, and he wore faded black Levis and a casual gray T-shirt. He turned slightly, and she froze, afraid to make any sudden moves lest he notice her.

Angular profile, no scraggly gray beard, not even one of those three-day scruffs she really did not like. They were fine to look at from a distance, but not up close and personal. Not with porcelain skin like hers. No potbelly, no tattered shirt with the sleeves ripped off, tucked into dirty jeans held up with a big-buckled belt. No faded tattoos of naked women up and down his arms.

Phoebe knew she was stereotyping, but this part of California was home to a huge community of bikers who made their two-wheeled vehicles a lifestyle. With summers that lasted more than nine months of the year, it was ideal for motorcycles. And many of the clubs were still made up of old schoolers, fitting the stereotype to a T.

But this guy?

His tousled hair looked like he'd run his fingers through it after removing his helmet, and his full mouth was set in a wide grin as he studied the phone in his hand. Phoebe let out a quiet sound of relief. He must have been laughing over something on his phone, not at her comment about licking Victor.

She lifted the gas nozzle from its slot on her side of the pump and began to fill her gas can, making as little noise as possible. She really didn't want to be caught in this predicament by anyone, no less by the handsome biker only a few feet away.

Phoebe breathed through her nose as she watched the two-gallon can fill quickly. She loved the smell of gasoline fumes; they always triggered memories of her father standing in the open door of their family van, talking to his girls while he filled the tank. It was one of the few vivid images she could conjure up of him after all these years, without the help of a photo, anyway.

She returned the nozzle, grabbed the receipt that the machine spat out in exchange, and crouched down to screw the cap on the can before picking it up. She took a step away from the pump, careful not to let the flat soles of her sandals slap loudly on the concrete under her feet.

"You need help with that?"

~ ~ ~

Read – or listen to – Phoebe's story in **Phoebe & the Rock of Ages.** It's available in print, e-book and audiobook, and you can find it at **Becky Doughty Books** or any of your favorite online bookstores.